UNSEEMLY HONEYMOON

BOOK 6 OF THE CONCORDIA WELLS MYSTERIES

K.B. OWEN

~

For my mom,
Agnes Belin
with love and gratitude

~

CHAPTER 1

*N*ew York City, July 5, 1899
Deighton's Book Shop

Some might consider it unusual for a new bride to bring her husband to a bookstore at the start of a thirty-day honeymoon tour, but Mrs. David Bradley—*née* Concordia Wells, formerly a literature professor at Hartford Women's College—loved bookstores almost as much as she loved Mr. Bradley. The hush of the space, the smell of paper and ink and bindings, the sight of heavily laden bookcases that reached nearly to the ceiling—all held the promise of new adventures to discover or old friends to revisit.

One old friend in particular.

"Why, it's Miss Concordia!" A thin, slightly stooped man on the far side of sixty set aside a stack of well-worn leather volumes and limped over to clasp her hand. "How long has it been? Ten years, at least."

"Longer than that. Before Papa died." Concordia's father, respected Greek and Latin scholar Randolph Wells, had brought her here as a child whenever they made the trip to New York City from Hartford. She had happy memories of this place.

The man smiled. "Your papa was my best customer." He tilted his head for a better look at the young lady. Even a casual observer would note the merry green eyes behind silver-rimmed spectacles, the charming flush that touched her freckled cheeks, the wisps of deep red hair that escaped her hat and clung to her damp neck, and the slightly plump but diminutive figure, smartly attired in a summer walking dress of navy linen.

Standing beside her was a smiling gentleman in his early thirties, dark-haired and dark-eyed—though at the moment his eyes were only for the lady, who seemed to return the favor.

"And who might you be, young man?" the proprietor asked.

Concordia started. "Where are my manners? This is my huh—husband, David Bradley." *Drat it*, she still stumbled over the word *husband*. "David, this is Mr. Deighton, owner of Deighton's Books."

David extended a hand. "Pleased to make your acquaintance, Mr. Deighton."

"Everybody calls me Rusty." He stroked his salt-and-pepper beard ruefully. "Not that you can tell why anymore." He turned back to Concordia. "So, just married, eh?"

"A few weeks ago." She self-consciously rubbed the ridge of the wedding band beneath her glove. "We are getting away only now. But how did you know?"

He chuckled. "Your young man's standing awfully close to you to be anything but a happy new groom, and you haven't been eyeing my shelves nearly as much as you've been eyeing *him*."

She felt the flush creep up her cheeks as David grinned broadly.

"Though I see marriage hasn't changed you much, since you're here and not down the street at McCreery's white sale picking out table linens."

She made a face at him. "It's cooler in here."

He threw back his head and laughed. "Fair enough. Looking for anything in particular?"

"Do you have any books of Antoine Lavoisier?" David asked.

"The chemist?" Rusty stroked his chin thoughtfully. "Hmm, maybe. I know we have several copies of *Traité Élémentaire de Chimie*, though I imagine you already have that."

David nodded. "It's standard reading."

"Well, I'll show you the section. There are bound to be hidden gems in there. Something might pique your interest. What about you, Miss—I mean—Mrs. Bradley?"

"I'll just browse." Concordia nodded toward the back corner of the store, where a narrow, spiral staircase led to the upper gallery. The left portion of the gallery had only a door that led to the private apartment where Rusty and his granddaughter lived, while the right section was crammed with more bookcases. "I assume your Romantic poetry section is still upstairs?"

"Very little changes here," Rusty said. "I'd never find anything otherwise."

As she perused volumes of Wordsworth and Keats, Concordia kept her eye on the men below. A smile tugged at her lips as she watched David, sporting a coat of camel pin-check cotton that fit smoothly across muscled shoulders, a linen crash hat tucked under his arm.

It still felt strange to know they were married now. There had been one difficult time during their courtship when they had nearly gone their separate ways. She had chafed against his protectiveness, while he struggled to understand her tendency to "meddle," as their friend Lieutenant Capshaw was fond of putting it. She understood David's concern, of course. She had been in very real danger on several occasions. But behind each of those problems, each of those tangled puzzles to be solved, there had been a person she cared about in desperate need of help. How could she walk away? Eventually, David seemed to accept that, and they had come to an understanding.

3

She fingered the telegram in her pocket. She hoped he would understand once again.

Once Rusty had left David to browse through the sciences section, she climbed down the steep staircase to intercept him in the far corner. He brightened at her approach. "Find something you like?"

She glanced over her shoulder to make sure David could not overhear. "Rusty," she said quietly, "I need to speak with you about your granddaughter."

～

After a pleasant afternoon spent exploring the hidden treasures of Deighton Books, Concordia came away with a slim, leather-bound volume of Keats's poetry, although she was also tempted by a three-volume, leather-bound, first edition of Wilkie Collins's *The Moonstone*. David was pleased with the chemistry volumes Rusty had found and selected several.

"Can you deliver these to the Gilsey House Hotel?" David asked.

"You're staying there?" Rusty let out a low whistle. "Pricey place, that."

David snorted. "Everything is *pricey* here."

Concordia smiled. "It's a wedding gift from David's parents."

"Claude won't be back until tomorrow," Rusty said. "Can it wait until then?"

She lifted an eyebrow. "Claude still works for you?" The man had been here for the past twenty years.

Rusty smiled. "Don't know what I'd do without him."

"That will be fine," David said. "We're staying several days in the city before heading to East Hampton."

"Ah, the Hamptons." Rusty's eyes brightened as he scribbled a note. "Nice place, I hear, and a sight cooler this time of year."

Concordia tucked a damp strand of hair beneath her braided straw hat. "We're looking forward to it."

In the carriage on the way to the hotel, David clasped Concordia's hand and leaned in to murmur, "Why we need *more* books, when the library at the Dunwicks' summer cottage is sure to be sufficient, is beyond me."

She chuckled. "You added more to your collection than I, Mr. Bradley."

He smiled. "Dr. Hayden's invitation to speak at the History of Chemistry symposium this fall has motivated me to become better acquainted with Lavoisier." He stroked her wrist just above the glove. "You are sure you don't mind me meeting him alone for lunch tomorrow? We have much to discuss. But I feel a bit guilty abandoning you. It is our honeymoon, after all."

"Don't worry. I'm meeting an acquaintance for lunch myself."

He raised an eyebrow. "I didn't know you had friends in town."

"It's Rusty's granddaughter. You remember Miss Lester? She was a freshman at the college last year but had to withdraw in March."

His brow cleared. "Ah, yes. Short, dark-haired, large eyes that held sort of a melancholy look?"

Concordia nodded. "The poor girl had every reason to be melancholy. Her mother became ill, and she left school to take care of her. Unfortunately, the woman has since died and the medical expenses have reduced the family finances. Miss Lester lives over the bookshop with Rusty now and cannot afford to return to school." Perhaps she could ask the bursar—when Miss Lester was ready to resume her studies, of course—about what scholarship money might be available for the young lady.

David settled back against the cushions. "Such a shame. What is she doing now?"

"Rusty said she's a switchboard girl downtown, at New York Telephone's central office." He could tell her little else about his granddaughter, except to acknowledge that she did seem preoccupied lately.

Rusty had said, "Maybe she'll talk to *you* about it, miss. She refuses to tell me what's bothering her."

The girl's telegram felt as if it were burning a hole in Concordia's pocket.

IN TROUBLE. NEED ADVICE. PLEASE MEET ME WHEN IN TOWN, ALONE.

Should she show David the telegram? She bit her lip as she glanced at her husband. He looked so relaxed, gazing idly through the coach window at the passing sights. Why worry him? Besides, all she was doing was meeting with a former student and giving advice. Something she did every day as part of her duties at Hartford Women's College.

Better to say nothing more on the subject for now. She could always catch him up later, if necessary.

∾

The Gilsey House Hotel lived up to its reputation as a luxury accommodation. Concordia stepped out of the cab, clutching her hat and arching her neck for a better look at the ornate, Empire-style French architecture with its cast-iron façade and three-story mansard roof.

She was so busy looking up that she stumbled over a gap in the sidewalk. David caught her and kept a hand at the small of her back. The doorman tipped his cap respectfully as they passed. "Felicitations to the happy couple! Enjoy your stay."

"Are we that obvious?" she whispered to David, blushing.

"I doubt that *I* have a poker face." David's grin faded as he caught her just before she tripped again.

"Drat these new shoes," she muttered. "They hurt my feet."

"Here, why don't you sit while I get us registered and check on our luggage. It should have arrived from the station by now." Once he had helped her into a comfortable chair of tufted green velvet, he hurried over to the marble counter, staffed by a young gentleman in a bright blue waistcoat.

She sat back with a sigh, looking around the lobby. She didn't know what to gaze upon first: the warm, glowing bronze chandeliers that hung from the vaulted ceiling, the tall windows swathed in gold silk draperies, the cozy groupings of velvet chairs, or the rich, rosewood-and-walnut trim of the paneling, polished and gleaming.

Soon David returned. "Our luggage was delivered from the station without mishap. The porter is taking it up."

Concordia stood. "That's a relief."

"One more thing I forgot. You have to sign the register."

With the desk clerk looking on, smiling impishly at both bride and groom, Concordia signed her married name in the ledger with a shaking hand. *Mrs. David Bradley.* She glared at the man as she handed back the pen. One would think he'd never seen a newly married couple before.

The bellhop led the way to their room, unlocked the door, and threw it open with a flourish. He pocketed his tip and left, with a wink in the groom's direction.

At last, they were alone. The quavering feeling in her knees, the pounding of her heart in her chest, and the hot flush of her cheeks returned, as they invariably did when David gathered her close. She wondered if they would ever fade. *Bridal nerves,* her mother had called them.

Fortunately, David always had a way of helping her get over them.

CHAPTER 2

*C*oncordia and David went their separate ways the next afternoon, he for Shanley's and she for the Macy's ladies' lunchroom. Despite it being a short ride along the Sixth Avenue elevated line, David hailed her a taxicab.

"You know I've taken the elevated to Macy's before," Concordia protested, as a cab pulled to the curb. "It's in the heart of the Ladies' Mile shopping district and quite safe."

His dark eyes crinkled at the corners as he smiled. "No doubt, my dear. You are simply humoring a protective husband." In the shadow of the carriage door, he leaned down to place a warm kiss upon her forehead before handing her in.

Concordia gave a contented sigh. She could get used to humoring her husband.

The vehicle crept along the avenue in stop-and-start increments as pedestrians and bicyclists breezed past. It certainly would have been quicker to take the elevated train to traverse six blocks in this lunch hour traffic, but at least it gave her time to think about Miss Lester. She closed her eyes and leaned back against the cushions.

What sort of problem would have the girl in such a panic that she would contact her former teacher for help? Victoria Lester was an intelligent, hard-working, sensible girl, not given to impulsive action. Concordia hoped the issue didn't involve a young man. Even after years of teaching and chaperoning female students, she didn't consider herself equipped to give advice in that area.

The second-floor ladies' lunchroom at Macy's was bustling at this hour, and the throng of chattering women stretched beyond the red-velvet rope line. Concordia shouldered her way through the crowded foyer and recognized the slender, brown-haired, square-shouldered young lady at the front of the line, shifting from foot to foot and gripping her scuffed clutch purse tightly. Miss Lester seemed thinner than she remembered. The shadows beneath her eyes hinted at a recent spate of sleepless nights.

Her forehead smoothed in relief as Concordia approached. "Thank heaven you've come." Her thinned lips barely curved in a smile.

"Of course I would come," Concordia said. "It is good to see you, dear. We miss you at the school. I hope you will return to finish your degree at some point."

The girl leaned closer and whispered, "I've had some opportunities here and there to make money, in addition to my regular job. I've been saving it all so I can come back."

"Most commendable. Perhaps we can also inquire about a scholarship when you are ready," Concordia said cautiously. She didn't want to hold out false hope.

Miss Lester met the eye of the waitress approaching them with menus. "We're ready, Millie. Definitely *not* the lunch counter. Someplace quieter, if you can manage it."

Concordia and Miss Lester followed the waitress to a secluded corner table beside a window, partly screened by a potted palm. "You know the waitress?"

Miss Lester nodded as Millie handed them their menus and

filled their water glasses. "She's a good egg." She glanced up at her friend. "Perfect, thank you."

Millie smiled. "You're welcome, dear. I'll be back soon to take your order."

Concordia wasted no time after she left. "All right then, Miss Lester, why don't you tell me what the problem is."

The girl twisted the napkin in her lap. "I'm sorry to have troubled you on your honeymoon, Miss W—uh, Mrs. Bradley. I'm at my wits' end."

"I'm happy to do what I can, though I am surprised you wouldn't turn to your grandfather for help."

"I—I would rather he not know. He has been through so much lately. Mother's death has been hard on him." She hesitated, then took the plunge. "You know I have a job as a switchboard girl for the New York Telephone Company?"

Concordia nodded.

"Well, during an afternoon shift, I overheard a conversation—" She broke off as a group of matrons brushed past their table.

Concordia shifted impatiently after they passed. "What about?"

Miss Lester looked from side to side then dropped her voice to a whisper. "Murder."

Concordia's mouth hung open for a moment. "You're sure?"

The girl nodded. "I heard him plain."

"Him? Who?"

"I don't know. The call I connected came from the lunchroom of a private club. It could have been any of the patrons."

"Who makes such a call in a restaurant?" Concordia asked.

Miss Lester shrugged. "I didn't hear any background noise. The instrument itself was probably in a booth or an alcove."

"When was this?"

Miss Lester sighed. "Last Monday. The twenty-sixth. I'd just started my shift, and it was hectic. The girl who was supposed to work the panel next to mine had been dismissed, so I had charge of both until they arranged for her replacement. Several calls were coming in at once. I thought I had disconnected my headset from the call, but I was mistaken. That's how...I overheard it." She hesitated as if to say more.

"What exactly did he say?" Concordia prompted.

Miss Lester closed her eyes briefly in concentration. "He said, 'He didn't die. I don't know if I have it in me to try again.'"

Concordia suppressed a shiver. "Who was he talking to?"

"A woman."

"Which woman? Couldn't you tell by the line you'd connected him to?"

She flushed and dropped her eyes. "It all happened so fast. It took me a minute to realize what I was hearing, you see. By that point, my supervisor was standing right over my shoulder. He must have suspected I was listening in. I—I panicked and disconnected, and then he started questioning me so sharply—while I was still trying to connect other lines—that by the time he'd moved away, the number had gone clean out of my head. All I can remember was it was an exchange in the Bronx."

Concordia could sympathize. It is not every day that one hears talk of murder. And then to be berated by a strict supervisor... little wonder the girl had been flustered. "What about the man?"

"I told you, I don't know who he is."

"He didn't identify himself to her? She did not refer to him by name?"

"No. It could have been anyone at the club."

Ah. Now they were getting somewhere. "You know the name of the club, at least?"

She nodded. "The Stock Exchange Luncheon Club."

Concordia frowned. "I'm unfamiliar with it."

"Naturally, I have never been there myself, but from what I understand, it's a restaurant where brokers from the New York Stock Exchange meet for lunch." Miss Lester looked up as Millie approached their table.

"Have you decided?" The waitress pulled out her pad.

Concordia glanced at the menu. "I'll have the tomato bisque."

Miss Lester passed over her menu without looking at it. "Just some tea, Millie. I'm not very hungry."

Millie frowned as she turned away.

"I admit, that's a most distressing thing to overhear," Concordia murmured. "How did the woman at the other end respond?"

Miss Lester looked up with anguished eyes. "That was the worst of all. She said, 'You must persist. With the suffering he has brought upon us, he has had it coming for a long time.'"

Concordia grimaced. "How horrible."

"So, what do we do?"

"We?" Concordia asked dryly.

Miss Lester blushed. "All right, then—what should *I* do?"

"There is only one thing to do, dear. Go to the police. Tell them what you know and leave it to them. They are the experts in dealing with such matters." Concordia suppressed a sigh. How many times had she not taken her own advice? Well, those days were over.

The young lady shook her head vigorously. "Impossible."

"Why?"

"For one, I doubt they will believe me. Only wealthy, well-respected investment brokers are admitted to the Luncheon Club. Who would take the word of a switchboard girl over someone like that?"

"It cannot do any harm to at least report it," Concordia objected.

Miss Lester sniffed as she fished out a handkerchief and dabbed her eyes. "I can't risk losing my position. We need the money."

"Would that really happen? After all, you over-listened by accident."

"You don't know how strict our supervisor is. Only yesterday, he fired a switchboard girl for leaning back in her chair and crossing her legs. Making public the fact that a telephone operator eavesdropped on a private conversation involving a rich businessman is sure to get the entire office in trouble, not just me. People are nervous enough that we might be listening in on their calls. This would confirm it."

"I see your point," Concordia said. "Well, then, I believe we are back to doing nothing."

Miss Lester narrowed her eyes. "I don't mean to be disrespectful, Mrs. Bradley, but I had hoped you could come up with a better solution than that. After all, I know you encountered several such problems and intervened when bringing in the police was not sufficient. *You* did not simply sit back and do nothing."

Concordia felt her cheeks flush. "Those were entirely different circumstances, Miss Lester, and in retrospect I am not entirely sure I followed the most prudent course."

The girl gaped in astonishment. Finally, she recovered her voice. "I never thought I would hear you say that. Where would Maisie Lovelace or Dean Maynard be if you had not stepped in last year? Marriage seems to have changed you."

"There is no call for impertinence," Concordia snapped. She gathered her belongings and put several bills on the table. "I must go."

Miss Lester face contorted in distress. "Please," she croaked. "I'm sorry. I did not mean to offend you. Please, stay."

Concordia gave a sigh and sat back down. "I know you are under a great deal of strain." And maybe, just maybe, the idea of marriage changing her had touched a tender spot.

Miss Lester leaned forward. "I have to do *something*. Perhaps I could send an anonymous note to the police, telling them what I know but not how I found out?"

Concordia shook her head. "I doubt that would be enough for them to conduct a serious investigation. An anonymous note could be explained away as spite. You would need to give the police more information, such as the name of the man who made the threat and, most importantly, the name of his intended victim."

Miss Lester sat up straighter. "You're right. I will have to learn more."

Concordia grimaced. That was not what she meant, at all. "No, no, Miss Lester, you are not to involve yourself further, you understand? It is too dangerous."

The girl raised a skeptical eyebrow.

"Besides," Concordia went on, hoping she was playing her final trump card, "you don't want to risk your position at the telephone company, do you?"

Miss Lester sighed. "I suppose not."

CHAPTER 3

"*H*ow was your lunch?" David asked.

Concordia gave a grunt as she rummaged through her trunk. "It was good to see Miss Lester again, although the poor girl seems overworked."

She was leaving out a great deal, but had already decided there was no point in going into detail. She would caution Rusty to keep an eye on his granddaughter. Beyond that, there was nothing else to be done. "Help me find my opera gloves, will you?"

"What do they look like?"

She stopped short of rolling her eyes. What else would opera gloves look like but...opera gloves? "They are black silk, long—extending to the elbow, with a row of tiny buttons down the side. They are my only pair. We cannot leave until I find them." A lady may as well attend the theater barefoot if she was to go without her gloves.

She continued sifting through the trunk. "Have you and Dr. Hayden finalized the symposium arrangements?"

He shrugged. "Mostly, except for the panel I am to present. And he wants to see a draft of my speech as soon as possible." He pulled open another drawer. "Ah! Found them." He handed them over. "They were mixed in with my socks."

She smoothed them out, checking that the buttons were still secure. Traveling with a husband created more chaos than her former solitary life had prepared her for.

"Any sign of the books Rusty was to have delivered?" David asked.

Concordia shook her head. "We should have expected them by now. Something must have come up. I'd like to stop by the bookstore again tomorrow anyway. We could retrieve them then."

David nodded. "Good idea."

As it turned out, they would not visit the bookstore for another three days. Concordia wondered afterward if that would have made all the difference.

It was a short drive to Hoyt's Madison Square Theatre at Twenty-Fourth and Broadway. Concordia felt a tingle of anticipation as they found their seats in the balcony and settled in for the performance of William Gillette's *Because She Loved Him So*. A professional theater production was a rare treat, particularly when her recent experiences were limited to directing student Christmas Revels and the senior Shakespeare play on the small stage at Hartford Women's College. But here—ah, the grandeur of the professional milieu took one's breath away: the orchestra, the stage set, the thrilled hush of the crowd as the lights dimmed—all of it created an atmosphere one could not get elsewhere.

David grasped for her hand in the dark, and she let it rest in his, strong and warm, for the entire first act.

When the lights came up for intermission, she pulled out her fan. The cooler roof air blowing in from beneath their seats—part of the Hoyt's famed air conditioning system—couldn't quite counteract the hot lights. She was glad her mother had insisted upon taking her shopping for a sleeveless, low-necked evening gown of emerald green to add to her wardrobe. David's bright, lingering gaze as he tried not to fix his eyes upon her décolletage suggested that he approved, too.

"Shall I get us some punch?" he suggested.

She nodded her thanks. "I'll come with you. I've been sitting for much too long."

It was difficult to maneuver in the reception area, crowded with patrons on the same mission of fresh air, a change of scene, and a cool beverage. Concordia stood in a corner, away from the crush of people, catching glimpses of her husband threading his way to the punch line.

"Concordia!" a female voice exclaimed. "How lovely to see you here." A young lady approached, dressed in a striking gown of burgundy satin. Every strand of her brown hair was smoothed in place, elegantly tucked at the nape. Such an arrangement served to emphasize her strong, square jawline.

"Charlotte, what a surprise!" Concordia said, clasping her hands. "I didn't know you were in town."

Charlotte Crandall had been a senior at Hartford Women's College during Concordia's first year as a professor. Shortly after graduation, the young lady had returned to teach at her alma mater and had stayed ever since. Concordia considered herself lucky to count her as a friend and colleague now.

Charlotte nodded toward the tall, gray-haired gentleman standing just behind David in line. "Uncle Anthony has business here these past few weeks and invited me to come along to see *Because She Loved Him So.* Mr. Dodson is among his favorite actors." She waved a hand back toward the open doors and the stage. "It's refreshing to attend a play done by professionals, isn't it?" She winked.

Concordia chuckled. "Enjoy it while you can."

Charlotte would be taking over Concordia's former duties at Hartford Women's College, which included directing the annual senior play, a chore Concordia certainly would *not* miss. Charlotte was also taking over her position as teacher-in-charge of one of the student dormitory cottages. A married woman could not possibly hold such employment. Concordia's mouth quirked at the thought of David—and then, *mercy*, children—living among those harum-scarum young ladies.

Children. The mere notion made her abdomen clench in a very uncomfortable way.

"Where's your aunt?" she asked, to take her mind off the subject. Lady Dunwick always enjoyed a good play.

"She went straight on to East Hampton. She said she needed a little time to herself and wanted to oversee the servants opening up the summer house for the season." Charlotte clasped her hands in excitement. "I am so happy that you and Mr. Bradley are coming to stay with us! We shall have such fun. Canoeing, hiking, fishing, surf-bathing, riding—both bicycles and horses"—she winked, all too aware of Concordia's antipathy to the beasts —"and of course, there are to be garden parties, dances, even an old-fashioned country fair."

"Sounds delightful," Concordia said with a straight face, wondering where her peaceful, quiet honeymoon had gone. She had not thought there would be a great many social events at a seaside cottage.

Charlotte frowned. "But we don't want to intrude upon your leisure. You aren't obliged to attend any of it."

"No, no," Concordia said quickly, "it was incredibly kind of your aunt and uncle to invite us in the first place. I'm sure we'll enjoy the activities."

David and Sir Anthony Dunwick returned with brimming cups of punch for everyone.

"It's good to see you again, sir," Concordia said.

Sir Anthony gave a little bow. "The pleasure is mine, Miss— Mrs. Bradley."

For a gentleman in his early sixties, he carried himself with the erect carriage and bright-eyed alertness of a younger man. He did seem to move more stiffly than she remembered, however, as he passed the punch cup to his niece.

Sir Anthony caught Concordia's look. With a self-deprecating laugh, he flexed the fingers of his right hand. "Got banged about in the carriage last week. Infernal city traffic. Good thing I have Pickering to dictate letters for me."

"Pickering?" David asked.

"A stenographer-typist who works for the brokerage firm I use. They have very kindly lent him to me, at least until I find a permanent assistant. I'm writing my memoirs, you see, now that I've retired from my law practice."

David moved closer to Concordia, adjusting her stole over her shoulder, for which she smiled her thanks. "I'm sure you have fascinating tales in that regard," he murmured absently.

Sir Anthony's bright blue eyes crinkled at the corners as he watched David. "Enjoying your stay in the city, I hope?"

"Yes, quite," David answered, giving his wife a warm glance.

Concordia blushed and changed the subject. "We are also looking forward to visiting you in East Hampton, Sir Anthony. It was most kind of you to invite us."

He waved a dismissive hand. "There's plenty of room. Stay as long as you like. We're getting a late start and won't be closing up the place until the end of September."

"We will have to return sooner than that," David said. "The fall semester starts at the end of August."

Concordia felt a prickle of excitement. Although she would miss living with her students at Willow Cottage, she was fortunate enough to have been awarded the position of lecturing fellow at Hartford Women's College this coming year, which meant she would be teaching a few seminars and supervising independent study projects. It was the first time in the college's history that a married woman held any sort of faculty position, although the school was keeping it quiet. If it were widely known, everyone would have an opinion, most of them stridently expressed.

"We're looking forward to it, all the same," David added.

Concordia hid a smile behind her punch cup. David didn't realize the bounty of activities that Charlotte had in store for them. They might need a rest from their holiday.

"What is your business in town, Sir Anthony?" Concordia inquired politely. "You mentioned a brokerage?"

"Terribly dull stuff, I'm afraid. Meetings with my investment broker to look over quarterly reports, shift some commodities that have been under-performing, seek out new prospects, that sort of thing."

David leaned forward in interest. "I have considered putting more money into my current investments and perhaps diversifying." He glanced at his wife. "With the possibility of starting a family soon, it would be wise to have a solid plan."

Concordia gave him a sharp look, and it wasn't about David expanding his stock portfolio. He smiled blandly. Easy for him to smile—he wasn't the one who would bear the children, feed them, and...well, whatever else was expected maternally.

There it was again, that feeling of unease. Would she even be a good mother? She had never been fond of children to begin with, although a woman should never say such a thing aloud. In her opinion, children were snotty-nosed, loud, messy, always needing something. Could she be unselfish enough to subsume herself to the needs of such a creature? Would she resent the loss of her freedom? She suppressed a sigh, realizing she had not been attending to the conversation.

"—plenty of opportunity to pick up some pointers during your stay in East Hampton," Sir Anthony was saying. "When we dined with my broker and his colleagues at the club last week, I invited the whole lot of them and their families to join us at the cottage."

Concordia started. Lunch at the *club*. Investment brokers.

Could this be the establishment Miss Lester had referred to? Here might be an opportunity to learn something.

"You'll be interacting with the best investment minds on the East Coast," Sir Anthony went on.

David frowned. "How many people can your summer cottage accommodate, sir?"

Charlotte laughed. "'Cottage' is rather a misnomer. The main house has eight bedrooms, in addition to the four cabins on the grounds. In fact, Aunt Susan plans to have our nicest cabin prepared for you two. Very secluded." Her eyes twinkled.

Had the lobby become warmer all of a sudden? Concordia plied her fan to her reddened cheeks. Time for a change of subject. "Where did you say you dined with your broker?" she asked Sir Anthony.

If he thought it a strange question, he was too polite to let on. David, on the other hand, raised a quizzical eyebrow.

"The Stock Exchange Luncheon Club, on Broadway," Sir Anthony answered. "It's a members-only establishment, but they bent the rules for me. Quite comfortable, and the prime rib is stuff of legend."

"I believe I have heard of it," Concordia said. "From what I understand, it has all the latest amenities, isn't that so?" She could tell by David's frown that it must sound strange to be discussing a venue she could never patronize.

"It opened less than a year ago," Sir Anthony said, "so naturally it has the modern conveniences one would expect."

"Private telephones, perhaps?" she pressed.

David's frown grew deeper.

Sir Anthony nodded and drew breath to speak when the gong sounded for the patrons to resume their seats. He held out his arm for Charlotte. "Shall we?" With a nod to Concordia and David, he added, "A pleasure to see you both again. I look forward to your upcoming visit."

"What was that about?" David hissed, as Concordia tucked her hand in his arm as they made their way back to their seats.

She widened her eyes. "What was *what* about?"

"That innocent look doesn't fool me. I know you too well," he murmured. "And your voice goes up just a bit when you're evading a question."

Drat. She'd have to work on that. Not that she wanted to deceive him, of course, but it could not be good for a relationship if one's husband always knew what one was up to.

The lights dimmed as he settled her into her seat. "I'll tell you later," she whispered. The curtain went up to a fresh wave of applause.

"I'll hold you to that," he whispered back.

CHAPTER 4

*T*he next few days were a whirlwind of activity for the newly married couple: museum exhibits, sightseeing, concerts, and—now that Charlotte knew they were in town— invitations to teas, dinners, and even a piano recital.

Finally, it was the morning of their last full day in the city before they were to leave for East Hampton. "It has been ages since I've been to Central Park," Concordia said, as the hotel elevator doors opened to the ground floor lobby. "You're sure we can rent bicycles there?"

David nodded. "I've already checked. We go to the main kiosk. We can have them for three hours."

"We should go to Deighton's Books afterward. We've put it off much too long."

"They must have forgotten about my books by now." He inclined his head toward the front desk clerk hurrying toward them. "Unless...perhaps here is news of them?"

The clerk tipped his cap politely. "Good morning, Mr. and Mrs. Bradley, I have something—"

"A package for me?" David interrupted.

"N-no, sir. There's a note for the missus." He fished in his tunic pocket, passing over a thin envelope with "Mrs. Bradley" scrawled across in a hasty hand.

"When was this?" Concordia asked, lifting the flap.

"Late last night. The night clerk considered it best not to disturb you." He shook his head. "He thought it passing strange that a young lady would be out alone at that hour of the night."

"An unaccompanied lady left it?" David asked.

The man nodded.

Concordia pulled out the slip.

I am being followed. He mustn't know where I live. Once I have managed to evade him, I will go home. Can you meet me at the bookstore in the morning? I fear I have made things worse. I'm sorry.

Concordia bit her lip. Despite her caution to Miss Lester about becoming further involved, the girl had obviously plunged head-long into this mess. "Miss Lester wants to meet me at the book-store as soon as possible." She slipped it in her pocket before he could ask to see it. "Do you mind if we postpone our bicycle excursion and go there first?"

David gave her a sharp look and steered her away from the clerk looking on in curiosity, through the lobby to the cab stand. "What is going on? Why would Miss Lester leave you a note in the middle of the night? If she wanted to see you today, she could have telephoned this morning. Why was she out alone at that hour?"

Concordia looked up at him, into those dark brown eyes now clouded with worry. Now was the time, it was past the time, to tell him. Why did she hesitate?

A cab pulled up. "Where to, mister?" the cabbie called out.

"Do you know Deighton's Books?" David asked. He helped her into the cab and climbed in.

"Yessir," the cabbie said, closing the door behind them. They set off at a brisk pace.

"Now then," David said sternly, "tell me what is going on with Miss Lester. I want the whole story."

There was no help for it. She took a breath and began her tale.

David's frown deepened into a scowl as she passed over the note for him to read. "So you knew, even before we arrived in New York, that she was in trouble? Why didn't you tell me?"

"I didn't know what sort of trouble it was. She asked for my advice. I thought it might be a romantic attachment or something equally confidential. I wished to respect her privacy."

He sighed. "Didn't you warn her how dangerous it was to meddle further?"

"Of course, I did," she snapped. "I used every argument I could think of. I even pointed out that her employment could be at risk. I never imagined she would continue."

"But you couldn't let it go yourself," David pointed out. "That was why you asked Sir Anthony about a telephone at the lunch club."

She put a placating hand on his sleeve. "I simply wanted to confirm if her story was plausible. Sir Anthony had dined at the same club where Miss Lester said she overheard a man talk of murder on the telephone. Surely you can see my reasoning?"

He covered her hand with his and squeezed gently before glancing at the note once more. "'He mustn't know where I live.' The would-be murderer, I assume."

Concordia nodded. "But how did he know about her?"

"Would she have been so foolhardy as to confront the man?" David asked.

"I don't think so."

David passed back the note. "I say we both speak with Miss Lester, instruct her to go to the police with her information. If someone is indeed pursuing her, he will stop once the authorities are involved. Then that will be an end to it." He clasped her hand. She shivered as he lightly stroked the fine bones of her wrist. "Besides, chasing a would-be murderer through the city streets is a poor way to spend a honeymoon."

They were two blocks from the bookstore when the street traffic came to an abrupt halt. The cabbie, after a quick interchange with a top-hatted gentleman on the sidewalk, got down and came around to their door. "Can't go any farther, sir. Seems to be a bit of trouble up ahead. The street's blocked off. Ya want me to take ya back?"

David and Concordia exchanged a look. "What sort of trouble?" she asked.

The man jerked a thumb over his shoulder. In the distance, a thin plume of smoke was visible. "One o' the stores burned down early this morning."

Concordia scrambled out of the vehicle as David hastily paid the driver. "Never mind, we'll walk from here."

~

Concordia's heart pounded in her throat as they hurried toward Deighton's Books. *Please, not the bookstore. Please.*

A crowd of onlookers impeded their progress, making it difficult for her to see ahead. David kept a firm grip on her elbow as they threaded among the press of people. Once they reached the corner of Eleventh Street, he stopped abruptly.

"Is it...Rusty's...store?" she asked, struggling to catch her breath. Several people blocked her view, but David was taller.

His jaw clenched as he gave a quick nod. "Looks bad, I'm sorry to say. Come on." He reached for her hand.

With a mixture of pushing and apologies, they muscled their way to the curb, where a policeman stood to keep the people back.

"Whoa, there." He put up his hands. "That's far enough, folks."

Concordia stared at what used to be the storefront of Deighton's, now a collection of sodden, charred wood, broken glass, and blackened pulp. Firemen were packing up their hose and axes, and rope cordoned off the sidewalk in front of the store.

She shivered, and David put his arm around her waist. "We're friends of the proprietor and his granddaughter," he said. "Are they safe?"

The policeman gave a mighty sigh. "'Tis a crying shame, that. Such a nice family. You better talk to the clerk. We let him go back inside, to get the till and whatever else looters might think to be stealin'. But don't stay long. It in't safe in there." He lifted the rope to let them pass.

With the acrid smell filling their nostrils, Concordia and David picked their way carefully. David held one of her hands to help steady her as she lifted her skirts in her other hand to avoid the shards of glass and navigate the charred, splintered bookcases across their path. "Claude?" she called out.

"Over here," came a subdued voice. They found a weary man in his fifties near the back corner of the store, crouched over a strongbox he was settling into a wooden crate. Thanks to the hard work and quick action of the fire brigade, this section of the store was undamaged by the fire, albeit damp and reeking of smoke.

Claude stood as they approached. His eyes widened. "Why, it's Miss Concordia! Rusty said you were back in town." He nodded toward David. "And this must be your young man." He held up sooty palms. "Sorry I can't shake your hand, sir." He swiped his cuff across his sweaty forehead.

"Claude"—Concordia's voice rose in her agitation—"where are Rusty and Victoria?"

"They took her to New York Hospital. Rusty's gone with her. I offered to do what I could here." His brows lowered. "She's in a bad way, miss."

Concordia's knees quavered. "Will she...survive?" David kept a strong, reassuring arm around her shoulders.

Claude's eyes filled with regret. "I honestly don't know. I pray she does. She's all the old man has left in the world."

"How did the fire start?" David asked.

Claude shrugged. "I only know what Rusty told me. When I got here, the fire was nearly out and the ambulance was getting ready to take her. He says it started in Miss Victoria's room early this morning. Heaven knows how. The sound of breaking glass woke him up—fire chief says the window blew out—and he found the room ablaze and her unconscious on the bed. By the time he dragged her out and a neighbor went for help, the upper floor and storefront under it were completely engulfed."

"How horrible." Concordia looked up at David. "We must go see them."

His warm brown eyes softened in understanding. "Of course." He turned to the clerk. "Anything we can do for you?"

The man shook his head. "There's not much left to do. Once the firemen open up the street, I'll send for a cart to load up whatever's salvageable, store it in my brother's shed. It won't be much, I can tell you. But that reminds me." He dropped to his knees and started shifting books around on the floor, plucking out a three-volume stack with David's name affixed on top. "I happened to tuck your books over here yesterday, so they mostly escaped damage, though they may smell a bit. Sorry about the delay in getting them to you, sir. We were so busy the last few days that I had no time."

"No matter." David tucked them awkwardly under his arm. "Thank you."

After a few blocks' walk, they found a cab to take them to the hospital. The ride was a quiet one, filled only with Concordia's mounting anxiety and the smell of damp smoke from the books at David's feet.

Concordia stared out the window, paying little heed to the streets as they rattled along. What had happened at the bookstore last night? Was the fire connected to the note Miss Lester had left at the hotel?

He mustn't know where I live. The words chilled her.

Every instinct screamed against this being a coincidence, even as she prayed that it was.

David touched her sleeve as the cab came to a stop. "We're here."

After paying the cabbie extra to deliver the books to their hotel, David and Concordia climbed the broad stone steps of New York Hospital.

They approached a desk littered with stacks of papers, staffed by a middle-aged woman in a starched apron and a personality to match. She looked at them over her wide spectacles. "Yes?"

"We are looking for a young lady who was brought in this morning," David said.

"Wrong desk," she snapped, tapping her pencil on the sign in front of her that said *Billing*. "Visitor check-in is over there." She jerked her pencil over her shoulder, where a long line had formed.

"Please." Concordia was unsuccessful at keeping the quaver from her voice. "Surely you can help us? Her name is Victoria Lester."

The woman's expression softened. "Poor girl. I saw her come in. You are family?"

Concordia shook her head. "Friends. I used to be Miss Lester's teacher. I believe her grandfather, Mr. Deighton, is with her?"

She stood and smoothed her apron with a sigh. "I'll fetch him. You can have a seat over there."

After what seemed an agony of waiting, Rusty crossed the lobby. Everything about the man sagged—head, jowls, shoulders— as if the floor beneath would swallow him whole.

Concordia rushed forward and clasped his hands, which trembled in hers. "Come, sit down. How is she?"

He shook his head, his eyes brimming with tears. "She passed away twenty minutes ago."

Concordia put a hand to her mouth.

"I suppose she inhaled a great deal of smoke," David murmured.

"That wasn't the only cause." Rusty drew a ragged breath, struggling for composure. "The doc found a wound on the back of her head. He believes someone struck her from behind. The police have been called. They'll be here soon."

Concordia's breath caught, and the floor tilted alarmingly. In an instant, David had his arms around her shoulders and helped her put her head between her knees. "Breathe. Slowly," he instructed.

Rusty leaned forward. "I'm so sorry. I didn't mean to distress you."

David's lips compressed in a grim line. "I'm afraid we have further distressing news, Rusty." He nodded toward Concordia as she straightened. "Show him the note."

~

When the police arrived, the woman at the billing desk thought it expedient to put them all in the director's office to talk. The sight of a uniformed officer and his patrolman standing in the lobby might alarm patients and visitors, after all. Rusty was called in first, then the Bradleys a short time later.

Lieutenant Oliver of the Fifteenth Precinct was a tense, sinewy man of small stature with flat, dark eyes that brooked no nonsense. He cut short the polite round of introductions and got down to business. "As I told Mr. Deighton here, the attending physician confirms my suspicion about the young lady's untimely end. We are looking at an assault."

Rusty's grip tightened on the armrest. Oliver licked his pencil, tested its point, and turned a fresh page. "Now then, Mrs. Bradley...you and Mr. Bradley are honeymooning here in the city?"

Concordia gave a puzzled nod as David shifted restlessly. "We've been here nearly a week. What has that to do with Miss Lester's death, Lieutenant?"

Oliver squinted at them through narrowed eyes. "I am trying to understand how you come to have what I've been told is crucial information regarding this case, when you are purportedly on your honeymoon."

"I can explain," Concordia said.

"Very well, ma'am. I am all ears."

She described the first telegram from Miss Lester, their lunch conversation, and then the final note that the girl had left for her the night before, which she now pulled from her reticule and passed over.

The lieutenant frowned over the slip of paper. "And how is it you know the young lady?"

"Until a few months ago, she was a student in one of my classes and lived in the dormitory cottage I oversaw."

Oliver's eyebrows nearly met his hairline. "You taught at one of those women's colleges? Well, at least you're married now and no longer indulging in such foolishness."

She had just taken breath to retort when David squeezed her hand in a silent plea. She let out a sigh. The things she did to keep her husband happy. Her restraint might not last for long, however, if the policeman continued in this vein.

Oliver glanced at Rusty and waved the slip. "Were you aware of your granddaughter's problem?"

"I knew she was upset and preoccupied these past—oh, I don't know, almost two weeks now. She wouldn't tell me what was troubling her." Rusty looked down at his hands. "It has been a difficult time for us, since her mother died a few months ago. I did not want to press her."

Oliver clucked his tongue. "I believe in keeping a firm hand on one's female relations. It is unfortunate that you did not insist upon learning what the young lady was up to. It could have saved you a great deal of heartache."

"Here now," David protested, as a gray-faced Rusty rested his head in his hands. "There is no call for such talk. You don't know what would have happened."

Concordia glared at the policeman. "Our energies would be best served in catching the man responsible for Miss Lester's death and the fire at the bookstore. It's obvious the conversation she overheard is connected to those events."

"It's not obvious to me," Oliver snapped. "You said yourself she did not know the identity of the man she heard on the telephone. It is more likely that a lover attacked Miss Lester in a jealous rage then set fire to the apartment to cover the deed."

"A...lover!" Rusty sputtered. "My granddaughter would never...she wasn't...there was no one, I assure you."

Oliver flicked his hand in a dismissive gesture. "Not that *you* know of. Begging your pardon, sir, but the young lady sounds like the sneaky sort. I don't doubt there were a number of things in her life you knew nothing about. We'll see. I'll need a list of her friends and co-workers at the telephone company, and we'll search her room—if there's enough left of it."

"But you *will* investigate the telephone call she overheard, in case there is a connection?" Concordia pressed. "The note she left suggests a stranger was following her."

Oliver's jaw clenched. "I will keep my own counsel as what the evidence suggests, young lady. We will pursue all promising avenues of inquiry."

"What about a prowler?" David suggested. "If she was struck from behind, that would make more sense than an, *ahem*, intimate acquaintance."

Oliver shook his head. "Amateurs," he muttered. He stood and opened the door. "If you will excuse us, I have more questions for Mr. Deighton. Thank you for your information."

Concordia gave Rusty an anxious glance. "We'll wait for you outside."

Oliver gritted his teeth. "I would remind you, Mrs. Bradley, your role in this is now over. Do not interfere further." His gaze flicked over to David, and Concordia could read his message just as clearly as if he had spoken it aloud. *Keep a firm hand on your wife.*

After another hour of tedious waiting, Rusty came out of the office, pale and shaken.

"Oh, Rusty," Concordia said, "I am so sorry."

"I know, miss." Rusty passed a handkerchief across his damp forehead with a shaking hand. "I wish you had told me what was going on sooner."

Guilt twisted her abdomen. "I was going to tell you, today, after the alarming note she left last night. Before that, I had no idea she was still pursuing the matter."

David steered them toward the door. "Let us go someplace where we can have something to eat and talk. I saw a coffee shop nearby." He gave Rusty a worried look. "I'm sure you could do with some sustenance. You look ready to collapse."

Once they were settled comfortably in a quiet booth and had strong coffee in front of them, Rusty cleared his throat. "I'm sorry for seeming to blame you, Miss Concordia. It's still such a shock."

"I know. I do wish I had said something sooner." The guilt had now established residence in the pit of her stomach.

"Where will you stay, now that the store has been destroyed?" David asked.

"Claude will put me up. Bless that man, he promised to take care of salvaging what he could from the store." He rubbed the back of his neck. "But I cannot imagine starting over, at my age."

"Are you insured against fire?" Concordia asked.

He nodded. "And I have a bit of money I've been putting by. I was going to give it to Victoria to use for tuition. She had some saved as well."

"That's right. I remember her saying she took odd jobs for extra money," Concordia said.

He leaned forward. "Such an enterprising girl. She had a second job—" He stopped abruptly, as if he had said more than he'd intended.

"What kind of second job?" she asked.

He looked down at his hands. "I suppose you should know, but I hope you won't think any less of her. One of the stockbrokers was paying her to listen to telephone calls placed from the Stock Exchange Luncheon Club."

Concordia gaped. So, Miss Lester had lied. She had *not* eavesdropped by accident.

David leaned forward. "I assume the man paying her had hoped to learn of business interests to exploit?"

Rusty nodded. "She passed along several bits of information that earned her bonuses. She also shared a tip with me that allowed me to place a profitable investment and increase my portfolio."

"Rusty!" Concordia chided.

He rubbed a hand over his salt-and-pepper hair, making it stand on end. "I know, I know, I'm not proud of it. I regret it now, especially after what happened to my poor girl."

"Which broker paid her? He could be in a lot of trouble," Concordia said.

Rusty dropped his voice. "Edgar Wynderhane."

David let out a low whistle. "Of Wynderhane, Gemmer, and Miles? A very prestigious firm."

The name meant nothing to Concordia. "Did you tell this to Lieutenant Oliver?"

"No, and I do not plan to. I can only imagine the kind of trouble I'd be in if a prominent man such as Wynderhane knew I'd told the police."

"Not to mention trouble from the authorities," David added,

"because you made investments based on illegally obtained information."

Concordia shifted in her seat. "But knowledge of Wynderhane's involvement could be crucial to finding your granddaughter's murderer."

Rusty fiddled with his spoon. "I know, but I daren't risk it." He gave her a pleading look. "Couldn't *you* find her murderer?"

Concordia blinked. "*Me?*"

"Absolutely not," David declared. "We must leave it to the police to solve."

"Victoria told me how you solved the mystery that cleared the dean last year," Rusty said, ignoring David. "I know it's a lot to ask, with you being on your honeymoon..." His voice trailed off.

"We are supposed to leave for East Hampton tomorrow," David said.

The old man swallowed. "That's it, then."

"Rusty, you must understand," Concordia began, "even if it were appropriate for me to become involved"—she ignored David's sideways look—"I wouldn't know how to begin. Stockbrokers, private luncheon clubs, telephone switchboards...what do I know about such things? The problem I helped with last year was at the college, involving people with whom I'm familiar."

They were all quiet for a moment, the only sounds the clinking of china and cutlery and the murmur of nearby conversations.

"There is one thing I can do," Concordia went on. "I have a friend—more skilled than I—with a great deal of experience in discreet inquiries, independent of the police. Penelope Hamilton. I can send her a telegram and see if she is willing and available to take the case."

Rusty's eyes brightened. "I would be most grateful."

Concordia heard David exhale softly in what she was sure was a sigh of relief. "I will send it today."

CHAPTER 5

*T*he next morning, Concordia and David took the Hunters Point ferry at the foot of Thirty-Fourth Street, then boarded the Long Island Railroad to East Hampton.

David helped his preoccupied wife to her seat as the porter stowed their luggage. "We must put this unpleasant business behind us, my dear. The police have the investigation well in hand."

Concordia looked up and suppressed a snort. "Lieutenant Oliver is pursuing an entirely wrong line of inquiry. Rusty kept him in the dark about the most important factor in this case. How is he supposed to find the murderer?" Her voice rose in her agitation, turning heads in their direction.

David sighed and took the seat beside her. "You sound like Miss Hamilton," he murmured. "Can we please forgo such terms as *line of inquiry, case,* and especially *murderer?* Not congenial to a honeymoon atmosphere," he added lightly.

She certainly couldn't argue with that. It was a nine days' wonder that David wanted to marry a lady who bandied about such terms. "You are right, of course. But I would have felt better if we'd gotten an answer to my telegram. I hated to leave, not knowing whether Penelope could help."

"I know. But we left our address with the concierge, and he will forward her message when it does come." He clasped her gloved hand. "Now is the time to relax and enjoy our holiday together."

She blew out a breath and turned toward the window, watching the water and then the sun-drenched landscape pass below, more blurred as the train picked up speed. Could she put aside the tragedy of Victoria Lester? Perhaps the change of scene would help her forget.

The trip along the Montauk branch of the railroad line took a couple of hours, although Concordia dozed through most of it. She had not slept at all well last night. Finally, they disembarked at the East Hampton station and followed the porter with their luggage across the wooden platform to the line of waiting carriages. She inhaled the fresh air—particularly welcome after her time in the city and on the train—and took in the quiet prospect of shingled buildings, picket fences, and wide, well-kept avenues. "It's lovely. Is the Dunwick cottage very far from here?"

David steadied her by the elbow as they reached the step. "I'm not sure. I only know they don't reside in the town of East Hampton proper. The cottage is closer to a neighboring village, called"—he pulled out a slip from his pocket—"Hassett Knoll."

"You are headed to Hassett Knoll?" a cheerful, female voice behind them inquired. "How propitious!"

Concordia turned to see a tall, solidly built woman in her early thirties just behind them, blond hair escaping the Leghorn hat that she clutched to her head in the breeze. An equally sturdy, flaxen-haired girl kept a tight grip on the lady's other hand. The girl was nearly of a height with Concordia, though the lingering chubby cheeks of adolescence proclaimed her to be much younger.

"You must be with the Dunwick party," the woman went on. "I'd heard they were expecting a number of guests."

"Here, sir?" The porter stood beside their luggage at the edge of the drive, where a carriage bearing the Dunwick crest waited. David nodded, and the porter helped the driver stow their cases.

"Yes, we are," Concordia said. "I am Concordia Bradley, and this is my husband, David Bradley." She didn't stumble over the word *husband* this time. Perhaps it was a learned skill, like bicycle-riding or ice-skating…or pretending one wasn't bored to tears at a faculty meeting. Although she hadn't quite mastered that last one. "Are you visiting the Dunwicks as well?"

The woman chuckled, a full-throated, lively sound that made Concordia smile. "*Mercy*, no, we live around these parts. I'm Gwendolyn Ambrose, and this is my niece, Susannah."

Concordia nodded toward the girl. "A pleasure to meet you, Susannah." The girl put her face in her aunt's shirtwaist.

"She's a little…shy. We call her Susie," Miss Ambrose added, smoothing the child's braid over her pinafore.

David touched his wife's arm. "The driver's ready whenever we are." He tipped his hat in Miss Ambrose's direction. "Is there somewhere we can drop you, miss? You are welcome to share our carriage."

Miss Ambrose smiled. "That would be delightful, Mr. Bradley. We live just outside the village of Hassett Knoll. It should not take you out of your way."

It was an open-air carriage, so Concordia clung to her straw bonnet and fixed her spectacles more firmly upon her nose as they rattled along the elm-lined, double-lane dirt road out of town. "It doesn't seem as dusty as I would have expected. Have you gotten rain recently?"

Miss Ambrose shook her head. "The East Hampton Ladies' Village Improvement Society has raised funds for a water truck to come daily during the height of tourist season and sprinkle the main roads. The dust will pick up once we're out of town, unfortunately. Hassett Knoll is quite tiny and has no funds for such extravagances. While it's no tourist destination, it's quite charming in its own way. I've taken many photographs of the area." She motioned toward the leather camera case at her feet.

"Ah, you dabble in photography," David said.

The lady snorted. "I do more than *dabble*. It is our bread and butter." At David's confused expression, she added, "I'm a postcard photographer, you see."

"How interesting!" Concordia exclaimed. "Have you been doing it very long?"

"Only the past two seasons. The shops in East Hampton, Bridgehampton, and Sag Harbor sell my postcards. I hope to get them into more of the shops along the railroad line."

"I should like to see your pictures," Concordia said.

"Stop by and visit us sometime. It's a short walk from the Dunwick property. I'll make you a cup of tea and show you my work."

"That would be lovely," Concordia said.

After setting down the Misses Ambrose at the crossroad of what looked to be an overgrown sheep track barely wide enough for a wheelbarrow, the carriage continued on to the Dunwick cottage.

A cooling shore breeze stirred the hair clinging to Concordia's neck and rippled the expanse of salt hay in the distance. She took a deep breath. "This is just what I needed."

David grinned and put an arm around her waist. "I knew it would be."

The road inclined as the carriage followed the split rail fence along its border, softened by a vigorous growth of wildflowers. It wasn't until they passed under a boxwood *parterre* that they had their first good look at the two-story, shingle-style house. The term *cottage* certainly did not seem apt, Concordia reflected, taking in the length of the structure—it appeared to be two houses pushed together—as their vehicle stopped along the graveled *porte-cochère*.

"Concordia!" Charlotte Crandall burst through a side door, running to hug her.

Concordia returned the embrace. "It's good to see you, dear. Did we interrupt you in the kitchen? I didn't know you cooked."

Charlotte laughed. "Not really, but I wanted to help our cook make your favorite pastry—"

"Lemon tarts!" Concordia exclaimed.

Charlotte nodded. "They're nearly ready. We'll have them with our tea. But first, let's get you settled and give you a chance to freshen up."

As the breezes had disarranged her hair and bonnet considerably, Concordia welcomed the chance to put things to rights. They followed Charlotte inside.

"I hope you don't mind a suite in the main house for a night or two," Charlotte said. "All of the cabins are still being aired out. They've been shut up since last October."

"That's fine," David said, "but aren't you expecting other guests?"

"They won't be coming until Friday," Charlotte said.

He nodded. "It's quite generous of you and your family to go to such trouble for us."

"After what you both had done for me last year, and for Randolph, it's the least we could do." Charlotte's eyes misted, and she gave a sniff as she flung open the bedroom door. "I'll leave you now. Come down whenever you're ready. We'll have tea in the parlor when Aunt Susan comes back from her walk."

But Lady Dunwick had not returned by the time David and Concordia came downstairs, and Charlotte was nowhere in sight. Concordia poked her head through a number of doorways until she found the library. "We may as well wait in here."

David's eyes brightened as he headed for the writing desk,

neatly stacked with newspapers. "Excellent idea. I can catch up on the local doings." He pulled out his spectacles and settled in to read as Concordia perused the shelves.

After a few minutes, she realized that he had stopped folding back pages and was frowning down at one item in particular. "What is it?" She leaned over his shoulder to read.

At first, he reflexively folded the paper shut, then sighed and spread open the second page of the *Suffolk County News.*

Island News Notes

The Reverend Isaiah Claymore has just returned from looking over the Tanner farm in Bridgehampton, with an eye to building an Episcopal church there.

The Jericho Turnpike has been macadamized from East Meadow to the Suffolk County line.

The largest sturgeon of the season thus far was caught by Captain Decker and Ike Hardwin, opposite East Moriches. It weighed four hundred and eleven pounds.

Concordia cocked her head at David. "What am I looking at, besides accounts of road paving and local fauna?"

He pointed farther down the column, and her eyes widened.

Sir Anthony and Lady Dunwick will be hosting Mr. Edgar Wynderhane, Wall Street investment broker for Wynderhane, Gemmer, and Miles, along with other guests at their summer cottage in Hassett Knoll.

"Wynderhane," she breathed. "*He* is staying here?" So much for getting away from this mess.

"Though it appears the event is less noteworthy than a record-breaking fish catch," David said lightly.

"I don't find this funny," Concordia snapped, pacing the room. "What are we going to do?"

"Do? Why, nothing."

"What? How can we do *nothing*?"

"Concordia. Sit down, please. We must approach this calmly."

She collapsed upon the settee. "I know. But we're talking about the man who may have murdered Miss Lester."

"I highly doubt that," he said quietly. "Certainly, he was instrumental in involving her in a sordid scheme that set in motion an unfortunate chain of events, but you know as well as I that he cannot be the man she overheard."

"What do you mean—oh!"

Yes, of course.

Wynderhane would have known the telephone line at the stockbrokers club was being monitored, since he was the one who paid Miss Lester to do so. He would never have made such a damning confession on that particular telephone.

David nodded as he watched his wife's brow clear. "So you agree with me. We say nothing of the matter."

She grimaced. "Shouldn't Sir Anthony and Lady Dunwick know what sort of man they are hosting under their roof?"

"It would be unfair to put them in such an awkward position. Sir Anthony is undoubtedly Wynderhane's client—you remember he told us at the concert that he had invited his broker, along with the firm's partners and families, to stay at the cottage? Wynderhane must be who he meant. What would you have the Dunwicks do, refuse their guests admittance and send them back by return train to New York City?"

Concordia sighed. "I suppose not."

"Besides, Sir Anthony is a man of the world. I would imagine he has few illusions about the scruples of Wall Street stockbrokers."

But Rusty's plea weighed heavily on her mind. She bit her lip as she thought. She and Wynderhane would be under the same roof. She should take advantage of the opportunity. "What if I spoke to him in confidence and told him what happened to Victoria? He might have information that would help the police find the man."

David was shaking his head emphatically. "No, Concordia." He held her gaze. "Please. Leave it be."

The maid walked in at that moment and gave a quick curtsy. "Mr. and Mrs. Bradley? Lady Dunwick and Miss Charlotte are waiting for you in the parlor."

The parlor was papered in a delicate striped pattern of cream and seafoam blue, the colors picked up in the candle tapers and in a eyelet throw on the gold settee. Sitting atop the polished black piano was a bowl filled with white roses that fragranced the room.

"How delightful to see you again, my dears!" The petite-figured Lady Dunwick, dressed in a light summer frock of paisley foulard, rose as they entered. She reached for Concordia's hands and held them warmly, with surprising, bony-knobbed strength for a woman of advanced age. "Come, sit down beside me, and tell me all about your trip so far. Charlotte says she saw you at the Gillette play. Did you have the chance to attend other entertainments? There is so much to do in the city."

Concordia met David's eye and suppressed a sigh. She knew he wanted her to omit any mention of Victoria Lester's death. As the tea was poured and passed around, she proceeded with an edited account of their time in the city.

Lady Dunwick plucked a sugar cube from the bowl. "I fear you will find the amusements here more subdued in nature."

"We would appreciate a more subdued vacation, believe me," David said.

Concordia shot him a quick look, unclenching her hands when she noticed Charlotte glancing her way.

"Aunt Susan," Charlotte said, "you are forgetting about the East

Hampton fair." She nodded toward the Bradleys. "It is quite the local event."

Lady Dunwick grimaced. "That was why I was late for tea. One of the village ladies cornered me on the path." She sighed. "You are now looking at the new chairwoman of the rummage sale."

Charlotte laughed. "And you thought you had escaped it this year! Wasn't Mrs. Anderson to be in charge?"

"Her daughter's baby was born ahead of schedule. She has already left for Richmond to be with them." Noting David's perplexed expression, she explained, "Every year, the Ladies' Village Improvement Society organizes an all-day fair—which includes a rummage sale and an assortment of food, craft, and activity booths—to raise money for civic projects such as street lights and road improvements."

He nodded. "Miss Ambrose mentioned the water cart, to reduce the dust in the roads."

"Ah, you've met Miss Ambrose!" Lady Dunwick said. "A rather...unconventional woman."

"I like her," Charlotte said.

Concordia nodded. The lady had an appealing, forthright air about her.

Lady Dunwick smiled indulgently at her niece. "You would. Although I'll admit, the woman is doing the best she can, under the circumstances. She hasn't had an easy time of it."

"Oh?" Concordia asked, as David passed her a slice of lemon tart. "Are you able to tell us about it?"

"It's a widely known story," Lady Dunwick said. "Gwendolyn Ambrose's family owned much of the land in these parts for generations, and at one point, the entirety of Hassett Knoll village. Made their fortune in the menhaden fishing industry. Built this house for one of the sons—Gwendolyn's father—about thirty years ago."

David leaned forward. "What happened?"

47

"A string of poor luck," Lady Dunwick said. "A hurricane destroyed their boats, and the insurance policy had lapsed. As they struggled to get back up and running, competitors had gained ground and undercut them. The family sold off buildings and parcels of land, this one to us about five years ago. All that's left of the Ambrose holdings now is the bayfront property adjacent to us. It is prime real estate, but Miss Ambrose won't part with it. Not that I blame her. The property and her twelve-year-old niece are all she has left of their family."

Concordia started. "What happened to her other relations?"

"Fire," Charlotte said, her voice subdued.

"Nearly four years ago," Lady Dunwick said. "You can't see the burned-out ruins of the former house until you're farther along the path. She never had it torn down. She and the girl live in a small cottage within sight of it."

"All of the family died? How many?"

"Eight in all, including Susie's parents. Only Gwendolyn and Susie escaped." Charlotte bit her lip. "The locals think the girl started it, as everyone slept."

Concordia felt a chill. "Deliberately?"

Lady Dunwick spread her hands in helplessness. "No one is saying that. But the girl is…well, I suppose feeble-minded would be the compassionate term to use. She has never been right in the head."

"I had no idea," Concordia said. "She never spoke a word, only clung to her aunt. I thought she was simply shy."

"Well, I for one do not consider her a threat to a single soul," Lady Dunwick said briskly. "It was a tragic accident, and by all accounts, Miss Ambrose is taking good care of her niece."

"And we try to help them out however we can," Charlotte added. "We buy vegetables and other goods from them, and Uncle Anthony has hired Miss Ambrose as our winter caretaker."

"Really?" David said. "A woman?"

"Indeed, some of the villagers made comments at the time, but it's none of their concern," Charlotte said.

"Do let's speak of happier things," Lady Dunwick said, looking at Concordia closely. "I believe we are depressing your spirits with such talk, my dear."

Despite feeling that very thing, Concordia was about to protest that she was fine when the maid came in with a slip of paper. "Excuse me, my lady, but this telegram just came for Mrs. Bradley."

Lady Dunwick gave a nod, and the maid handed it to Concordia.

Concordia tore it open and quickly glanced at it.

REGRET THAT I AM UNABLE TO HELP. OCCUPIED IN
S.F. WILL WRITE MORE LATER.
~PENELOPE

She swallowed her disappointment. Now what? "Thank you," she said to the maid, who gave a quick curtsy and left.

"Nothing troubling, I hope," Lady Dunwick said.

"Just news from an old friend." She shoved the telegram in her pocket and stood. David, who had been watching her closely, sprang to his feet as well.

"Would you excuse me, Lady Dunwick? I'm feeling a bit...tired. I believe I shall lie down."

Lady Dunwick's brows creased in concern. "Not at all, my dear."

Concordia showed David the telegram when they reached their rooms. "I'd hoped she could look into the matter, for Rusty's sake." She struggled to maintain her composure, but David bundled her into his arms.

"My dear, you have done all that you could," he consoled. "We cannot fix all the troubles of this world. I know it's hard to let this go, but it is best to step back now. The police have the investigation in hand. They will learn the truth."

She dried her eyes with the handkerchief he passed her. She wasn't at all confident of Lieutenant Oliver's line of inquiry, but what could she do?

"You should write to Rusty," he said, "and let him know Miss Hamilton's answer."

She nodded. "I will. But first, I'd like to take a walk and clear my head."

He smiled. "I have textbook reading to catch up on, so I shall leave you to your solitude."

After a tour of the grounds to admire the rose garden and lily pond, Concordia took the path that ran parallel to the shoreline beyond the dunes, passing several of the cabins belonging to the Dunwicks. A workman repairing a window ledge tipped his cap politely as she passed, but she was absorbed in her thoughts.

Wynderhane will be here. Despite David's objection, she fully intended to approach him for information. Perhaps she could appeal to his sense of honor—at least, she hoped he had *some* sense of honor—of righting a wrong and bringing a murderer to light. There could be no harm in making the attempt. Even if she were unsuccessful, she would know she had done all she could.

Concordia paid little heed to where she was going until she passed a stand of elms and came upon a hulking, blackened skeleton of a structure ahead. She must be on the Ambrose property. She shivered, her imagination playing out the terrible scene. How could Gwendolyn Ambrose and her niece live within sight of such a horrid memory?

Perhaps the expense of tearing it down and hauling it away was more than they could manage.

The sound of full-throated laughter drifted over a rise in the path. She followed it.

Beyond the rise was a small, three-room cottage. Neatly

trimmed ivy clung to the shingles above the porch and provided shade to the front windows. Bright geraniums bloomed in a cracked pot beside the rain barrel.

Before she had a chance to call out a greeting, a gray kitten scampered through the open door, Susie quick on its heels. "Kitty!" she cried, then stopped short at the sight of Concordia.

"Hello, Susie," Concordia said, as the kitten came up and batted at her skirts.

Gwendolyn Ambrose came through the door next, drying her hands on a dishtowel. "My goodness! Mrs. Bradley, hello!"

Susie ran back to her side.

"It's all right, dear," Miss Ambrose said. "This is Mrs. Bradley. We rode in their carriage today, remember?"

Susie gave a slow nod, her eyes fixed upon the kitten.

Concordia scooped it up and approached the girl. "Would you like it back?"

Without a word, Susie snatched the animal and ran inside.

"I apologize," Miss Ambrose said. "She's not adept at conversation. But it is good to see you. Have you come to look at my pictures? We've already had tea, I'm afraid, but if I can offer you something—"

"No, thank you," Concordia interrupted quickly. "I've had my tea as well. It was quite by accident that I arrived at your doorstep. I was out for a walk. I cannot stay long."

"Well then, you must come back some other time to see the photographs."

Concordia inclined her head toward the cottage. "Are you sure that won't be an inconvenience? I don't wish to distress the child."

"It's not distress, exactly. I think it's more a matter of...confusion." Miss Ambrose hesitated. "Has anyone told you of our situation?"

Concordia nodded. "Lady Dunwick and Charlotte. I hope you don't mind."

"Not at all. It saves me having to do it. And the Dunwicks have been quite kind over the years." She gestured toward the tiny cottage. "This used to be a gardener's shed, can you imagine? After the fire, Sir Anthony sent his workmen and materials over and had it converted into a cozy home for us."

"They are a generous family." Concordia bit her lip. "You may think me terribly forward to presume upon our recent acquaintance, but I wondered about…" Her voice trailed off.

"You wondered about Susie, and what exactly is wrong with her." Miss Ambrose gestured toward a pair of benches that overlooked the path and shoreline. "Come, let us be comfortable."

They sat side by side, facing the view. Concordia waited, watching the breeze ripple the stalks of dune grass upon the land break in the distance.

Miss Ambrose smoothed her apron over her lap. "I wish I could tell you what is wrong with my niece. Even the doctors are perplexed. She seemed normal for the first two years of her life, singing, talking, quick to learn, attentive to the world around her. Then she had a fever, a dangerous one. We thought we would lose her. It lingered for weeks. After that…" She looked down at her hands in her lap.

"Is there no hope of recovery?"

She gave a wry smile. "I will never believe there is 'no hope.' However, it has been ten years."

Concordia nodded. "I was surprised to learn from Lady Dunwick that she is only twelve years old. She is tall for her age."

"People often mistake her for someone older, but they are quickly disabused of that impression when they try to converse with her. She speaks some words and seems to understand when a person talks to her simply and directly. She is quite adept at sketching. I believe it is a means of communication for her. Most of the time, however, she is absorbed in her own world, where I— I cannot reach her." She choked out the last words and took a ragged breath.

Concordia gave her time to compose herself. "She enjoys animals, I see."

Miss Ambrose nodded. "That she does. And she is good with them. We have quite a menagerie in the backyard: chickens, ducks, goats, several fat, lazy cats, a new litter of kittens, and even a hedgehog she nursed back to health in the spring. I console myself with the knowledge that she is happy."

"Then you have done well."

"But what of the future? What will become of her when I am gone? I am twenty years older."

Concordia bit her lip. There seemed no good answer to that.

The lady gave a remorseful laugh. "I'm sorry, Mrs. Bradley. You are bearing the brunt of my solitude. The first chance I have for a sympathetic woman's ear, and I go on and on." She nodded toward the long slant of light coming across the sparkling waters of the bay. "It is getting late. They will be wondering about you."

Concordia got up and clasped the lady's hand. "It was a pleasure seeing you again, Miss Ambrose."

The lady smiled. "Please, call me Gwen."

"Then you must call me Concordia."

"Ah, you were named after the Roman goddess of harmony?"

Concordia nodded. "My father's idea. He was a scholar of classical Greek and Latin texts."

"Excellent. Well, then, Concordia, be sure to stop by whenever you wish, for tea and a perusal of my photographs."

Concordia gave a little wave and turned down the path. This time, she did not slow as she passed the blackened house.

She found David ensconced on the screened porch, notes and books scattered happily about, extinguished pipe clenched between his teeth as he frowned over the book in his lap. She withdrew before he could become aware of her and headed to the library to compose her letter to Rusty.

The house was quiet, which would change, of course, when Sir Anthony and his other guests arrived at the end of the week. The library itself had a special sort of hush to it, the result of the wood paneling, deep Turkish carpet, and the long drapes closed against the late-afternoon sun. She pulled them open a bit before drawing out a sheet of stationery and a pen from the writing desk.

Dear Rusty,

I'm writing to inform you of Miss Hamilton's answer to my telegram. Regrettably, she is unavailable to take on the case. Please know that I share your disappointment.

I hope by the time you receive this that the police have made progress in the investigation, and that you have begun to recover from the dreadful fire that devastated your shop. Recovering from the loss of your granddaughter is another thing entirely, I know. Please accept my deepest condolences once again.

Concordia hesitated, tapping the end of the pen against her cheek as she considered what to say next. She wanted to offer something in the way of assistance, so Rusty knew she had not abandoned him...

Yes, that was it. She could tell him about Wynderhane.

As you know, we are staying with the Dunwicks in East Hampton. I've learned that Sir Anthony has invited Edgar Wynderhane and his family to stay at the cottage as well. I have resolved to speak with him privately about the arrangement he had with Victoria and ask him what he may be able to conjecture about the man responsible for her death. If he was at the club that day, he may even remember who used the telephone.

I do not wish to hold out false hope, but I wanted you to know I am doing everything in my power to help, even from this distance. The arrival of Wynderhane on my very doorstep, so to speak, is an opportunity I will not neglect.

Yours,

Concordia Bradley

She re-read it twice, then folded it up in an envelope, sealed and addressed it, and put it in the stack of envelopes to be mailed.

She felt better for having a plan of action. With a lighter heart, she went back to the porch to retrieve David and dress for dinner.

~

Over the next two days, Concordia and David gave themselves over completely to enjoying their holiday. They sun-bathed and picnicked along the bay, rode bicycles with Charlotte, and picked raspberries in a thicket beyond the pond.

On Friday morning—Sir Anthony and the remaining guests were due that afternoon—Lady Dunwick proposed a shopping excursion to Hassett Knoll while the staff moved Concordia's and David's belongings to the cabin. "By the time we've returned," she said, "all should be ready for you at Crosswinds."

"Crosswinds?" Concordia asked.

Lady Dunwick nodded. "That's how we keep them straight. Each of the four cabins has a name."

Concordia smiled to herself, wondering what it was like to have so many holdings on one's property that it was difficult to keep track of them all.

"I look forward to getting a taste of local life," David said.

"Hassett Knoll is nowhere near as grand as East Hampton," Lady Dunwick explained, "but it has its own charm, nevertheless. I want a word with the baker about supplying some of her specialties. Her pastries are light as a feather. It will also ease Marie's workload."

While Lady Dunwick took care of her errand, Concordia and David explored the well-trafficked main street of the village, passing a general store, a vegetable stall, a blacksmithy, and a butcher's shop. Some sported welcoming wood porches and rockers, which local patrons took advantage of, rocking and chatting amiably. Nearby window boxes spilled over with blooming flowers.

"What a lovely little town," Concordia said.

He pointed to a brightly striped awning on the corner. "Look, there's a café. Let's go in. I'm starving."

"You're always hungry," Concordia teased. "But I could do with a glass of lemonade. It's getting hot." As Hassett Knoll had no water truck for its streets, the dust kicked up by the road traffic was palpable. It seemed to lodge in the back of one's throat.

The bell dinged as they entered the shaded space. A buxom woman in a gaudy floral apron stepped around from the tiled counter. "Welcome. What can I get you?"

"Two lemonades, and"—David glanced at the chalkboard propped on the counter— "a chicken salad sandwich, please." He turned to Concordia. "You're sure you don't want any food?"

She shook her head with a smile. She had no appetite in this heat.

"The lemonade will be a few minutes," the woman said. "I was just about to make a fresh batch. You're welcome to sit, or"—she gestured to the left end of the shop—"browse our souvenir art tables. One-of-a-kind items for sale, all by local craftsmen. We have a thriving art colony, you know. No mass-produced curios here."

They headed over to peruse the offerings. Ceramics, wood carvings, wire sculptures, paintings, and watercolors of every size and configuration littered the tables. Any attempt at order had collapsed some time ago.

Except for one smartly ordered display in the far corner of the room, where David now lingered. *Captain Decker's Wooden Decoys*, the hand-painted sign proclaimed.

Decoys? What could possibly capture his attention there? Concordia went over to look. Atop a smooth, blue tablecloth sat four rows of wooden duck decoys, lined up neatly, beak to tail, from smallest to largest. It resembled a veritable duck army. Or more aptly, a navy.

David picked up a decoy that resembled a mallard, turning it over in his hands. "Look at the workmanship, Concordia. So smooth. The wood positively glows. And notice the delicate curve of the neck, the detailed painting of the feathers?"

She realized her mouth was hanging open. "Umm, yes. Very nice."

He set that one aside and picked up a smaller one of reddish-brown, painted with gray speckled feathers.

Not knowing her duck species all that well, she couldn't even guess at what this one was supposed to be. "Since when have you taken such an interest in decoys?"

He grinned. "I carved a number of them as a boy. Never with such skill, of course. My brother and I used to set them afloat in the fountain at city hall square. These bring back happy memories." He hefted them both in his hands and carried them over to the counter, where their hostess had just set out a pitcher of lemonade and glasses on a tray.

The woman's eyes brightened. "You've found something you like, I see."

David nodded and turned to his wife. "And I know exactly where they will go in our new home."

Concordia held her breath. *Please, not in the parlor.*

"On the mantel in my study," he went on.

She blew out a relieved sigh.

He stroked the beak of the larger decoy. "An ideal spot, don't you think?"

Behind him, the shopkeeper bit her lip to keep from laughing. Concordia shot her a look before giving her husband a half smile. "Words fail me, dear."

"I should like to meet Captain Decker sometime," he said. "In fact, I have a project in mind I would like to start on. Perhaps he can give me a few pointers."

The woman nodded. "He comes in most ev'ry day, around three o'clock. Likes to keep his display tidy, see if any o' them have sold. He'll be right happy to discover someone has bought *two*! I'm sure he'd be glad to help." She carefully wrapped his purchase in old newspaper.

That reminded Concordia of something. "Captain Decker... was he the one who caught the sturgeon that we read about in the paper?"

The lady puffed up proudly. "Indeed it was, along with my boy, Ike."

Concordia smiled.

Lady Dunwick came into the café, cheeks flushed, hat slightly askew. "Ah, I thought you would be here."

David reached for the twine-tied boxes that threatened to slip out of Lady Dunwick's arms. "Allow me."

"Thank you, dear." She righted her hat and dabbed at her neck with a handkerchief. "Rosie, another glass, please."

The three of them sat and sipped their lemonade—David devouring his sandwich in no time—and watched the street traffic: pedestrians, bicyclists, farm carts, and a carriage or two. "This really is a nice little town," Concordia said.

Lady Dunwick set down her glass. "East Hampton tends to divert the tourist traffic, but there's plenty of opportunity here, if the village would invest in a hotel, some more shops, and expand the public dock. On the other hand"—she winked—"there is the advantage of us having the area to ourselves, without tripping over tourists at every turn. A purely selfish consideration, of course." She gestured to David's bundle. "I see you've done some shopping. Did you notice Miss Ambrose's work for sale?"

"I must have missed that," Concordia said, blaming the ducks. "Postcards?"

"No, the general store sells those for her. I mean her original watercolors and pen-and-ink sketches. She's quite talented."

Concordia excused herself and went back to the souvenir tables. She found them at last, behind the gaudy sunsets of another artist.

Miss Ambrose's muted watercolors, mounted simply on

eggshell mattes, depicted the usual local subjects: umbrella-dotted beach scenes, sailboats on the bay, and sweeping ocean vistas. However, there was nothing typical about their execution. There was a slightly unfocused quality that soothed the eye as one was drawn to the subject's focal point. Concordia set aside three that would look lovely in the parlor of their new home, including a delicate watercolor of what was labeled *Hassett Pond Windmill*.

As she replaced the others, she came upon a stark charcoal sketch mounted on cheap cardboard, this one signed in clumsy letters *S. Ambrose*. Susie?

The sketch was of a stubbled clearing that trailed wisps of fog or smoke. A black huddle in the distance was undoubtedly the burned-down Ambrose mansion. Though skillfully done, it was a stark, disturbing composition. Why would Gwen Ambrose submit such a piece for sale? Had she done it to please Susie? Who would buy it?

Concordia shivered and put it back.

CHAPTER 6

*C*oncordia and David were sitting out on the front porch of their Crosswinds cabin shortly before tea-time when Sir Anthony and the remaining guests arrived. At the moment, David was softly dozing in the rattan rocker, a rough block of wood in his lap and a scattering of wood shavings at his feet. Concordia smiled to herself as she sifted through the bowl of shells she'd gathered for her nieces. He'd wasted no time borrowing the materials he needed to start on his "project," which she assumed would be a duck decoy to join the ones he'd purchased. *Mercy*, they'd have an entire fleet of them at this rate.

The sounds of carriage wheels on the gravel drive in the distance and the chatter of voices roused him. "Huh?" He turned and gave her a sheepish smile. "Sorry to fall asleep. It is not the company, I assure you."

She laughed. "I think it has more to do with the sun and salt air."

He set aside the wood, brushed off his trousers, and pulled out his pocket watch. "They made good time. Shall we go greet everyone?"

She cocked her head. "By the sound of it, there are quite a

number of them. There's bound to be a jumble of valises and people milling about, not knowing where to go next." A high-pitched wail followed. "And crying infants," she added, wincing. "Why don't we wait until the hubbub has died down a bit? We'll have a chance to meet them at tea."

He stood and stretched. "I suppose. I'm quite anxious to meet these brokers and pick up a tip or two."

She kept her head bent over her task of brushing off sand from the shells. Perhaps if he didn't bring up Wynderhane, she could avoid lying to him about her plans.

"Are you all right?" he asked. "With Wynderhane being among the guests, I wondered..." His voice trailed off.

Drat. Well, there was no help for it. She met his eye. "I'm fine."

He raised a skeptical brow. "I would have thought you'd be angry about his presence here, but you act as if—" He hesitated. "You intend to speak with him about Miss Lester, don't you?"

"Yes."

"After I expressly told you that I wanted you to let it go?" His voice rose.

She blinked as panic gripped her. Was he really talking to her this way? Was this to be the other side of married life, to be told what to do and what not to do? She knew many women who had found it so but thought that, surely, it would never be that way for her and David.

Mercy, what had she gotten herself into?

She took a calming breath. No need to get carried away with suppositions. She brushed off her hands and stood. "I was not aware that you were *forbidding* me to do so. Are you?"

His eyes widened. "Of course not. I would never do that." He glanced down at his hands. "I'm sorry for raising my voice. It seemed as if you had not considered my wishes in making your decision."

"David, of course your wishes are important to me. I know you are concerned. It is just that—well, when I wrote to Rusty that

Penelope could not take on the investigation, I wanted to offer *something* in the way of help. If Wynderhane has any information of value, I will merely pass it on for Rusty to share with the police. Nothing more. It would be impossible to do more than that, anyway. We are over a hundred miles from the city. But perhaps whatever I can pass along would help."

David's brows lowered in skepticism, but he said nothing.

"When that one small task is taken care of," she went on, "I can feel easy in my mind for the rest of our stay. That is the goal, is it not? To relax?" She looked searchingly into his face.

His expression smoothed. He reached for her waist and drew her close. "Indeed, it is," he murmured in her ear.

Tea was served in the gazebo, and Lady Dunwick did not seem in the least surprised that Concordia and David were late to the gathering, which looked to be entirely ladies. Where were the men?

"Allow me to introduce you." Lady Dunwick inclined her head toward a woman in her early fifties, clad in an unbecoming shade of yellow muslin. "Mrs. Wynderhane, may I present Mr. and Mrs. David Bradley."

The lady nodded politely. "You know Lady Dunwick from Hartford, I presume?"

"Yes," Concordia said. "Her niece Charlotte was a student of mine at Hartford Women's College."

Mrs. Wynderhane's eyes widened. "You are a...a *teacher*? But you are a married woman."

David stepped closer. "*Recently* married."

Mrs. Wynderhane gave a satisfied grunt as she reached toward the tea tray and shifted the sugar bowl so that it aligned with the cake plate. "Ah, I see."

Concordia resisted the impulse to explain that she was still employed at the school, though perhaps the less said about that the better. President Langdon was on shaky ground when it came to keeping her on.

"You met at the school, then?" the lady asked.

David gave his wife a wide smile. "Indeed, we did."

Concordia knew he was recalling that first day, when she had run him down—well, *nearly* run him down, he'd dodged just in time—with her bicycle. She wrinkled her nose at him, and he winked. The less said about that the better, as well.

Lady Dunwick continued, introducing Mrs. Gemmer, the wife of one of Wynderhane's business partners, a stout, heavily-corseted lady of indeterminate age with dark, snapping eyes. Next was Mrs. Eleanor Reese, grandmother of Wynderhane's business secretary, James Reese, a rounded woman with fluffy salt-and-pepper hair piled high and a ready smile as she nodded and resumed her knitting.

Charlotte was chatting with a uniformed young woman beside her, who was occupied with bouncing an infant on her knee while wiping raspberry jam from the face of a white-frocked, five-year-old girl.

Charlotte looked up as David and Concordia took seats across from them. "I was wondering where you two were! This is Miss Farraday, the Gemmers' nurse."

The woman was quite pretty, with a broad, intelligent fore-head atop a heart-shaped face, wide gray eyes, and blond hair peeking out from beneath her cap.

"Pleased to meet you, Miss Farraday," Concordia said.

She gave a quick nod of greeting before returning to her charges.

"Will the gentlemen be joining us?" David asked, accepting cup and saucer from the maid.

Mrs. Wynderhane shrugged. "They have gone to the dock to inspect Sir Anthony's new sailboat, so who knows?" She fussed with the tea service again, this time straightening the sugar tongs on the dish.

"Sailboat? I don't remember a sailboat," David said.

"It was just delivered this morning," Lady Dunwick explained, eyeing Mrs. Wynderhane's rearrangement.

Mrs. Wynderhane finally sat back with a sigh. "Another toy for my husband to covet." She glanced across at Lady Dunwick. "Edgar has long extolled the virtues of a malaria-free summer residence, replete with bracing ocean breezes. Ever since Sir Anthony invited us to your summer house, he has been keen to buy property in the area."

Mrs. Gemmer nodded. "He spoke of little else on the way here."

"Do you know of anything for sale?" Mrs. Wynderhane asked.

Lady Dunwick took a sip of her tea before answering. "Not around these parts, although I hear property in the Montauk area is selling fast, now that the railroad has extended out there."

"Oh, that would not be nearly as convenient as here." Mrs. Wynderhane smiled. "We wish to be close to you."

Was that a grimace Lady Dunwick hid behind her cup? Concordia couldn't tell. Perhaps she feared Mrs. Wynderhane would rearrange all of her kitchen cupboards if she lived any closer.

Mrs. Reese roused herself from plying her needles and gestured along the coastline to their right. "Who owns that area? It looks quite wild and neglected. No one can be living there, surely. Perhaps an absentee owner who would wish to sell."

Concordia grimaced. The Ambroses' tidy little cottage, vegetable garden, and animal pens were out of sight of both the road and the Dunwick holdings. From this perspective, the property did look overgrown. Obviously Miss Ambrose, occupied as Susie's caretaker and the sole breadwinner of the family, had not the time or the means to care for the rest of her land.

Charlotte exchanged a quick glance with Lady Dunwick. "The owner is not selling."

Mrs. Wynderhane laughed and waved a be-ringed hand. "Oh, my dear, everything has its price. Perhaps Edgar could have a word with the gentleman. Do you know how to contact him?"

They were spared a reply by the arrival of Sir Anthony, accompanied by five other gentlemen. After a quick bow to the ladies, one of the younger men in his mid-twenties pulled up a wicker hassock to sit beside Eleanor Reese. Likely her grandson James, Concordia thought. His fair hair, a bit long at the top, was combed straight back and fell in a part down the middle, which would have given him a younger look if not for the full, pale-brown mustache that extended past his upper lip. The old lady gave him a quick smile before turning her work and beginning the next row.

Sir Anthony made the proper introductions—his brokers Wynderhane and Gemmer, along with their secretaries Reese and Nash, and lastly Pickering, his temporary assistant—but Concordia ignored the rest and focused upon Edgar Wynderhane. He certainly looked the part of an investment broker, or at least what she conceived of one: a brown-haired, balding man of middle years, with a portly stature, pale complexion, and dark eyes that assessed its subject, for good or ill.

She would have to watch for an opportunity to speak with him in private while still observing the rules of propriety. If only David would accompany her, but she knew he was dead-set against the idea to begin with.

As if aware of her gaze, Wynderhane turned to look at her, raising a dark eyebrow in mock inquiry. David nudged her, and she broke eye contact to turn to him.

"Stop staring," he whispered fiercely.

"Sorry," she murmured back. She was beginning to envy Mrs. Reese's knitting occupation.

He reached for the tea tray and passed her a slice of pound cake. "Have some, it's delicious."

She smiled and picked up her fork. It did look quite appetizing.

"Are you pleased with the boat, dear?" Lady Dunwick inquired.

Sir Anthony smiled. "It's a lovely gift, thank you. I hope we can take it out tomorrow, if the weather holds. Some of the fishermen down at the dock think we're in for a shower."

"A gift?" Mrs. Reese raised an eyebrow.

"In celebration of their fortieth anniversary," Charlotte explained, passing a napkin to her uncle.

"Anthony was most generous as well." Lady Dunwick held out a graceful hand, though spotted and knobby with age. Around the wrist was a gold-and-ruby bracelet. Its clear red stones glittered in the light.

"Lovely," Mrs. Wynderhane breathed, leaning in.

Mrs. Reese's eyes clouded in an expression Concordia could not fathom—envy? No. Disapproval, perhaps?—before turning back to the fluffy yellow yarn between her nimble fingers.

Edgar Wynderhane gave the bracelet a passing glance then shook his head at his wife. "We shall have to economize, my dear Maud, and refrain from more baubles if we are to buy a summer home out here."

"Oh, Edgar, that reminds me," Mrs. Wynderhane said, "the lot adjacent to this one"—she waved a vague hand in the direction of the Ambrose path—"looks untenanted. You should see if the gentleman is willing to sell."

Lady Dunwick was quick to intervene. "I doubt she would be willing to sell."

"*She?*" Mrs. Wynderhane repeated. "Ah, a widow then. Even better."

"No, no, not at all," Lady Dunwick began, only to be interrupted by her husband.

"My dear, Miss Ambrose is barely managing. Perhaps a

generous offer by Wynderhane here could be just the opportunity for her and her niece to make a fresh start."

At that moment, a blur of white whizzed past Concordia's knees and upset her teacup in her lap. It was the young Gemmer girl, making good her escape from her nurse.

"Serena, stop this instant!" Miss Farraday commanded, shifting the infant to her hip. With a muttered, "Excuse me," she all but climbed over Concordia and David in order to give chase.

Mrs. Gemmer watched her progeny for a moment as the child flung herself upon the lawn beyond the gazebo and began to roll around on the grass, Miss Farraday reaching for the nearest flailing limb she could grasp. The matron sighed and settled back. "It is *so* difficult to get qualified help these days."

"Quite right, my dear," Hans Gemmer harrumphed. He was a completely bald man with a precise, thin mustache and goatee that quivered in his agitation. "That nursemaid of yours has her nose in a book whenever she gets the chance. She should be folding baby clothes and straightening the nursery when the children are sleeping, not poring over *The Mysteries of Udolpho*."

"True enough, although the children adore her," Mrs. Gemmer said. "It would be more trouble than it's worth to find a replacement. Young ladies these days want to be typists and switchboard girls rather than nannies." She sighed again, this time more dramatically. "Motherhood can be a trial."

Mrs. Wynderhane chuckled, this time fussing with the teapot, turning its handle outward—would the woman never leave anything out of place? "Ah, Marta, I cannot tell you how delightful it is when they are grown and out of one's hair. The chaos in the meantime is quite a strain on the nerves."

Marta Gemmer nodded. "It cannot come soon enough."

"So, we were speaking of Miss Ambrose's property," Wynderhane went on, with barely a glance at the domestic tableau now playing out upon the lawn. "What can you tell me about the lady's situation?"

Concordia stood. "If you will pardon me, I should attend to this." She gestured to the tea stain on her skirt. It was as good an excuse as any to avoid hearing Miss Ambrose's unfortunate life story again, this time with the New York City elite to exclaim over the salacious bits.

"Oh dear," Charlotte said, also getting up. "I'll help you with that."

David started to rise. Concordia put out a hand. "I'll be fine. We'll return shortly."

Charlotte led her around to the door of the kitchen. "A bit of white vinegar and a rinse should take care of it." She looked back over her shoulder, watching the nurse as she set down the baby to toddle in the grass, out of sight of the gazebo's occupants. "Poor Miss Farraday. She has her hands full."

Concordia watched as Miss Farraday smiled and accepted a dandelion flower that Serena had plucked from the grass. She hoped the nursemaid would continue to find any chance to read that she could, no matter what her employer might think.

Once the stain was removed and the skirt blotted dry, Concordia and Charlotte wandered over to the porch swing rather than return to the gazebo. Concordia was quiet for a while, watching the afternoon sun play out upon the fields in the distance.

"Is something bothering you, Concordia?"

"I am concerned about the Ambroses. Especially now that the Wynderhanes seem fixed upon the idea of buying their property." She turned to Charlotte. "I visited her cottage, you see."

"Oh? When was this?"

"The first afternoon we were here. I was idly following the path and came upon them quite by accident."

Charlotte nodded. "They are making the best of things, but it isn't easy. I wish she would tear down that burnt wreck of a house. It must cast a pall over everything."

"That would be quite expensive, would it not?"

"But people are beginning to talk. She is getting a reputation as an eccentric recluse."

"That hardly seems fair," Concordia protested.

Charlotte shrugged. "Fair or not, it's true."

"What about the Wynderhanes? How much pressure do you think they will exert to get her to sell?"

Charlotte brushed away a leaf that had settled on her skirt. "Gwen is a strong-minded woman. I'm sure she will have no difficulty turning down any offer Wynderhane makes. Unless she *wants* to leave, of course."

"Susie seems happy here," Concordia said. "I cannot imagine Miss Ambrose uprooting her niece. I do wish there was some way we could help."

"Why don't we go see her tomorrow? We can at least give her advanced warning about Mr. Wynderhane." Charlotte jumped up and reached for Concordia's hand. "But for now, I see they are setting up for croquet. Let us forget about other people's troubles for a while, shall we?"

There was something to be said for the welcome distraction of whacking a wooden ball across an open lawn. David gazed on in mock despair as Concordia sent his ball rolling clear off the course, where Serena Gemmer proceeded to knock it about with her child-sized mallet.

As the sea breeze ruffled her hair and cooled her neck, Concordia felt the pleasant vigor of fresh air and exercise.

Daniel Pickering, Sir Anthony's secretary on loan from his duties at the brokerage, had been paired up with Charlotte. He was an agreeable-looking fellow, tall and lean with fair hair, deep-set hazel eyes, and a high, wide forehead that bespoke intelligence. At the moment, however, the man barely seemed to know which end of the mallet he should be swinging, prompting Charlotte to patiently coach him on more than one occasion. Concordia suspected he wasn't giving it his full attention. He kept glancing over at Reese and Wynderhane, who weren't playing but looking on as they conversed.

For a subordinate, James Reese seemed perfectly at his ease in Wynderhane's company, laughing and joking, with the stockbroker nodding in approval and even smiling. As Concordia turned back to Charlotte and Pickering, she noticed the white-knuckled grip the young man had on the mallet, the clenched jaw and dark look directed toward Reese, so quickly masked Concordia wasn't sure she'd seen it at all.

A quiet giggle drew her attention to Miss Farraday. The nursemaid was enjoying herself, as Gemmer's assistant William Nash good-naturedly held the baby when it was her turn to play. He was certainly a handsome young man, Concordia realized, only now noticing the cleft chin, sharp jaw, and dark hair, a shock of it falling into his eyes occasionally, which he would brush back in a careless gesture. He exchanged a warm, lingering look with the blushing nursemaid.

Ho-ho, Concordia thought. Mrs. Gemmer wouldn't like that at all.

CHAPTER 7

*C*oncordia had no opportunity to speak with Mr. Wynderhane after dinner that evening, as the gentlemen, David included, retired to the billiard room with their cigars and brandy snifters. After an hour or so of cards and coffee with the ladies, Concordia pleaded fatigue and made her way back to their cabin. She stirred briefly when David, still smelling faintly of tobacco, returned and snuggled beside her. She smiled in the dark.

After breakfast, David returned to his textbooks. Concordia and Charlotte packed a small basket of sweets for Susie—honey sticks, lemon drops, and macaroons that Concordia had bought in town—and set out for the Ambrose place.

"We may be too early," Charlotte warned. "Gwen often goes out with her equipment to catch the morning light."

Concordia glanced at the clouds banking near the shoreline. "I suspect the sunlight won't last. The fishermen were right—it looks like rain. That's a shame. David was looking forward to going out on Sir Anthony's new boat today."

Charlotte waved a dismissive hand. "Plenty of time for that, I'm sure. You two will be staying until the end of July, you said?"

Concordia nodded. "If you'll have us that long."

Charlotte shifted her basket and linked an arm through Concordia's. "It is quite self-serving of me, actually. I have been recruited along with Aunt Susan to help with the fair. I am to be in charge of the posy booth. I was hoping you would help."

"Of course. What is it you need me to do?"

They approached the fork in the path. One branch extended past the main house toward the cabins. The other hugged the coastline dunes and led to the Ambrose property. Eleanor Reese stood upon the dune, a satchel at her feet, taking in the view of the harbor. At that moment, a stiff breeze came up and blew the bonnet clean off her head.

"Mrs. Reese, hello!" Charlotte said, bending to retrieve it. "If you wish to sunbathe, I can ask the staff to bring you a blanket and other items for your comfort."

The lady laughed and reworked the pins in her bonnet. "Oh, I am much too old for such pursuits, dear. Thank you all the same." Her sweeping gesture took in the shore, the boats bobbing upon the deepening gray of the water and the gulls swooping overhead. "As a confirmed city-dweller, sights such as these don't come my way all that often. I decided to bring out my knitting and take in the view before the rain." She rubbed her elbow and winced. "I can always feel when that's coming." She nodded toward the basket over Charlotte's arm. "Isn't it a bit early for a picnic, dear?"

"We're heading to see Miss Ambrose and her niece," Concordia explained. "We're bringing treats for the child."

"Ah! Would you mind some company? I could do with a bit of a walk."

Concordia stifled a smile. She doubted it was a walk the woman wanted, but rather a chance to satisfy her curiosity about the Ambroses after hearing their story. Still, Mrs. Reese seemed a pleasant enough sort. She didn't look down her nose at everyone the way the Wynderhanes and Gemmers did. Concordia read no malicious curiosity in her aspect.

"I suppose that would be all right," Charlotte said hesitantly. "We're not even sure if they are home. We may have to return later."

"Fine, it's settled, then," Mrs. Reese said, picking up her bag. With Concordia's help, she scrambled back down the dune to the path and brushed the sand from her skirts. "Ready."

When they came within sight of the burnt house, Mrs. Reese let out a soft exclamation and stopped. "Lordy. It's a miracle any of them made it out alive." She shook her head. "Poor lambs."

As they approached the cottage, they met Gwendolyn Ambrose, tripod and camera in tow, coming down the other end of the path. She stopped short with a frown. "Hello. Is there something I can do for you, ladies?"

Charlotte introduced Mrs. Reese. "I hope you don't mind us coming unannounced. Concordia and I wanted to speak with you about something, and Mrs. Reese came along for the company."

Miss Ambrose shook her head. "Not at all, though I won't introduce you to Susie just now, if you don't mind, Mrs. Reese. She had a difficult time of it last night. Best to leave her in the backyard with her animals." She gestured toward the Adirondack chairs grouped beneath a large elm. "Please, make yourselves comfortable while I put things away."

She returned a short time later, bearing a tray with a pitcher of iced tea and glasses. When they had helped themselves, she sat back in a chair. "Now then, what did you want to talk about?"

Mrs. Reese fished out her knitting as Charlotte explained the conversation in the gazebo about the Wynderhanes' interest in buying her property.

Miss Ambrose's frown deepened. "So, all of the guests know our sad story." She gave Mrs. Reese a sharp look of inquiry, but that lady kept her head bent over her needles, pausing to count her stitches.

"Anyone who comes down this path can extrapolate at least some of it," Charlotte said dryly. "Is it not time to tear down that wreckage, dear? I'm sure there are neighbors willing to pitch in. I could ask my uncle to help with the expense—"

"No," Miss Ambrose cut across. "He does enough, buying eggs and produce from our garden and hiring me in the winter months. This is my business, and I will tend to it when *I* decide."

Charlotte sighed.

"Speaking of produce, I've cut a quantity of rhubarb—the last of the crop before it bolts in the heat. Lady Dunwick says Sir Anthony is quite fond of Marie's rhubarb pie. Would you take it back for me?"

"Yes, of course." Charlotte gestured to the basket at her feet. "And we brought a few treats for Susie."

Miss Ambrose's expression softened. "That was kind, thank you. I'm sure she will enjoy them."

The silence stretched. Mrs. Reese raised her head, as if suddenly aware of the awkwardness and seeking a remedy. She cleared her throat. "You are a photographer, Miss Ambrose?"

Concordia raised an eyebrow. It was an abrupt change of subject, but at least it diverted them.

If Miss Ambrose was equally surprised, she gave no sign. "Do you find that objectionable, Mrs. Reese?"

The old woman shook her head. "Not under the circumstances, although I would advise you to find a husband as soon as you may."

Miss Ambrose's lips twitched as she sipped from her glass.

"My grandson James dabbled in photography when he was younger," Mrs. Reese went on, grimacing. "Oh, the smells!"

Miss Ambrose nodded toward a tall, wooden shed. "I have a separate area for developing the photographs. One must be very careful with the chemicals. Many of them are poisonous. Fortunately, Susie knows not to touch them."

"May we see your photographs?" Concordia asked. "I didn't have a chance during my last visit. Although I have seen your artwork at the café in town. I purchased several of your watercolors. They are quite lovely."

Miss Ambrose flushed a becoming pink. "I am flattered."

"There was one marked S. *Ambrose* as well," Concordia added.

"Is that Susie? She is quite talented for a child her age."

Miss Ambrose started. "So that's what happened to it," she murmured. She stood. "I'll fetch the binders."

After the photographs were brought out and examined, the ladies took their leave. It was fortunate that there were three of them, Concordia reflected, as the vast quantities of eggs, zucchini, and rhubarb, along with jars of raspberry preserves and honey, would have been impossible to carry otherwise. Even Mrs. Reese was pressed into service, stowing several jars in her knitting bag.

"Good thing Miss Ambrose keeps her photographic chemicals separate from her kitchen," Mrs. Reese joked, "or I'd be looking askance at the items from her larder."

As they walked back to the Dunwick cottage, Concordia recalled an earlier topic that Charlotte had raised. "You said you needed my help with the fair?"

Charlotte sidestepped a small garter snake sunning itself on the path. "Aunt Susan will need both of us to help her sort through the rummage sale items, tag them, and make small sewing repairs: a missing button, a dropped hem, and so on. The farm cart is bringing the donations today."

Concordia nodded. "I can help with that."

"Many hands make light work," Mrs. Reese said. "When is this fair?"

"In eight days. I know it seems like a lot of work, but it's great fun," Charlotte said. "They begin with a bicycle parade down Main Street, and then in the afternoon there's a baseball game. This year it's to be Hassett Knoll versus East Hampton. They are expanding the booth offerings to include more activities for the children: a puppet show, ring-toss games, and a petting enclosure.

Then once the fair closes, everyone goes home for supper, changes into their best attire, and attends the country dance at the Maidstone Club."

Concordia wondered when these people took a vacation.

CHAPTER 8

"*H*ere's another that needs buttons," Charlotte said, shaking out a waistcoat and setting it aside.

The cart of donations arrived mid-morning, and Lady Dunwick, Charlotte, and Concordia had already been at the task of sorting and folding for the past couple of hours. And not only clothes had been donated. A set of wood duck decoys, four in all, had been contributed by Captain Decker, whom Concordia had mentally dubbed—though hoped she would never say it aloud —"Captain Decoy."

She combed through Lady Dunwick's sewing basket. "Where are your buttons?"

Lady Dunwick inclined her head toward the dresser. "There's a large tin of them in the top drawer."

As Concordia fetched the button box, Charlotte opened a tissue-paper wrapped parcel. "*Oooh*, how sweet!" She held up a lacy baby's bonnet, booties, and a gown.

In spite of herself, Concordia came over for a closer look. The booties, done up in cream satin and lace cuffs, seemed impossibly tiny. Her heart clenched with a sensation she didn't recognize. *Mercy*, what was so special about small clothes, anyway?

Lady Dunwick nodded. "The pastor's wife promised she would finally go through her old cedar chest for items to donate. That layette must be forty years old. It has held up quite well." Lady Dunwick paused. "Have you any infant clothes in your trousseau?"

Concordia realized she'd been absently stroking the gown and, cheeks flushed, snatched her hand away. Here she was, cooing over something as banal as baby clothes. "Not yet. No doubt my mother has some items from when Mary and I were small."

Lady Dunwick nodded toward the stack of clothes atop the armoire. "Concordia, dear, would you mind bringing that over? Those are Anthony's donations."

As Concordia turned to fetch them, Lady Dunwick tucked the layette under a pillow.

"You're giving these away?" Concordia picked up a gentleman's suit coat and matching trousers of ecru crash linen. "They are quite nice."

Lady Dunwick chuckled. "My husband grew overly fond of Cook's stroganoff last winter. Now he finds he cannot fit into his favorite summer suit. I'd better check the pockets." She held out a hand, and Concordia passed them over. "The man is notorious for stuffing things in there and leaving them behind." A crackle of paper rewarded her efforts, and she triumphantly drew out an envelope. "*Aha*, see?"

She grew quiet as she withdrew the contents from the envelope. All Concordia could see from her angle was a dark-colored, pressed flower and a small slip of paper. She could not make out the single line of writing.

Lady Dunwick hastily tucked it all into a skirt pocket without a word and turned her attention to smoothing and folding the suit. The silence lengthened.

Concordia and Charlotte exchanged a glance.

"Aunt Susan, is something wrong?" Charlotte asked.

"No, no. Not at all." She straightened and surveyed the piles on the bed. "Although I remembered something I must take care of. Would you mind finishing up?"

"Of course," Charlotte answered, "there isn't much left, so—"

Lady Dunwick had already left the room.

"What do you suppose is in the envelope that troubles her?" Concordia asked.

"I rarely see her flustered so." Charlotte bit her lip. "Did that look like a pressed flower enclosed in the envelope?"

Concordia nodded. "Is it significant?"

"Only that I saw something like it this morning, before we left for the Ambrose place," Charlotte said. "I was catching up on my mail. Some of Uncle Anthony's correspondence had become mixed in with mine, but I didn't realize it until I had slit open one of his letters." She hesitated, brows drawn.

"And?" Concordia prompted.

"Enclosed was a single, pressed flower. An iris."

A flower… Was Sir Anthony engaged in an unseemly correspondence with a lady who was not his wife? Concordia hoped not. It didn't seem at all like the man. "Was there a note?"

"There was. I know what you're thinking, but no, it was not a missive of a romantic nature." Charlotte grimaced. "Although he was quite angry to find that I had opened it. He refused to explain. I was scarcely in the position to demand an account. I was in the wrong for violating his privacy, after all."

"What did the note say?" Concordia was barely keeping her impatience in check.

"It said, 'July twenty-second. You have much to answer for.' That's all. No signature."

"Does that date have any meaning for your uncle?"

Charlotte shrugged. "None that he would say. I am not aware of any significance."

"So the envelope your aunt pulled out of his suit just now," Concordia mused aloud, "could have been a similar letter, sent to him—when? Last summer, perhaps?"

"It's possible. But that implies that someone is sending him a pressed flower on a yearly basis. Why?"

Concordia gave Charlotte a steady glance. "I believe your aunt knows." She was willing to bet every decoy in the captain's collection that Lady Dunwick was having an earnest discussion with her husband at this very moment.

～

After a delightful picnic lunch in the gazebo, most of the guests lingered out of doors, taking advantage of the weather before the expected rain.

"Shall we go for a walk down by the shore?" Concordia asked David, as he helped her from the bench.

He grimaced. "Professor Hayden has been waiting for the draft of my symposium speech. I was hoping to finish and send it off by the afternoon post. Sir Anthony said I could work in his study. I will catch up with you later, dear." With a quick clasp of her hand in apology, David headed to the house.

Concordia wandered the grounds, unsure how to occupy herself. A rare sensation after years of teaching lively, irrepressible young ladies. A dip in the water? Too much trouble to clean up and change afterward. The rose garden? Too hot. The shaded koi pond? That might be nice.

As she approached the pond, she realized she wasn't the first to come up with the idea. Hans Gemmer and his secretary already occupied the benches, Gemmer dictating in a flat, droning voice while Nash bent over a stenographer's pad upon his lap and scribbled rapidly. A hunk of dark hair fell across the young man's forehead but did not obscure the clenched jaw. Poor Mr. Nash. Gemmer did not believe in vacations, it seemed.

She slipped away without disturbing them, deciding to borrow a book from the library and read on the back porch swing instead.

As she stepped into the cool hush of the Dunwick library, she realized she wasn't alone here, either. Perusing a low bookcase beside an overstuffed armchair was the nursemaid.

"Hello, Miss Farraday," Concordia called out.

"Oh!" The young lady gave a start and tumbled sideways over the arm of the chair.

Concordia helped extricate her from the cushions. "I beg your pardon. I didn't mean to give you a fright."

Miss Farraday smoothed her apron. "I'm the one who should apologize, Mrs. Bradley. I shouldn't even be here, but I'd hoped to borrow a book while the children were down for their naps. I finished what I brought with me, you see."

Concordia smiled. "I understand perfectly. What did you have in mind? I hear you enjoy the works of Ann Radcliffe."

Miss Farraday raised a surprised eyebrow. "True, but I read more widely than that. I am particularly fond of modern fiction— Verne, Wilde, Kipling, but I didn't imagine Sir Anthony would have any of those. I'd hoped he might at least have a collection of Dickens I could re-read. So far I have only found biographies and legal treatises."

"I'll help you look. I was in search of something to read myself."

As they scanned their hosts' impressive collection of biographies, histories, legal treatises, and classical works, Concordia asked, "Have you considered getting your degree and perhaps teaching someday, Miss Farraday?"

She shook her head. "I'm an orphan without any other means of support. I have always had to work for my living, ma'am. Besides, I'm too old now. That sort of endeavor is better suited to vivacious nineteen-year-olds."

"You'd be surprised," Concordia called over her shoulder, crossing to the other wall of shelves. "Ah! Here we are. An entire set of Dickens, along with Collins and Braddon." Below that was a shelf of periodical magazines—Charlotte's influence, no doubt.

With a quick nod of thanks, Miss Farraday made her choice

—*David Copperfield*—and was about to hurry back to the nursery when she stopped in the doorway and put a finger to her lips. "You won't tell anyone I was here, will you?" she whispered.

Concordia chuckled. "Your secret is safe." And with that, Miss Farraday slipped away.

After settling upon a Braddon novel, she hefted it under her arm and stepped outside.

She was surprised to find the porch occupied. Edgar Wynderhane sat alone on the swing, dressed in a creased, sage-green seersucker jacket, smoking a pipe and staring out at the view. A yellow slip of paper lay crumpled in his lap.

Concordia stopped. Had he heard them talking in the library? She didn't want him reporting back to the Gemmers and getting Miss Farraday in trouble. "I beg your pardon. Am I disturbing you, Mr. Wynderhane?"

The gentleman removed his pipe from between his teeth and looked her up and down. It was a gaze that surveyed its subject, weighing what potential use could be gained. She did not like it at all.

"Mrs.—Bradley, is it not?" He shifted over on the swing. "Please, be comfortable."

Although she had no intention of sitting beside the man, she realized that here was her chance to speak with him alone, even if she had to stand over him the entire time.

She took a breath for courage and set aside her book. "I believe you knew a friend of mine," she began.

"Oh?"

"Her name was Victoria Lester." She watched him carefully. He blinked a bit rapidly but gave no other sign of recognition.

The moment passed. He leaned back in his seat, stretching his legs with a casual air. "*Was?*" he repeated. "Something has happened to your friend?"

"I'll get to that in a moment." Concordia hesitated, tipping her head toward the window to the library that adjoined the porch.

Had she heard a sound? Her imagination, surely. Miss Farraday had left ahead of her, only a couple of minutes ago. "You paid her to eavesdrop on the telephone line at the Stock Exchange Luncheon Club, did you not?" She had little time for anything subtle.

He tried to light his pipe, but his hand quavered. He gave up and set it aside. "I have many sources of information. Only the best service for clients such as Sir Anthony." He seemed to sneer bitterly at his own words.

"I doubt that federal regulators would approve," she retorted.

He raised an irritated eyebrow. "Are *you* going to turn me in, my dear woman?"

"Don't be absurd." Although she hadn't ruled out the possibility that Sir Anthony should be told. But that was a decision for another time. "However, Miss Lester is dead, and you bear some responsibility for that."

He folded his arms across his wide chest in a defensive gesture. "How am *I* to blame?"

"She eavesdropped upon a conversation that got her killed."

Wynderhane hesitated. "This is the first I've heard of it. Sit down please, Mrs. Bradley, and tell me what has happened."

Concordia sat upon the wide railing across from him. A gentleman such as David would have stood and relinquished his seat, rather than allow a woman to find a makeshift perch. Wynderhane's manners left a lot to be desired.

"Miss Lester asked my advice," Concordia said. "She was deeply troubled by a conversation she overheard a few weeks ago. A man placed a telephone call from the Stock Exchange Club and told the woman at the other end of the line that his plan to murder someone had not worked."

Wynderhane sucked in a breath. When he made no comment, she went on. "Although I tried to dissuade Miss Lester from getting involved further, it troubled her so greatly that she did not heed my advice. She must have learned something of import, because she left a most disturbing note for me with the hotel clerk late one night."

"What did it say?"

"It said: 'I am being followed. He mustn't know where I live. Once I have managed to evade him I will go home.' She asked me to meet her there. By the time I saw it, it was too late. She had been attacked during the night, and the building she lived in had been set ablaze." Concordia clenched the railing in an effort to maintain her composure.

Wynderhane was quiet for a long while. "She tried to reach me as well," he said finally.

Concordia raised an eyebrow in surprise. "She did? When was this?"

"Last Friday."

Concordia nodded. The day after their lunch.

"She came to the office while I was out," he went on. "My receptionist thought she was just there to turn in her weekly transcripts. But she said the girl was troubled to learn I wasn't in. She pleaded that I send for her when I returned. Said it was urgent."

"Did you?"

He shook his head. "I didn't return for my messages until Monday. Besides, everyone in my business says it is *urgent*. I was not about to set aside my schedule for a switchboard girl. Although now...I rather wish I had." He closed his eyes. She couldn't tell if he was dozing or thinking.

"Perhaps you can make up for the lapse," she said. "Can you remember back to the afternoon of June twenty-sixth? That was the date of the call. Did you happen to dine at the club that day?"

He opened his eyes, but they seemed unfocused as he retrieved the memory. "Hmm, yes, I was there. It was a Monday. I remember the club being particularly well attended. Several of us used the telephone. It is situated in a booth, for privacy." He looked across the lawn, lost in thought, muttering to himself. Concordia could barely make out the words. "Yes, I think he...but no, that can't be." He roused himself, rubbing his eyes, which Concordia could tell, even from this distance, were reddened. He stood. "I have to consider this further. I do not wish to idly speculate, particularly when so much is at stake."

Concordia shifted, impatient at the delay. "Miss Lester's grandfather is devastated by what happened. I would be grateful for whatever information you could share."

He was silent for a long minute, giving her the same appraising look he had earlier. "How grateful, my dear?" He quickly crossed the distance between them, placing a hand on her shoulder.

Concordia froze. His breath smelled of tobacco and whiskey as he leaned in and reached for her waist.

She shrieked in protest and landed the sharpest kick to his shin that she could manage at close quarters—his yelp confirmed it had hit home—then pushed hard against his chest. As she ducked under his arm to get free, a hair pin caught on his cuff and pulled out, sending her long hair tumbling over her face. *Bother!*

Although she could not see, the next roar of a male voice could only be David's. "Get away from my wife, you vile lout!"

By the time she had swept the hair from her eyes and attempted to restore it to rights, David had grabbed Wynderhane's collar and was shaking him. She watched, mouth open. Here was a David she had never seen.

James Reese, followed closely by Mrs. Reese and Mrs. Wynderhane, burst upon the scene next. "Here, now!" Reese protested, attempting to pry David's grip from the man's collar. "That's enough!"

David abruptly let go, sending Wynderhane off-balance and sprawling to the ground. Turning his back upon the man, David came immediately to Concordia's side, putting an arm around her anger-stiffened shoulders. "Are you all right? Did he hurt you?"

Before she could answer, Mrs. Wynderhane, clutching protectively at her husband's arm, pointed accusingly at her. "My Edgar would never do such a thing! It's this—this college woman, with her radical notions. *She* tried to lure him away! I know your kind," she added, jaw clenched, "you harridans who wear trousers and espouse free love, votes for women, and other evils! You're all alike."

Concordia blinked. While true that she favored women's suffrage and had once worn trousers—it had been an emergency —she certainly didn't espouse those other notions. Free love —*mercy*! From her short time thus far as a married woman, she suspected that one man was enough work for a woman's lifetime. She didn't know whether to laugh or cry.

David tightened his arm around her.

"I'm sure this is all an unfortunate misunderstanding," Wynderhane's secretary said quietly, although he flashed an uneasy glance at his employer, who was smoothing his hair and straightening his collar with as much dignity as he could muster.

Eleanor Reese had been standing out of the way all the while, taking in the scene. She unsuccessfully stifled a snort. "I raised you better than to believe *that*, James." He flushed and looked at his feet.

She turned her back on them both, plucking at Concordia's arm. "Come, my dear. Let us go to the kitchen for a nice cup of tea. We will leave them to sort it out."

David folded his arms as he glared at Wynderhane. "Good idea," he said over his shoulder.

"But—I never—but he—" Concordia protested, as Mrs. Reese led her away. She sighed and gave up. She could do with a cup of tea.

Mrs. Reese guided Concordia to a chair in the cool, stone-floored kitchen. She murmured something to the cook, Marie, who clucked sympathetically as she heated the kettle.

Soon Marie had the steaming cups set in front of them, along with a plate of ginger crisps. "This will fix you right up, ma'am."

"Thank you," Concordia said, reaching for the sugar.

"Don't you worry, now. That one has a roving eye, for sure."

Marie shook her head. "In the house for barely a day, and he's already pinched the parlor maid, who tells me he's been trying to corner the Gemmers' nurse, too." With a sigh, Marie went back to her work.

Concordia sipped her tea, a chamomile blend that soothed her jangled nerves. After a while she glanced at Mrs. Reese, who was watching her closely. "There is one thing I cannot understand. How could his wife defend him so vociferously?" She could not imagine doing that. Of course, David would not behave so.

The old lady shrugged. "Some women do not want to believe what's right before their eyes, especially if it stings their pride. Besides, Wynderhane has given her a good life. She'd be giving up a lot more than a philandering husband if she left him."

Concordia would much prefer a faithful husband to a rich lifestyle, but perhaps not everyone had that choice. After all, how much did a lady really know about the man she was marrying before the fact? The etiquette of courtship was too constrained for much in the way of self-revelation.

David came into the kitchen, his face smoothed back to its usual calm expression, though the muscle twitch in his jaw suggested otherwise. "Are you feeling better?"

She nodded. "We should talk." She got up and turned to Mrs. Reese. "Thank you for keeping me company and suggesting the tea."

"Any time, dear."

Concordia and David didn't exchange a word until they were back at Crosswinds, sitting upon their porch.

"I appreciate you defending me. I regret it was necessary," Concordia said.

His lip quirked. "From my vantage point, you didn't need much in the way of defending. It was probably a kindness to Wynderhane that I intervened. He was still rubbing his leg when I left."

She felt a heathenish twinge of satisfaction at the news but said nothing.

He picked up his block of wood—only with a great deal of imagination did it resemble a decoy at this point—and whittling knife. "Still, I wish you had told me you were going to talk with him. If I had accompanied you, the entire fracas would have been avoided."

Concordia's eyes narrowed. "This was not some meeting with overtones of a secret assignation," she retorted. "Land sakes, I was speaking to the man out on the open porch. Someone could have come along any minute, as you and Mrs. Wynderhane and the Reeses did. I am not to blame."

He kept his gaze upon his work. "I know, dear. It's just that you needlessly place yourself in difficult situations."

Needless? It was all too necessary, although her chance of extracting any more information from Wynderhane was unlikely now. "Since when have you been willing to participate in a conversation with Wynderhane about Miss Lester's death? You were dead set against me bringing it up with him, as I recall."

He was silent for a long minute, his hands stilled in his lap. She held her breath. She did not want another argument. Heavens, this was supposed to be their honeymoon. Did all newly married couples struggle so?

He set aside his task and clasped her hands in his. "You are quite sure he didn't hurt you?"

She nodded. "What happened after Mrs. Reese and I left?"

He sat back against the step and stared out at the hedge beyond their gate. "Wynderhane's secretary settled them both down—I suspect he's rather practiced at that, poor fellow—and after Wynderhane stammered an apology for what he termed the *misunderstanding*, his wife led him away to lie down."

Concordia frowned. "I didn't hurt him that badly."

"You didn't. The man was corned. He could barely stand

upright, and here it is only mid-afternoon. Sir Anthony would do well to reconsider his investment broker."

"So now what do we do?"

David sighed. "After the Wynderhanes left, Reese begged me not to say anything to the Dunwicks about the incident. Apparently his employer has been under a great deal of stress lately. Reese also confided in me that he is leaving the man's service once they return to the city. Gemmer has offered to promote him to be his assistant."

"His assistant? But what of Nash?" The dashing young man with the cleft chin and the shock of dark hair that fell across his eyes. The one Miss Farraday was so taken with. Concordia could see the appeal.

"Nash is merely Gemmer's business secretary, though he is bound to resent being passed over for the promotion in favor of Reese. Yet another reason for the fellow to keep quiet about it."

"I know someone else who resents Reese," she said. "Pickering."

David raised an eyebrow. "Really? Why?"

She shrugged. "It was just an impression. As to the 'why' of it, well, he could be jealous of Reese's position, or of how well Reese and Wynderhane get along."

"Pickering seems to be settling in just fine with Sir Anthony."

"I'm guessing he wants a higher position than personal secretary, and a more permanent one."

"You may be right about that. Being pulled off the firm's payroll for a short stint in private employment may be a setback for his ambitions."

"Is it generally known that Reese is making the job change? Pickering may be in a good position to take his place," she said.

David shook his head. "Reese is feeling guilty about leaving. He says he hasn't found the right time to break the news to Wynderhane. He doesn't want to add to his employer's troubles."

"Troubles? What sort of troubles?"

"I found this under the porch swing after everyone left." David passed over a wrinkled slip of yellow paper.

She recognized it as the one Wynderhane had been holding. She smoothed it out. As she had guessed, it was a telegram.

D'S STOCK IN PORTFOLIO C BOTTOMING OUT. STAY OR SELL? NEED IMMEDIATE REPLY.

"Oh, dear. I assume 'D' is Dunwick?"

"That would be my guess."

"Does Sir Anthony know?"

David shrugged. "Difficult to say, but it explains why Wynderhane was dipping into the bottle so early in the day."

"Surely, that cannot be all of the Dunwicks' investments," she said. "The family is incredibly wealthy on both sides. What is 'portfolio c'?"

"Likely a code name," David said. "It would be unwise for a firm to broadcast a particular company stock as failing in a telegram that others could see."

"You're right about that."

He resumed his whittling. "No matter how diversified the Dunwick holdings may be, it will still be a blow. Would you be willing, under the circumstances, to keep this morning's incident to ourselves? I hate to add to our host's woes."

"What of Mrs. Reese and the cook? They are bound to circulate the tale."

"Reese said he would speak to both his grandmother and Marie. And we won't have to put up with the Wynderhanes much longer. They plan to stay only another week, until the fair is over."

Concordia stifled a sigh. It was bound to be a strained week. And then there was the issue of what further information

Wynderhane could provide. She had only one new tidbit to go on: Victoria Lester had tried to speak with him at his office.

But what could be done with that? She needed to learn the identity of the man who made the call at the club. And she was sure Wynderhane knew who it was.

Yes, I think it's...but no, that can't be...

He would never tell her now.

CHAPTER 9

Concordia checked her reflection in the mirror as she reached for yet another hairpin. Drat this hair. Although she had long ago accepted that the bright-red tint would never deepen to a more fashionable auburn, its thickness and stubborn waves consigned her to madly pinning its bulk into place. The result lasted all of an hour before she had to re-work the pins. She tried to sigh, but the effect was mitigated by the tight bodice of her emerald silk.

Dinner that evening was to be a formal affair, as the Dunwicks had invited several local personages to join them. Since the incident with Wynderhane yesterday, she had managed to keep clear of his company. There was no avoiding him now. Perhaps it was just as well. She would have to face him sooner or later. He was bound to be on his best behavior in such a public gathering.

Once again she wished she could have pressed him further about what had gone on at the club. She reached for the letter she had received just this afternoon, from Rusty's assistant Claude.

Dear Mrs. Bradley,

I'm concerned about Mr. Deighton. He is mighty agitated about his granddaughter's death. Just before he got your letter, he learned that the police have suspended the case for lack of progress.

He talks now of coming to the Dunwick cottage to confront Wynderhane about his role in this tragedy. I have managed to convince him to think on it awhile, but he will not be content to wait much longer. He is sure to go there himself and seek answers. Or revenge, I am sorry to say.

As soon as you know anything, please write to him immediately. I have never seen him so distressed, and I do not know what he might do.

Yours Sincerely,

Claude

The last thing they needed was Rusty Deighton and Edgar Wynderhane in the same room together. There was bound to be a brawl. She could not let that happen. But how could she get Wynderhane to tell her more?

A knock on the bedroom door brought her back from her thoughts. David came in and drew a breath at the sight of her. "I am wed to the prettiest bride in all of Long Island."

Concordia laughed. "I will settle for the fairest in the cabin, my dear."

David looked quite handsome himself, in his black tie and smooth-fitting black dinner jacket, which emphasized his wide shoulders and the dark, wavy hair that just brushed the collar. "What's that?" he asked, nodding toward the envelope.

She handed him Claude's letter. "I only now had a chance to catch up on today's correspondence. Do you think Rusty will come and make a scene? It would put the Dunwicks in a difficult position."

He frowned as he read. "I understand your concern, but you needn't worry. If Rusty does come, I'll take charge of him." He shrugged. "Besides, what more is there to get from Wynderhane?"

"That's right, I forgot to tell you that part." She described the man's hesitation, the barely mumbled words of recollection, and his promise to consider the matter further.

David's eyes widened. "So he does know something."

"He was careful not to phrase it that way. He said"—she closed her eyes to recall his exact words—"'I do not wish to idly speculate, particularly when so much is at stake.'"

David let out a low whistle. "We must speak with him again."

Although she felt a rush of gratitude at his use of *we*, she couldn't imagine coaxing more information from Wynderhane. "How will we get him to tell us anything?"

"Perhaps we can play upon his regret over yesterday's incident. Or at least prevail upon his sense of gratitude for us not mentioning it to the Dunwicks." He winked. "Or you could always kick him again."

She laughed. "I will call upon you, my good sir, should it come to fisticuffs." She picked up her wrap and her fan. "Ready?"

Merry Chinese lanterns festooned the Dunwicks' front portico, flickering in the growing dusk as they approached the house. A carriage stood in the graveled drive, where a liveried, white-gloved footman helped the occupants descend. She couldn't see much more than the shapes of two men and two women from this distance.

"I hope it won't be one of those tedious dinners," David whispered, "replete with boring local gossip. Who is coming again?"

"Local gossip may be unavoidable," Concordia murmured. "The Dunwicks are expecting the pastor and his wife, along with a former schoolteacher who is the librarian of East Hampton's Reading Room, and"—she paused for dramatic effect—"Captain De...Decker." She managed to avoid saying *decoy*, just in time. Really, she must stop thinking of the man that way.

"Splendid!" David said, brightening. "I've wanted to meet the fellow."

She smiled to herself in the dim light. So long as they did not bring home any more decoys, her husband could chat about wood-carving to his heart's content.

They were the last to arrive. The maid ushered them into the parlor, where a sideboard of hors d'oeuvres had been set up, along with bottles of sparkling cider in linen-wrapped brass urns to keep them cool. Flanking the buffet were bright vases of cut flowers and matching-color satin bows.

"Ah, now I can introduce you to the Bradleys," Lady Dunwick said. She crossed the room and clasped Concordia's hands in a warm greeting. "Welcome, my dears."

Lady Dunwick was dressed in a cross-bodiced lavender silk that set off her silver hair most becomingly. A smile crinkled the lines beside her light eyes as she drew them over to the group of newcomers. "Reverend and Mrs. Claymore"—the couple inclined their heads in greeting—"may I present Mr. and Mrs. Bradley."

"A pleasure," the minister said, extending his hand to David.

"And this is Miss Winston, in charge of our local reading room. Mabel, dear, you and Concordia are bound to have a great deal to discuss, as she is a former teacher as well." Miss Winston's eyes lit up in interest.

Lady Dunwick turned to the grizzle-bearded gentleman standing beside Miss Winston. "Captain Decker, may I present Mr. and Mrs. Bradley? I believe Mr. Bradley in particular has wanted to meet you."

David extended a hand to the captain. "A pleasure, sir. I've recently admired your woodworking skills."

The man's craggy cheeks crinkled as he grinned widely. "Have you now? Are you the chap who bought two of my ducks? You have a good eye there." He leaned forward conspiratorially. "Not that I should say this aloud, but those two are my best ones. I'm quite proud o' them."

The two moved off. Lady Dunwick excused herself and went to join the Gemmers and Wynderhanes, who clustered around the piano. Mrs. Reese was picking out a tune, with her grandson, Mr. Nash, and Mr. Pickering lending their tenor voices to the song.

"Have you visited our reading room yet, Mrs. Bradley?" Miss Winston inquired. She was a petite, bespectacled woman, with iron-gray hair pulled back into a tight bun, although the effect was softened by a cream lace collar and the delicate pink-shell cameo at her throat. "I staff the place most days, but I don't recall seeing you there."

"Regrettably, I have not had the chance," Concordia said. "I hope to soon."

Charlotte joined them, handing her glass of cider. "We should have the opportunity to visit tomorrow, in fact. Mrs. Bradley and I are delivering items for the rummage sale and bringing back more donations to sort through."

"Wonderful!" Miss Winston clasped her hands together in delight. "I believe you will enjoy our offerings. We have a complete set of the works of Shakespeare, Milton, and all of the major eighteenth century philosophers, along with the Enlightenment poets."

"Impressive," Concordia murmured, although eighteenth century philosophy was not quite in her line. She favored the Jacobeans and the Romantics.

"Should that be too dry for your tastes, we do have the novels of Bulwer-Lytton and Sir Walter Scott. Quite exciting."

Charlotte's snort turned into a polite cough. "Those aren't circulating nearly as rapidly as the popular periodicals: *Harper's Weekly, Godey's Lady's Magazine,* and *Lippincott's.* Lately, I have been catching up on Mr. Doyle's detective stories. I was first intrigued after reading an old *Strand* issue of Uncle Anthony's."

Miss Winston wrinkled her nose. Concordia suspected the lady was a purist when it came to what she considered suitable reading.

Movement out of the corner of her eye distracted her. Hoping it was David, she turned briefly to look. No, not David. James

Reese had broken away from the group at the piano and had drawn Wynderhane aside. He was whispering earnestly into his employer's ear. Hans Gemmer looked on with a frown.

"So, Mrs. Bradley, will you be staying for the East Hampton Fair?"

Concordia, only half-attending to the question, and not awake to the trap being laid for her, nodded. "We are looking forward to it." She craned her neck beyond Miss Winston's shoulder. Where had David gotten to? She couldn't see him but noted that Daniel Pickering was now approaching Wynderhane and Reese.

"Excellent! I was hoping to impose upon you to help with the play we are putting on at the fair."

Uh-oh. "Play?"

"Oh, not an *entire* play, merely a selection of key scenes from *Julius Caesar.* The East Hampton Ladies' Drama Guild will have a tent with a platform and viewing benches set up near the baseball field. We'll be giving morning and afternoon performances."

Concordia froze, frantically wracking her brain for a graceful way to decline.

"Oh, it should not take up much of your time," Miss Winston added quickly, likely noting Concordia's stunned expression. "You would still have plenty of opportunity to enjoy the fair."

It seemed she could never dodge involvement in a play production. She grimaced at Charlotte, who had turned away slightly, her face reddened in an effort not to laugh. That young lady knew all too well Concordia's futile attempts to extricate herself from such endeavors in the past. No help there.

The maid came in to announce the meal.

"Allow me to consider my time constraints, Miss Winston," Concordia said, as David materialized—where had he been?—and offered his arm. "Charlotte and I will stop by the reading room tomorrow, and I will let you know then."

The librarian took a breath as if to say something more, but Sir Anthony came over to escort the lady to the dining room.

Looking back, Sir Anthony gave Concordia a meaningful look and a quick wink.

Bless the man, Concordia thought, before turning her attention to David. "Did you have a nice chat with Captain Decker?"

David grinned. "Indeed, yes. We have arranged to meet tomorrow morning in his shop. He has any number of tools that should make my project easier and produce better results."

"Oh? Where is his shop?"

"Right in Hassett Knoll, on the way to East Hampton. I thought you and Charlotte could give me a ride tomorrow."

"We'll have to wedge you in between a number of rummage sale boxes," Concordia warned, taking his arm. They followed the couples into the dining room.

The space was just large enough for such a gathering, and the table was beautifully draped in ivory linen overlaid with a peach lace runner. Crystal goblets shone in the candlelight and picked up the gold rims of the china place settings.

Sir Anthony had just finished seating Miss Winston and came around to Lady Dunwick to pull out her chair. He stiffened. Concordia followed his glance, as did his wife.

In the middle of the table was a tall, cut-glass vase, wrapped in lavender ribbon and filled with long-stemmed blue irises. Lady Dunwick's face paled. The other guests were too occupied with finding their chairs and settling in comfortably to notice, but Concordia could see the quick glance between Sir Anthony and his wife, the quiet shake of her head, and the whispered conversation with Pickering, who returned quickly with the housekeeper.

Concordia straightened. *Irises.* A coincidence, or connected to the anonymous notes Sir Anthony had received? His reaction indicated the latter. She cocked her head in an attempt to listen. *Drat*, their voices were too low for her to hear much, although at one point she did make out *Miss Farraday.*

A few others sensed a disturbance of sorts and began to attend to the whispered conversation. Charlotte, seated across from Concordia and David, watched her aunt and uncle, a frown tugging at her brow. Concordia tried to catch her eye, but Charlotte was too absorbed. Mrs. Reese, at the far end of the table beside the Wynderhanes, watched the Dunwicks with narrowed eyes. The minister and his wife—closest to the Dunwicks—had that air of studied preoccupation that suggested they were actively listening while trying to appear not to.

The housekeeper gave a nod, leaned over the table, and removed the centerpiece, taking it to the kitchen.

Mrs. Wynderhane, currently occupied with adjusting the angle of the butter knife beside her neighbor's plate, started. "What on earth—?"

Lady Dunwick gave a self-deprecating laugh as the house-keeper returned with an elaborate centerpiece of glazed fruits and salmon-tinted roses. "A miscommunication among the staff. They set out the wrong centerpiece. My apologies."

"No need to apologize," Marta Gemmer said. "You could have left the other one. It was an attractive arrangement. Do you grow irises in your garden?"

"Yes, we do," Charlotte chimed in, when the distracted Lady Dunwick didn't answer.

As the soup was served, the conversation turned to local doings.

"We have quite the thriving art colony here," Reverend Claymore said, looking proudly at his wife. "It is what originally brought many of our current residents to this locale. My Patsy has several items for sale at a nearby gallery."

"A gallery? Where?" Marta Gemmer asked.

"Right in East Hampton," Mrs. Claymore said. "They are looking to expand the space and bring in talent from New York City."

Concordia nodded. "We have already seen some lovely items in the village of Hassett Knoll. Gwen Ambrose is quite gifted. I purchased several of her watercolors. I also saw a sketch of Susie's that seems quite advanced for a child of her age."

Mrs. Claymore grimaced. "Tragedy has made that family quite...odd," she said hesitantly.

Concordia bristled. "How do you mean?"

She waved a hand. "I don't mean to be unkind, dear. I'm sure Miss Ambrose is doing her best under the circumstances. But they are certainly a reclusive pair, not interacting much with the neighbors or attending any of our social events. Oh, I know the child cannot speak normally, poor thing. I'm referring to Gwendolyn...tramping around alone at odd hours, hardly ever smiling or chatting with the locals when she comes into town. Fetches her supplies and leaves. Why doesn't she try to make a better life for herself? Find a good man to marry?" She shook her head. "Once people are rebuffed one time too many, they stop trying."

Concordia didn't know what to say, but it was obvious that Charlotte's concern for the Ambroses' reputation had a legitimate foundation. She opted for a change of subject. "Do you display your pieces elsewhere besides East Hampton, Mrs. Claymore? I don't recall seeing your work at the café in Hassett Knoll."

Mrs. Claymore gave a quick glance toward Captain Decker, occupied in conversation with Mr. Nash and Mr. Reese. Nonetheless, she dropped her voice and leaned in. "The café is not quite the...um...ideal venue. There is insufficient space to really showcase one's work there, and it becomes quite a jumble. I'm a potter, Mrs. Bradley. Perhaps you'll have occasion to visit the studio when you're in East Hampton tomorrow. It's on West Road."

"Any other sights you would recommend in the area?" David asked. "We have already enjoyed surf-bathing and are looking forward to going out in Sir Anthony's new boat. I may even try my hand at some fishing," he added, giving Concordia a mischievous glance.

"Only if you intend to clean and prepare what you catch," she shot back.

Sir Anthony laughed. He seemed more at ease now, sitting back in his chair, hand loosely grasping his wineglass stem. "We have a man who takes care of all that, Mrs. Bradley. We shall certainly take the *Susan D* for a day of fishing. The weather has been a bit unsettled lately for that sort of lengthy excursion."

"The *Susan D?*" Concordia repeated.

Sir Anthony glanced fondly at Lady Dunwick, who did not return the look, her attention elsewhere. "It's what I've decided to name the boat. In honor of my lovely wife."

Captain Decker turned his head. Perhaps it was the repetition of the word *fishing* that had finally got his attention. "If you want to catch sturgeon, you'd best go beyond the mouth of the bay. Yer more likely to have success."

"Well, you certainly did, Captain," David said appreciatively. "We read the newspaper notice about your record-breaking catch. Congratulations."

"What about land pursuits?" Mrs. Reese asked. "I'm afraid boats do not agree with me." She grimaced.

Concordia could see her point. Simply imagining the rocking motion of a boat upon the water was making her feel a bit queasy. She pushed away her consommé and picked up her roll instead.

"There's some interesting history around these parts," Mrs. Claymore said. "The windmill that you can see from the gazebo is nearly one hundred years old and was in use as recently as ten years ago. It's worth a look at the structure, which has a small house attached. Indian arrowheads have turned up there, too. A stream runs just past it—perfect for a picnic—and there's a lovely view of the surrounding countryside from the top floor, where the turbine mechanism is located. You can see for miles. I know several landscape artists who have gone up there to sketch the view."

Lady Dunwick nodded. "A great many people tramp through there."

"The owner does not mind?" David asked.

Lady Dunwick shrugged. "The place was bought by an investment firm in the city. No one has bothered with it recently. As long as no one vandalizes it, the local constabulary doesn't mind that we trespass on occasion."

Charlotte looked up from buttering her roll. "Aunt Susan, we should organize a picnic excursion to the windmill. It would be such fun!"

Lady Dunwick hesitated. "We have much to do before the fair."

"*Pshaw*, we have plenty of time," Charlotte countered. "Besides, do we not have a responsibility to our guests to ensure they are having a pleasant time?"

Lady Dunwick gave her niece a skeptical look. "Very well, but I shall leave you to organize it. I have enough on my hands."

"Wonderful!" Charlotte cast her eye on the company. "I shall firm up the details and send 'round invitations in the next day or so. I hope you all can come."

As the conversation turned to other topics, Concordia's thoughts wandered. She looked toward the end of the table where the Wynderhanes were seated, recalling the conversation she'd had with David before coming here. So far, Edgar Wynderhane was polite but subdued. She had noticed the broker casting a few anxious glances toward Sir Anthony, but she was fairly confident that the Dunwicks knew nothing about the incident on the porch yesterday. His anxiety might stem from the telegram David had found. Had Wynderhane lost a large portion of the Dunwicks' money? Had he told his client yet? Sir Anthony seemed at his ease, now that the irises were gone. Not at all like a man who had lost a fortune. She noticed he did not engage the Wynderhanes in conversation, however, as he was doing with the Gemmers.

Edgar Wynderhane was his own island this evening. His wife was ignoring him, his host was ignoring him, and he studiously rebuffed Reese's attempts to engage him. Pickering was paying covert attention to Reese and Wynderhane as well, even as he made desultory conversation with Miss Winston.

Concordia glanced at David tucking happily into the main course. *Where does he put it all?* While the stuffed flounder was quite tasty, she seemed to fill up quickly these days.

David caught her look, glanced over at Wynderhane, and gave a brief nod. They were in agreement. David would try to corner Wynderhane alone when everyone got up from the table.

The time came soon enough for the ladies to head for the parlor for coffee and the gentlemen to the study for port and cigars. Concordia lingered in the hallway, pretending to examine a landscape painting of cows.

Out of the corner of her eye, she saw David follow Wynderhane, but then Captain Decker came up behind David and clapped him on the shoulder. "Well, now!" Decker cried, "What were we talking about before the dinner bell? Ah, yes, my last sea voyage. Well, we had quite the time of it, I must say..." Their voices faded as they entered the study.

Drat. So much for that plan. But where had Wynderhane gotten to? She hadn't seen him join the gentlemen.

In the silence, she heard a sharp voice through the hall window. Someone was on the porch. She crept closer. No, there were two men on the porch, Wynderhane and Reese. She could see the back of the younger man's blond head in the moonlight and the silhouette of his trim figure.

After a quick glance down the corridor to be sure she was unobserved, she tipped her head to listen.

"—you think you can simply walk out on me?" Wynderhane's voice rose in his agitation. "I gave you your first break. You wouldn't be in this business without me."

"You must understand, sir," came Reese's quiet voice— Concordia leaned as close as she dared—"I have to look after my own best interests. It's a substantial increase in salary. I would accompany him on his trips to Amsterdam—"

"You are despicable, selling yourself out in such a fashion!"

"You could always match his offer."

Wynderhane gave a bitter laugh. "'Match his offer'? My offer is much less pleasant for you, my good fellow. What if I told you—"

"Concordia!" The distant voice sounded like Charlotte's. The men stopped abruptly.

Concordia, startled, clutched the sill, managing just in time to keep from falling into the window in a most unladylike manner. Reese's back was to her, so thankfully he saw nothing, but Wynderhane may have caught sight of her before her hasty retreat. She couldn't be sure.

She passed the closed library door and hesitated. Did the knob turn, ever so slightly? On impulse, she pushed it open, sending a startled Daniel Pickering tumbling to the floor.

"I beg your pardon!" she exclaimed, as Pickering brushed himself off with as much dignity as he could muster. "I didn't expect anyone here." The room was dark, the only light coming through the window facing the porch. The window had been cracked open for air...or was it to listen to the same conversation she had overheard?

"No matter." Pickering reached for the pipe that had fallen to the floor. When he glanced back at her, his deep-set hazel eyes were carefully neutral. "Sir Anthony had mislaid his pipe. If you will excuse—"

"Concordia!" Charlotte's voice was closer now.

With a quick bow, Pickering headed for the study to join the gentlemen.

Concordia hurried toward the parlor. "Where have you been?" Charlotte asked. "We have been missing you for a while."

"I just needed some fresh air," Concordia said.

Charlotte frowned and looked at her closely. "Are you unwell? You looked a bit pale at dinner."

"No, no, I am fine." Concordia smoothed her skirts. "I'm sorry to take you away from the gathering in search of me."

"Oh, never mind that," Charlotte said. "The conversation was getting tedious. It's all talk of the fair and summer fashions. Fortunately, the gentlemen will be joining us soon."

When the men rejoined the ladies in the parlor, however, it was not quite the relaxed atmosphere one might expect at such a function. Besides the antipathy between Reese and Wynderhane—for which Concordia and perhaps Pickering understood the reason—the Dunwicks seemed ill-at-ease in one another's company, circulating in separate parts of the room and only exchanging the occasional stiff glance. After one such interchange, Concordia looked questioningly at Charlotte, who gave a silent shrug.

But the mood of the evening unraveled completely when Miss Farraday joined the group after she had tucked her charges into bed. She had no sooner seated herself and was handed a cup of tea by the maid when Sir Anthony strode over and sat across from her.

"So, Miss Farraday," he broke in abruptly, much to the frowning consternation of Mrs. Reese, who had engaged the young lady in conversation. "I hear you have been cutting flowers in our garden today." His light tone was belied by lowering brows and narrowed eyes. An attorney by training, he leaned forward to more closely study Miss Farraday's facial expression, as if ready to pounce upon the slightest prevarication.

Madeline Farraday shrank back a little. "I—I asked permission first, sir. I wanted some flowers for the nursery. Your gardener said you wouldn't mind."

"Oh? Which flowers were they?"

"Serena and I cut some pink mop-head hydrangeas. The gardener said they could do with a bit of pruning anyway, and the child is fond of them." She bit her lip. "Is something wrong?"

He ignored the question and plowed ahead with what could only be construed as a cross-examination of a reluctant witness. "You are telling me, my good miss, that you did not cut the irises and arrange them in a vase for the dining table?"

Mrs. Reese's mouth dropped open. "Is that what this is about? What is it that disturbs you about those irises, Sir Anthony?" She raised an eyebrow, her curiosity awakened.

He sucked in a sharp breath, suddenly aware of how clearly he had revealed his agitation. Charlotte, Lady Dunwick, and David, conversing nearby, stopped and stared. The Gemmers looked back and forth between their employee and their host, unsure how to intervene.

But the Gemmers' other employee, William Nash, had no such qualms. The young man pulled up a stool beside the red-cheeked young lady and raked a hand through the shock of hair that had fallen once again across his eyes. "Is there any way I may be of assistance, Miss Farraday?" he murmured. She shook her head mutely, looking down at her hands.

Nash looked up at his host. "No disrespect meant, Sir Anthony, but you seem to be distressing the young lady."

Sir Anthony Dunwick spread his hands in apology. "I regret my sharp tone, Miss Farraday. I merely wished to get to the bottom of the matter, and my housekeeper told me you had been cutting flowers in the garden."

Madeline Farraday stood. She smoothed her skirts with hands that trembled, whether with anger or fear, Concordia couldn't tell. "I know nothing about any irises, Sir Anthony. And, as you know, I dined with my charges rather than the general company. I fail to see how it would be any concern of mine to decorate your table. If you will excuse me, I should check on the children."

As she left the room, Mrs. Reese grimaced and set her cup aside. "I believe I shall retire as well. Good night."

"I'll accompany you," Nash said quickly, offering his arm.

Concordia watched them leave. They crossed the room with hasty strides. She wondered if one or both of them were attempting to catch up to Miss Farraday and make sure she was all right.

"Dashing Nash to the rescue once again," Pickering murmured

caustically, before sidling up to the stiff-shouldered Sir Anthony. "I'll be in the study organizing your files, sir, if you need me."

Sir Anthony gave a distracted nod.

David was watching the whole. She caught his eye. A dignified retreat at this point would be wise.

After thanking their hosts, Concordia and David headed down the dimly lit path to Crosswinds. "What an evening!" David said. "Sir Anthony acted as if he had Miss Farraday on the witness stand. I do not understand it."

"Irises are a sensitive subject with Sir Anthony," Concordia said. She filled him in on what they had found in the pocket of his old suit and what Charlotte had said of her own discovery.

David didn't speak until they had entered their cabin and turned up the lamps. "So you believe the irises on the table today are connected to the anonymous letters that Sir Anthony has received?"

Concordia shrugged. "It doesn't matter what I believe. Sir Anthony believes it."

"It would be impolite to speculate further," he said. "It is obviously a private matter. We should not intrude."

She sighed, wondering if they would have that luxury.

CHAPTER 10

*C*harlotte and Concordia set out for East Hampton the next morning in the pony cart, with David perched precariously atop the boxed piles of sorted rummage sale donations. They stopped at the crossroads to Hassett Knoll's Main Street to let him off.

He grabbed his satchel of wood-carving materials and gave them a wave. "I'll get back to the cottage on my own when the Captain and I are done. You ladies have fun."

Charlotte shook her head as she flicked the reins. "It's going to be a hot walk back."

Concordia fanned her face. It was warm already. Theirs wasn't the only vehicle on the road. Many people were out and about, getting their errands done before the full heat of midday set in. The wheels from carts, wagons, carriages, and bicycles sent choking clouds of dust along the road.

But she didn't want to converse with Charlotte about the weather. Now was the time to find out more about Sir Anthony, if she could. She drew a breath. "Your uncle seemed quite upset last night."

Charlotte sighed, keeping her gaze upon the road ahead. "As was Aunt Susan. I wish—" She broke off.

"The flowers on the table—they're connected to the pressed irises your uncle has been receiving?"

Charlotte nodded.

"So the person responsible is here," Concordia mused aloud. She wondered about Miss Farraday. She had mentioned she was an orphan. What else might be in the young lady's background that connected her to Sir Anthony? Some perceived wrong done to her in a court of law, perhaps?

"I know for a fact that the person is here," Charlotte said.

"Because of the centerpiece?" Concordia sat up straighter. "Who is it?"

Charlotte was silent for so long that Concordia wasn't sure she would answer. Finally, Charlotte gave her a quick glance before fixing her eyes back upon the road. "I'm not talking about the centerpiece. I've been thinking more about the envelope I told you about—the one I accidentally opened the other day. I'd noticed at the time that it had no postage, but assumed the staff had removed the outer envelope that letters sometimes arrive in to keep them clean."

Concordia nodded. The practice was dying out, though it was still done for more formal invitations and announcements.

"But something bothered me about that," she went on. "I realized later it was because I'd received an invitation in the same batch of mail, and the outer envelope of that one was still intact. So I decided to ask the staff about it."

"And?"

"No one had removed any outer envelopes. Everyone was too busy with guests these last few days to sort through the mail."

"What about Mr. Pickering? Perhaps your uncle put him in charge of his personal correspondence."

"I thought of that. Pickering says he has been explicitly forbidden to handle Uncle Anthony's letters."

Concordia felt a chill, despite the morning's warmth. The conclusion was undeniable. Someone in the Dunwick household was responsible...but for what, exactly? "Charlotte, no threat was made in the letter you saw, correct? So perhaps there is nothing to worry about."

"Have you read any of the Sherlock Holmes stories?" Charlotte asked.

Concordia frowned in confusion at the change of subject. "Huh? A few, I suppose. Why?"

"What about 'The Adventure of the Five Orange Pips'?"

"I honestly don't remember. How is that significant?"

"It's a story of a man—several men, actually, who each receive an anonymous envelope containing only five orange pips. But these men know it's a warning—a warning that they will be killed for their betrayal of a secret organization. And upon each occasion, they are later found dead."

Concordia shivered. *A secret organization*...surely, the Inner Circle, disbanded and rendered powerless some time ago, could not be responsible for the irises. She shook herself. No, a single person with a personal grudge made more sense. "You think Sir Anthony is in danger? If so, why has it not happened already? He gets the same envelope, year after year. How long has it been going on, do you know?"

"I asked Aunt Susan about it. That's the only question of mine she would answer. She said she began noticing the envelopes three years ago."

"She told you nothing more? Nothing about who is doing this?"

She shook her head. "I don't think she knows. Heaven help me, I would do anything to find out... Well, never mind that. But I'm convinced my uncle knows much more than he's telling. Perhaps not who is responsible, but certainly why he has been getting these. It's just a feeling I have. What worries me most is the date: July twenty-second. That is only six days from now."

Concordia nodded. "The day of the fair. You are concerned something will happen to Sir Anthony on this year's anniversary of the date?"

"I do not know. All I can be certain of"—a look of determination crossed the young lady's face—"is I shall not leave his side the entire day."

~

They made good time to East Hampton. The volunteers waiting at the feed store warehouse, where the supplies were being collected for the fair, quickly unloaded the rummage sale items and promised to look after both pony and cart until the ladies returned from their errands.

"We are headed to the Reading Room," Charlotte warned. "We may be a while."

"Take your time," one young lady said, lending them an extra parasol against the strong sun. "Miss Winston is excited to have you visit and review the play. She talked of nothing else over at the coffee shop this morning. I imagine the entire Ladies' Drama Guild is there, waiting for you."

The East Hampton Reading Room was a simple white clapboard structure with a steep-pitched, shingled roof. "It used to be a boarding house," Charlotte explained, "and there are two upper floors that have yet to be used. Plenty of space to expand the collection later on and set up meeting rooms for local clubs."

Miss Winston was, indeed, eagerly awaiting them, along with three other women from the guild, each clutching a copy of *Julius Caesar*.

"Mrs. Bradley, Miss Crandall, how kind of you to come! We are missing a few ladies, but we were hoping for your expert advice—Miss Crandall tells me you have a theater background. We also wondered if you would mind taking over the role of

Brutus. Mrs. Graves has a nasty summer cold and is confined to her bed."

Concordia flashed a look at Charlotte and murmured, "My *theater* background?"

Charlotte chuckled.

"Miss Winston," Concordia began, "the role of Brutus is a formidable part—"

"Oh, I am sure you are equal to the task," the lady interrupted. "Both Miss Crandall and Lady Dunwick have such nice things to say about you and your time over at the women's college." Miss Winston thrust a copy at her.

Charlotte, her eyes twinkling in amusement, touched Concordia's arm. "I'll be reading in the back room. Come fetch me when you're done."

It was quite a while before Concordia was finished, but she felt confident in her part by that point and made suggestions about simplifying the scenes they were to portray. "The most important issue is that we project our voices from the stage. There will be a great deal of bustle and noise going on around us."

With a promise to return for two more rehearsals in the coming days, Concordia followed Charlotte back out to the hot street.

Charlotte checked her watch. "Are you hungry? It's past time for lunch."

Concordia realized she felt quite famished. "Good idea. Where would you recommend?"

Charlotte looked around to get her bearings then inclined her head. "This way. There's a sandwich shop around the corner. Their roast beef is superb."

Soon they were perched upon stools at the sandwich counter and had placed their orders. Concordia dabbed at her damp neck with her handkerchief and glanced idly through the large storefront window. Across the street was a barber shop, whose window featured poster pictures of various men's hairstyles, and several short hairstyles for women, too. She sat up a little straighter. Short hair...did she have the nerve to do it? What would David think?

"What is it?" Charlotte asked.

Concordia gestured to the barber shop. "What would you think of me with...short hair?"

"Really?"

"Well, if you think it's a bad idea...oh, I don't know." Concordia sighed. "It was just a thought. I know some would consider it rather daring."

Charlotte shook her head. "Not really. I was just startled at first. You know"—she gave her an appraising glance—"I believe short hair would look quite becoming on you. But what about Mr. Bradley?"

Concordia waited until their waitress, who had just set the plates before them, walked away. "That is the one factor giving me pause."

Charlotte picked up her sandwich. "If he doesn't like it, you can always grow it back. It's not a permanent change, after all."

"I don't know how I would feel about having a man cut my hair," Concordia said, frowning.

"Oh, that won't be a problem. The gardener told me—he gets his hair cut there—that the proprietor added a woman barber at the beginning of the summer season."

Concordia's eyes widened. "A *woman* barber?"

Charlotte laughed. "It's a small town, and the owner has a competitor a few blocks away. He's cut his prices and hired a woman, hoping to bring in more customers."

"Has it worked?"

"I haven't heard about that. It's early days yet." She gave a mischievous wink. "Why don't we go over after lunch and find out?"

Concordia smiled. It wouldn't hurt to go over there and merely *inquire* about getting her hair cut.

The lady barber was a kindly soul, the short, stout, motherly type. She cooed over Concordia's red hair, ushered her to a chair, and set to work releasing all of her hairpins. "There, now, what beautiful hair you have! Let's give it a good brush and see what we have to work with."

"I haven't decided yet about cutting it," Concordia warned, as the barber plied the brush. Reflexively, she closed her eyes as the brush strokes massaged her scalp and relaxed her.

"Dunna worry, dearie. If you change yer mind, I'll pin it right back up, and no harm done."

Once her hair was brushed out, spilling over her shoulders and into her lap, the barber examined the locks with a critical eye. "You have such a nice wave to yer hair. Without all this weight pulling it down, you'd have no problem getting it to curl nicely behind your ears." She paged through a well-thumbed fashion magazine until she found the picture she wanted. "See this bob? Nice and light, and frame your face right pretty, it would."

Charlotte leaned in to look. "Charming," she breathed.

"It *does* look quite becoming," Concordia said. She didn't have the cheekbones and dark, dreamy eyes of the lady in the magazine, though. Would it look as good on her? Would David like it?

The barber nodded. "You're quite lucky, miss, to have hair with a wave like this." She jerked a thumb toward Charlotte. "Yer friend here, her hair's too straight for such a style to come easy. She'd have to use curlers and such-like."

"Oh, Concordia, you should do it," Charlotte urged. "It's 1899, after all. We are nearly into a new century! You shall have a more modern look with which to greet it."

Concordia viewed her reflection in the mirror—one last look at the long, red hair that had been a nuisance to deal with all of her adult life—and let out a deep sigh. "All right, then. I'm ready."

They stepped out to the sidewalk some time later, Concordia feeling light as a feather. Not a single pin in her head, except for the hat pin. *Heat? What heat?* She felt quite giddy as she turned her head this way and that.

Charlotte kept giving her sideways glances. "I feel as if I'm walking beside a different woman."

A laugh bubbled out of Concordia, and the two of them giggled together.

"That was quite a tip you pressed into her hand," Charlotte said, when she could catch her breath.

"She deserved every penny. I feel wonderful." Concordia reached a hand to the base of her neck and patted the bob again, feeling it spring back below her hat.

"We should retrieve the pony cart and head home right away, or else we shall be late for tea." Charlotte grinned. "I cannot wait to see how everyone reacts when they first lay eyes upon you."

Concordia suppressed a sigh. That she could wait for.

CHAPTER 11

*S*he had to admit to some trepidation when she and Charlotte parted ways to freshen up before tea. She headed for the cabin. David should be back by now. Best to get this over with.

He was sitting on the porch, whistling as he bent over his wood-working project. A case of new tools lay near his feet. He looked up at her approach. "Hello, dear, did you have a good—" He broke off. "What on earth have you done to your hair?" He dropped his knife and stood.

She took a deep breath and carefully removed her hat so as not to muss the style. "A woman at the barber shop cut it for me. I am quite happy with it. What do you think?"

He came up close, walking around her to inspect it from all sides. Concordia stayed still, hoping...

"She did an excellent job," he said at last. "Just like the sketches in the fashion pages of the newspaper."

She exhaled. "You aren't disappointed, then?"

His mouth quirked in a half smile. "I admit I wish I'd had a little warning, but no, I think it looks quite becoming. It will take getting used to, of course." He reached up to tuck a strand behind her ear and leaned close. "But there is still plenty for me to run my hands through—"

Concordia ducked out of his grasp. "Oh, no you don't. I don't know how to fix this yet when it's mussed, and we'll be late for tea."

He chuckled. "Whatever you say, my dear. Heaven forfend I defy a modern woman."

She laughed.

Soon they were headed to the cottage and encountered Miss Ambrose on the path. She huffed up the hill, awkwardly carrying a large canvas bag with both hands.

"Here, allow me," David said.

Miss Ambrose gratefully passed it over. "Thank you, Mr. Bradley. Those are jars of rhubarb jelly, along with pick—" She caught sight of Concordia and stopped dead on the path. "Oh, my."

Concordia flushed. "It was rather spur-of-the-moment, when we were in town today."

"It looks quite charming. Funny, though. I didn't see you as the type." Miss Ambrose continued trudging up the path.

"'The type'? What type?" Concordia asked. She looked at David, who shrugged and followed behind.

"Oh, I didn't mean anything unkind by it," Miss Ambrose called over her shoulder. She knocked on the Dunwicks' kitchen door. Marie pulled it open and with barely a glance of greeting went back to her kneading.

As David put the jars in the pantry, Concordia asked again. "I'm not offended, Gwen, but what do you mean by 'type'?"

Gwen Ambrose chuckled. "You said you used to be a teacher. I have always pictured them as rather prim and serious, and not at all inclined to act on impulse. Besides, as a new bride, you have a husband's sensibilities to consider now. Most women would be quite cautious in that regard."

Concordia looked down at her wedding ring. She doubted marriage would cure her of acting on impulse.

Miss Ambrose leaned close and whispered, "Frankly, I think it makes you all the more interesting." She nodded toward David. "I hear it's good to keep one's husband guessing. One does not want to be too predictable."

They were interrupted by the gurgle of—was that an infant?—behind them. Concordia turned. Strapped to his high chair beside the sink was the Gemmer baby, his sister Serena spooning him what looked to be strained peaches. The nanny was nowhere in sight.

"Where is Miss Farraday?" Concordia asked Marie.

The cook looked up and swiped the back of her hand across her brow, leaving a white smear of flour. "She needed a bit of a break from the little 'uns, so I said I'd watch 'em for a while. That Mrs. Gemmer is a slave-driver, she is. Has the nurse doing sewing and mending during what's supposed to be her off-time. The poor lamb doesn't get an hour to herself."

Concordia turned away, hiding a smirk. Miss Farraday obviously exaggerated her situation a bit. After all, she found the time to squeeze in some leisure reading.

Marie grabbed a dishcloth to wipe the baby's cheeks. "Miss Farraday seemed a mite upset today."

Concordia nodded. "Sir Anthony's behavior last evening, most likely."

"Oh? What happened?" Miss Ambrose asked, accepting the now-empty canvas bag from David with a murmur of thanks.

He raised an eyebrow at his wife. "We should join the others in the parlor."

Concordia knew he disliked gossip. "You go on ahead. I'll be there shortly. I want to ask Marie for her lemon tart recipe."

With a dubious frown, David left.

Gwen Ambrose squinted at Concordia. "You don't want the recipe."

"On the contrary," Concordia said, "I am quite fond of lemon tarts. But first I'll tell you about Sir Anthony." She recounted his reaction to the vase of irises and his cross-examination of Miss Farraday after dinner.

Miss Ambrose frowned. "Why would irises trouble him so?"

Concordia drew her farther out of earshot of the cook. "Can you keep a confidence?" She was hoping that Charlotte would not mind. The Dunwicks obviously considered Miss Ambrose trustworthy enough to act as their out-of-season caretaker, and she certainly didn't spend her time gossiping with the locals.

Miss Ambrose leaned closer. "Of course."

Concordia sketched in the details of the anonymous pressed irises the man had received over the years, including the one Charlotte had found yesterday without a postage mark.

Miss Ambrose pursed her lips thoughtfully. "So that means it is someone in or near the house."

"Exactly. Of course, there has been no threat made, so it's difficult to know if this is truly a matter for worry."

"And Sir Anthony suspects Miss Farraday?"

Concordia nodded. "Of the vase centerpiece, at least. She denies it, and it's difficult to imagine what possible motive the lady would have. Of course, I know little of her background. She mentioned she is an orphan, but that's all I know."

"Perhaps the date is a clue. What was it?"

"July twenty-second." Concordia watched a grimace flit across Miss Ambrose's face. "Does that mean anything to you?"

"Our house burned down and our family was killed on that date. It will be four years ago next week. But that is merely a coincidence. The Dunwicks had nothing to do with our tragedy."

At that moment, the kitchen door flew open, and Miss Farraday rushed in. "Thank you, M—" She stopped. "Oh, hello, Mrs. Bradley. Miss Ambrose." Her voice was breathless, her hair coming out beneath her cap. She reached up a self-conscious hand to tuck away the strands.

Concordia checked her watch. "I should be going in to tea."

Gwen Ambrose nodded. "I should be getting back as well. Susie is waiting for me outside."

Concordia hurried into the front parlor, where David, Charlotte, Lady Dunwick, Mrs. Wynderhane, and the Gemmers waited. David and Hans Gemmer stood politely as she entered.

"My apologies for being late." She paused. Why was everyone staring? *Ah.* Her hair.

Lady Dunwick was the first to recover her voice. "No matter, dear. We are a scattered group today, although we expect the Reeses any moment." She patted the sofa cushion beside her, David shifting over to make room. "Come, sit by me. I want to hear all about this new...style you have decided upon." She glanced over at Charlotte, who was grinning ear to ear. "Although a certain person could have warned me in advance."

"What, and miss your priceless expression?" Charlotte countered.

Lady Dunwick wrinkled her nose at her niece. "Incorrigible girl."

Mr. Gemmer leaned forward to pluck a sugar cube from the bowl. "Is this what we have to look forward to in the coming century—women chopping off their hair and picketing in the streets?"

"Picketing?" Concordia asked.

Gemmer tapped the newspaper on the end table beside him. "Ladies' Garment Workers, marching for something or other."

"What has that to do with a woman's hairstyle?" David asked.

Gemmer waved a disparaging hand. "These young ladies and their modern, outlandish behaviors: smoking cigarettes, getting jobs, marching for 'causes,' wearing bloomers...where is the end of it?"

Maud Wynderhane nodded. "Quite right." She glared at Concordia and only looked away when Marta Gemmer set the plate of scones on the tray between them. In a purely reflexive gesture, Mrs. Wynderhane shifted the plate to the tray's precise center. Mrs. Gemmer looked away with a smile.

Charlotte shifted impatiently. "Why shouldn't women protest injustice when they see it, no matter their attire or length of their hair? Take care that the new century does not leave you behind, clutching nostalgic, irrelevant notions."

Both Concordia and Lady Dunwick gaped at Charlotte, who plucked self-consciously at the folds of her periwinkle silk tea gown. There was a difference between knowing one's own mind and speaking so strongly that a guest was made to feel uncomfortable. Given the dusky flush suffusing her neck and cheeks, Charlotte was aware she had stepped over that line.

James and Eleanor Reese entered the room just then, providing a welcome distraction from what was sure to be either a fractious discussion or an awkward silence. After Reese made sure his grandmother was settled comfortably, he turned to David with a wink. "I hear you have been recruited as well, Bradley."

David laughed. "Indeed. Captain Decker asked me today. Naturally, I couldn't refuse. The man took the time to help me with my project, even lent me tools."

"What is it you are working on?" Charlotte asked.

David glanced at his wife. "It's a surprise."

Hmm, not a decoy, then. "Getting back to this recruitment," Concordia prodded.

Reese smiled, the corners of his blond mustache curling up. "There is to be a baseball game the afternoon of the fair. The Hassett Knoll gents are down in numbers and asked us to join them against East Hampton. Nash will be playing as well. Pickering managed to weasel out of it. Trick knee or some such."

Charlotte grimaced. "I forgot they were still looking for able-bodied men. I should have warned you."

David chuckled. "I don't know how 'able-bodied' I will be. My skills are sadly lacking. I haven't played in ages."

"I know what you mean," Reese said. "At least there are a

couple of practices scheduled between now and the game. That should dust off the cobwebs. And I scavenged a bat and ball, Bradley, if you want to get in some extra batting practice. Nash is interested."

"Good idea," David said. "Decker tells me these locals are a competitive bunch when it comes to baseball. Speaking of Nash, where is he? And I haven't seen Pickering around, either."

"No idea about Pickering—the man seems to slip in and out of rooms so unobtrusively I'm not really sure he was ever there," Reese said, waving a dismissive hand. "Nash said he had papers to work on."

"Indeed, we had to completely revise the report we're sending to Miles in Amsterdam," Hans Gemmer chimed in. "Nash had better look lively if we're to send it off by tomorrow."

Lady Dunwick glanced at the mantel clock with a frown. She rang the bell for the maid, who came quickly. "Yes, ma'am?"

"Has Sir Anthony returned?"

"I can't say as I seen him, Lady Dunwick. I'm sorry. Can I get you anything?"

Lady Dunwick waved a hand. "No, that will be all." The maid left. Noticing Charlotte's quizzical look, she explained, "Your uncle is tending to his boat."

Charlotte shook her head with a smile. "You are the one who gave it to him, you know."

"Yes, yes, but he should not have been gone this long."

Charlotte shifted uneasily and glanced at Concordia, who knew exactly what she was thinking.

Concordia nudged her husband. "Would you mind going to the dock and seeing if Sir Anthony needs a hand?"

David set his napkin aside and stood. "Of course."

Reese got up as well. "I'll go with you."

The room grew quiet after they left, Gemmer returning to his newspaper, Mrs. Wynderhane smoothing the doily lining the tea tray, and Charlotte fidgeting in her seat.

Concordia searched for a topic, anything, to distract them. "Did you know the Ladies' Drama Guild will be putting on scenes from *Julius Caesar* at the fair?" she asked, of no one in particular.

Charlotte had just drawn breath to respond when James Reese burst in, perspiring and out of breath. "We must fetch the doctor. There has been an accident."

CHAPTER 12

*C*oncordia followed Charlotte as she bolted out of the room, leaving the others to sort out the details of getting the doctor and extracting information from Reese. She knew that Charlotte could not bear to sit and wait for news, especially when she had feared her uncle might come to harm.

When they reached the dock, they saw the elderly man slumped over the prow with David kneeling beside him, applying an already-bloodied handkerchief to the side of his head. Concordia's heart lurched at the sight.

David looked up and frowned at the two ladies hurrying towards them. "You shouldn't be here," he called.

With the ease of practice, Charlotte stepped across the gap and into the boat. She crouched beside them. "What happened?"

David gave her a long look before replying. "You are just as stubborn as my wife."

Charlotte glared back. "Are you going to answer my question or not?"

"He must have tripped." David pointed to the coiled rope peeking out from under the hatch. "Watch out for that," he said sharply to Concordia, who was awkwardly climbing into the vessel to join them.

"Tripped?" Charlotte repeated.

"And then he hit his head on the railing as he fell," David said.

Concordia pulled out a fresh kerchief and passed it over to her husband. "How badly is he hurt?"

David nodded his thanks and applied it to the gash. "He looks to be coming around now." He shifted his weight to get an arm under the man.

Sir Anthony gave a groan and moved to sit up. David supported his shoulders, easing him upright against the cockpit, where he promptly slumped back and closed his eyes.

"Uncle," Charlotte said anxiously, chafing his wrists, "can you hear me? What happened?"

"I doubt he's in any condition to give a cogent answer," David said.

Sir Anthony blinked rapidly and turned toward his niece, frowning in an attempt at recognition. His brow cleared. "Ah, Char—Charlotte," he mumbled.

He shifted his gaze to Concordia, squinting in confusion. "Is that—Concordia?" He looked over at David. "I must—I must have hit my head worse than I thought. Where is the rest of—her hair?"

David chuckled. "You're going to be fine, Sir Anthony. The doctor is on his way."

Concordia and David lingered in the library, waiting for news once the doctor had finished with Sir Anthony, who was now tucked comfortably into bed and attended by Charlotte and Lady Dunwick. The others were milling about as well, in the parlor, sunroom, and billiard room, ears attuned to when someone would come to tell them news. Concordia was grateful that she and David had the library to themselves. The tension in the house was palpable, and she was in no mood for desultory chit-chat.

David seemed ill-disposed to converse as well. He paced back and forth, from window to bookcase and back again, never standing still for long.

A maid came, shuffling through a stack of letters. "A letter for you, Mrs. Bradley." She passed it over. "Can I bring either of you anything?"

Concordia shook her head. "No word yet from the doctor?"

"No, ma'am." She turned to leave, but David stopped her.

"There is something you can do for me...Agnes, isn't it?" The woman nodded. "Intercept the doctor before he leaves and ask him to come see me here? There is something I would like to discuss with him, regarding Sir Anthony's condition."

A puzzled frown tugged at the girl's brow, but she merely bobbed a curtsy and left the room.

Concordia looked over at him in curiosity. "What was that about?"

He sighed and flung himself into a chair. "The more I think about it—Sir Anthony's posture when Reese and I found him on the boat, slumped forward like that—the less sense it makes. His wound was here"—he pointed just above and beyond his right ear, towards the crown—"but that was not the side he had collapsed against. There was only the winch nearby his head, which could have caused the gash, but I saw no blood upon it. There should have been. Scalp wounds bleed a great deal. There was no blood anywhere but where he lay."

She hadn't seen blood anywhere else, either. "You believe someone struck him? With what?"

He shrugged.

"We saw nothing nearby," she mused aloud, "although it would be simple enough to dispose of a weapon by tossing it into the water."

"That's what I'm thinking."

"So you wish to confirm your theory with the doctor?"

"And discover if there is some innocuous explanation that I had not considered." He nodded toward the envelope in her hand. "Who's that from?"

She glanced down. "Rusty." She slit it open.

Dear Concordia,

Your silence has me most anxious. As the police have suspended the case, there has been no further progress here. I cannot bear that whoever is responsible for Victoria's death is walking away a free man. I can only assume that Wynderhane is evading your questions. He may not be taking them seriously, coming from a woman. I am resolved to come and talk to Wynderhane myself. I have made arrangements to arrive in East Hampton on the twenty-first and stay at a local inn.

Please do not think I am ungrateful for your efforts. It is simply time for me to step in.

Yours Sincerely,

Rusty

She passed it over to David. "I should have insisted that we try again to speak to Wynderhane and not be put off." Guilt twisted her abdomen. Instead of gallivanting around downtown East Hampton, eating sandwiches, play-acting, and getting her hair cut, she could have cornered the man, demanding answers for a grieving grandfather.

David handed it back, his eyes softening at her troubled expression. "Don't blame yourself, dear. I doubt Wynderhane would tell us more. Perhaps Rusty *should* come. It may make him feel better to take action. And the appeal of a relative might carry more weight with Wynderhane."

"What if the confrontation turns violent?" she asked. "Can you control him?"

He folded his arms. "I can handle one old man. Don't worry."

A knock on the open door interrupted them. It was Charlotte, accompanied by the doctor.

"He's going to be all right," Charlotte said. "He just has to rest for a few days. He's sleeping now."

Concordia grasped her trembling hands and led her to a chair.

The doctor, a short, broad-chested man with graying hair and bushy brows, shifted impatiently. "I must return to my rounds." He looked over at David. "I was told you wished to speak with me about Sir Anthony?"

With a backward glance at the women, David inclined his head toward the door. The doctor followed him out, closing the door behind him.

Charlotte leaned back and pinched the bridge of her nose. "What was that about?" she asked wearily.

Concordia explained David's observations about Sir Anthony's head wound and the lack of a nearby surface that could have caused it.

Charlotte sat up. "I feared that might be the case. But Aunt Susan is worried enough. I would prefer we keep this to ourselves for now."

"With your uncle bedridden and constantly attended by staff and family members, I doubt he is at further risk."

"For the moment. But what of the future? We cannot be with him at all times."

"If we are correct in assuming that his attacker is someone staying here, perhaps we can narrow it down." Concordia bit her lip as she thought. "At the time your uncle was alone, tending to his boat, there were a number of people unaccounted for at tea-time." She ticked off the list on her fingers. "Mr. Nash, who was purportedly doing paperwork for Mr. Gemmer—we should check on that; Mrs. Reese, although an elderly lady catching your uncle unawares and knocking him over the head on a bobbing sailboat seems highly improbable; Mr. Reese, certainly young and strong like Nash, but Reese and his grandmother came into the parlor together." She stopped. Was that everyone? No. "Wynderhane wasn't in the parlor, either."

"His wife said he was indisposed," Charlotte said.

"Hmm, that's convenient. What if that was just an excuse? Perhaps he went to the boat to speak with your uncle, and they had an argument over the stock losses—" Concordia put a hand to her mouth. *Uh-oh.*

"Stock losses?" Charlotte exclaimed. "What do you mean? This is the first I've heard of it." She gave her a stern look. "Come now, out with it."

Concordia explained the telegram to Wynderhane, leaving out the part about the man making advances toward her. She'd already said too much as it was.

Charlotte bit her lip. "I don't think Aunt Susan knows about that. She would have told me."

"But surely Wynderhane has told your uncle. He got the telegram several days ago." She hesitated. "I'm sorry for blurting it out."

"Well, I'm not going to worry about it right now," Charlotte said briskly. "We need to get to the bottom of how my uncle came to be injured and if he's in danger. Is that everyone who could have struck him?"

Concordia took a moment to collect her thoughts, remembering whom she had seen today. "On our way to tea, we encountered Miss Ambrose on the path to the kitchen. That path also branches out to the dock—"

"You cannot imagine that Gwen attacked Uncle Anthony!"

Concordia sighed. "I am merely considering every possibility. Gwen is young, tall, and strong for a woman." As was Susie, who had been standing farther along the path, but that was a ridiculous notion. Just because the poor girl had mental difficulties and did not behave quite like a typical child did not mean she was capable of violence, despite the village gossip.

"But why would *any* of them hurt him?" Charlotte asked. "Except for Wynderhane, given what you've told me, although I doubt knocking my uncle over the head is the best way to get back in his client's good graces."

"It could have been in the heat of the moment," Concordia pointed out.

Or perhaps Wynderhane was intoxicated again and couldn't control himself. She frowned. Yes, that was possible.

Charlotte blew out an exasperated breath. "None of this makes sense. These people have only a business connection to my uncle. There is nothing personal going on."

Nothing personal. Concordia's eyes widened. She had considered Sir Anthony's problems as entirely separate from the death of Victoria Lester. And whenever she'd reflected upon Miss Lester's death, she had focused on discovering the caller's identity rather than the potential victim he'd spoken of.

That caller had been working up the nerve to try to kill a man. No, she corrected herself, to try *again*. And based upon the woman's reply at the other end of the line, the motive was quite personal. *With the suffering he has brought upon us, he has had it coming for a long time.*

She had no proof that Sir Anthony Dunwick was the target. But as she aired out the details in her mind, she could see the connections—between the club, the caller, the switchboard girl, and Sir Anthony. What would have been the *first* attempt on his life?

Then she remembered. At the play, Sir Anthony had alluded to getting "banged about" in his carriage. *Infernal city traffic,* he'd said.

The attempt had obviously failed. What if the killer had then followed them out here, perhaps manipulating an invitation from the all-too-generous Sir Anthony? He would be at his leisure to look for opportunities, to slip the anonymous envelope containing the iris in among a stack of letters, to catch Sir Anthony alone.

"Concordia?" Charlotte broke into her thoughts.

"Huh? I'm sorry, what were you saying?"

"I said, if only we could find what Uncle Anthony had been struck with. That might point us in the right direction. Then we would know it was deliberate, as disagreeable as that is."

"David thinks any weapon is under six feet of water by now. What would be of most benefit is learning what those anonymous irises mean. The motive lies there, I'm sure of it." She was tempted to share her thinking with Charlotte, to tell her about Victoria Lester, but the young lady looked overwhelmed enough at the moment. "I wish we could talk with your uncle."

Charlotte shook her head. "He is in no condition to answer any questions. We'll have to wait."

Concordia grimaced. *Waiting* was not her strong suit.

"Have we considered everyone who had an opportunity to catch him alone on the boat?" Charlotte asked.

"Hmm." Concordia pursed her lips as she thought. "There is also Miss Farraday. When she returned to the kitchen to retrieve her charges, she appeared quite flustered. And she does have a motive. Remember, your uncle upset her with his accusations last night." Back to the irises again. Yes, that seemed promising.

"I doubt that is sufficient cause to hit him over the head," Charlotte said.

"If she is indeed the one who set out the vase of irises, then it makes sense," Concordia said. "She could be the person sending him the anonymous letters."

Charlotte looked down at her hands. "I have a confession to make about those irises last night."

Concordia blinked. "Wait—*you* did that? Whyever would you do such a thing?"

"I did not intend for Miss Farraday to be falsely accused," Charlotte said defensively. "I hadn't realized she was cutting flowers from the garden that afternoon and might be viewed with suspicion."

Mercy, there seemed to have been quite a bit of traffic around

Lady Dunwick's cutting garden yesterday. "You still haven't answered my original question."

Charlotte wouldn't meet her eye. "I feel a bit silly."

"Well, it's done. You may as well tell me."

"My aunt and uncle refused to tell me anything about what was going on. Once I knew for sure that the most recent anonymous letter came without postage and the person responsible was here, I wanted to prompt the culprit to—to give himself away. I thought the sight of the irises upon the table might do the trick."

"You mean, get him to stand up and make a public confession, ideally before the soup course?" Concordia asked dryly.

Charlotte shot her a look. "Of course not," she snapped. "But I'd hoped for perhaps a guilty start of surprise, an uneasy look, something like that."

"I take it you were not successful."

The girl gave a miserable nod.

A creak sounded, just outside, but the door didn't open. *Someone was listening.* Concordia quickly crossed the room and flung open the door. Unfortunately, creaky floorboards work both ways, and the eavesdropper had already fled down the corridor. She had only a glimpse of the man's hounds-tooth jacket before he turned the corner. It was enough. She sighed and closed the door.

"Who was it?" Charlotte asked.

"Pickering."

"Ugh, he is such a nosey Parker," Charlotte said. "What a disagreeable man."

Concordia suddenly felt quite weary. The events of the afternoon must be catching up with her. A nap was in order.

She picked up her hat. "I should go. We'll know better how to proceed once your uncle is feeling well enough to talk. In the meantime"—she couldn't resist a small smile—"I would suggest you alter your reading habits. Those stunts in the Sherlock Holmes stories don't work in real life. After all, this is not 'A

Scandal in Bohemia.'" If she remembered the story correctly, Holmes had used a smoke bomb to trick the guilty person into revealing her hiding place. It wasn't a *bad* idea, *per se*, but fiction and reality were two different things entirely. Heaven forfend Charlotte tried something as drastic as that.

Charlotte gave a start of surprise. "I thought you hadn't read them."

Concordia chuckled. "I haven't read *all* of them, dear." With a wave, she left the library to seek out David.

CHAPTER 13

*S*ir Anthony recovered rapidly over the next few days, although Lady Dunwick kept a close eye and would let no one but Charlotte and the servants near him. However, when Charlotte tried to bring up the subject of the pressed irises or the idea that the blow to his head was no accident, Lady Dunwick banished her as well.

Charlotte wasn't the only one asking the question of how Sir Anthony came to injure his head. The guests—no doubt fueled by Pickering's gossip about what he had overheard—speculated among themselves when Lady Dunwick and Charlotte were out of earshot.

There was a restless air among the guests. Charlotte postponed the picnic at the windmill. It would have been too strenuous for her uncle, who wasn't equal to boating excursions, either. As Lady Dunwick was disinclined to host entertainments that would take her away from her husband, the group became a less cohesive whole, each off to his own pursuits. Edgar Wynderhane returned to the city alone, simply saying he had urgent matters to take care of and promising his wife he'd be back in time for Saturday's fair. Concordia wondered if he was trying to put Sir Anthony's investments to rights. Why not take Reese with him? Perhaps the broker was still angry at his secretary's pending defection.

Concordia stayed out of the gossip chain, finishing up with the rummage sale items and making trips into East Hampton to rehearse with the Ladies' Drama Guild. They should be ready for the fair in two days' time.

Of course, she continued to speculate about Sir Anthony's injury. Who was to blame? Wynderhane? Reese? Nash? Pickering? Miss Farraday? Or heaven forbid, Miss Ambrose? The names went around and around in her head.

David, Nash, and Reese kept busy, joining the locals for practice at the ball field in Hassett Knoll Park. David came home so tired from these excursions that he frequently fell asleep in his chair, his wood project untouched in his lap. Concordia would rouse him enough to get him to bed and tuck him in. They took most of their dinners at the cabin, too. Concordia was feeling tired herself, and her appetite was fickle these days.

David noticed. "You are pushing yourself too hard, helping out with the rummage sale and the play."

Concordia sighed. "It is just a couple more days."

Of course, not all were ill-disposed to stay put. Mrs. Reese seemed to find any place agreeable so long as she could knit. The Gemmer progeny enjoyed playing in the sand and water, and even Miss Farraday seemed more relaxed. Concordia at first thought it was because the children had settled into a routine, but she soon discovered another reason why.

The day before the fair, Concordia had awoken early to watch the sunrise and was strolling along the path beside the dunes. The crisp morning air felt wonderful, the quiet disturbed only by a chorus of birdsong and her own soft footfalls. As she gazed idly ahead, she saw movement behind the gazebo on the hill above. It was Miss Farraday, who headed for the house, tucking her hair tidily under her cap and smoothing her apron.

Concordia stopped and was about to call out a greeting when

another figure stepped into view and, with a wave to the young lady, hurried toward the opposite side of the house. William Nash.

Concordia's mouth hung open. Madeline Farraday and William Nash?

Not so far-fetched. Both worked for the Gemmers. They were bound to have encountered each other upon numerous occasions, especially if Hans Gemmer brought his work home with him as frequently as he did while vacationing at the Dunwicks' cottage.

A dalliance between the two would be a less sinister explanation of why Miss Farraday was unaccounted for during the time when Sir Anthony was injured. It would also explain the lady's tousled aspect when she had returned to the kitchen that day. Concordia felt a bit of relief at the possibility. Better some inappropriate dalliance than attempted murder. It likely cleared Nash as well.

She wasn't the only one who had observed the pair. At the sound of an old lady's chuckle, she whipped around.

Mrs. Reese had come from the path that led to the Ambrose property. "My, my, that is the third morning this week! Of course, young people are apt to throw caution to the wind."

"You haven't said anything to anyone?" Concordia asked.

The woman's expression turned wistful. She shifted her knitting bag upon her arm. "Who am I to interfere? They are grown adults."

"That is surprisingly broad-minded," Concordia said, falling into step with her.

"'Surprising,' you say?" The woman raised an eyebrow. "We old people are far less rigid than you believe, young lady. Only a few things in life are worth fighting for. Family, for instance."

"I can see your point," Concordia said. "I would say that one's principles are worth fighting for as well." In a change of subject, she asked, "Were you up early enjoying the sunrise?"

The lady tipped her head back toward the path behind her. "I like to walk when it's cool. Lately, I've found myself visiting the

Misses Ambrose in the morning. I believe young Susie is finally starting to warm up to me. Her aunt is grateful to have someone to keep an eye on her while she goes down to the shore with her camera."

"That is quite kind of you."

Mrs. Reese shrugged. "They feed me toast and jam. I am well recompensed."

"How is Susie?"

"Well enough, though I'm glad Edgar Wynderhane has gone back to the city for a while. His visits have upset the girl."

Concordia stopped. "He's been seeing them? Is he still trying to buy the property?" Gwen had made no mention of that yesterday.

"James tells me that Wynderhane's wife is most insistent. She is desperate to cultivate a friendship with Lady Dunwick. It would be quite a feather in her cap, although that is purely conjecture on my part." She gave a self-deprecating laugh. "I hardly move in such circles myself. A two-time widow with no fortune is not exactly sought-after company."

"Your grandson seems quite up-and-coming," Concordia said. "To be working for Wynderhane is prestigious enough, and now to be moving up—" She stopped, realizing this was information she shouldn't know. That seemed to be happening quite often lately. She returned to the previous subject. "I don't think it will matter what Wynderhane offers. Gwen won't sell."

"She may have no choice. He is threatening to have the land repossessed by the county. Miss Ambrose just received a letter from Wynderhane's lawyer yesterday to that effect. If that happens, Wynderhane could buy it even more cheaply and easily." The woman sighed. "It seems the man doesn't even need to be in the vicinity to cause harm to that poor family."

"Repossessed? Why?"

Mrs. Reese grimaced. "Apparently, the lady is behind in her property taxes—ever since she took possession, in fact. The county sends her reminders but, out of compassion for the family, had let the matter lie."

"And Wynderhane would simply swoop in and take her land? How beastly."

Mrs. Reese looked at her with troubled eyes. "I implored her to go to Sir Anthony and see what could be done—he is an attorney, after all—but she won't, given what the poor man has gone through recently."

Concordia bit her lip as she thought. Something must be done. They could not allow the Ambroses to be kicked out of their home.

She had just parted ways with Mrs. Reese and was heading for the house when she saw Nash and Reese step off the porch. She waved. "Skipping breakfast this morning?"

Nash had changed clothes since she'd caught sight of him at the gazebo with Miss Farraday. He nodded and brushed back the hair from his brow. "We'll get breakfast later. We want to get in some batting practice first." He elbowed his companion. "Reese here may be at leisure until Wynderhane gets back this afternoon, lucky fellow, but I have quite a stack that could keep me at my desk all day. Best do it now. We're going to see if your husband wants to join us."

Concordia nodded. "I'm sure he will. He was still at Cross-winds when I left."

She was about to go past them when Reese stopped her. "You haven't by any chance seen a baseball bat along your walk? I thought I left it on the porch yesterday."

She shook her head.

Nash chuckled. "You're always leaving things behind, my good man. I found your notepad by the fish pond the other day. The bat could be in the dunes for all we know."

Reese winced. "I'd hate to lose such a good bat. Ash wood, you know."

She knew very little about the merits of one wood over

another, especially for a baseball bat. "If it was left out, perhaps someone found it and put it in the tool shed."

Reese shrugged. "It's as good a place as any to start."

Out of curiosity, she followed them to the shed and waited outside—it was a bit cobwebby in there—as the men searched.

"Ah, here it is!" Nash came out, brandishing it in triumph, Reese close behind.

"What's that on it?" she asked, pointing to a piece of paper wound around the handle.

Reese frowned and unfolded it. Nash, reading over the shorter man's shoulder, let out a whistle.

"This is...outrageous," Reese whispered between thinned and pale lips.

"Indeed it is," Nash said indignantly. "I never imagined he'd sink so low."

"What? What does it say?" Concordia reached for the note. Reese hesitated, then silently passed it over.

Reese—I know you tried to kill him.

She gaped at the bat in Reese's hands. Were they looking at the weapon used against Sir Anthony? Was the culprit holding it now? She suppressed a shiver.

They had imagined the weapon would be under six feet of water by now. Not if it were a crucial piece of sports equipment, something not easily replaced and needed in just a few days' time.

"May I see the bat?" She reached for it, and Reese reflexively snatched it away.

"Come now, man, we know you didn't do it," Nash coaxed. "Let's see." He took the bat out of the man's nerveless grip.

Her stomach clenched at the sight of several dark, reddish brown stains near the widest end. "What are those marks?"

Nash shrugged. "I don't remember noticing them before, but who inspects a bat? Clay mud stains, probably."

She frowned.

Reese's jaw clenched. "Someone is trying to place the blame on me." He snatched the bat and stalked to the house.

Concordia looked at William Nash. "Am I to assume he's referring to Pickering?"

He scowled. "The man's been angling for James's position for quite a while. Always slinking around, listening in on conversations... Still, I wouldn't have thought he'd do something so underhanded."

She sighed. She and Charlotte had given Pickering the ammunition he needed when he had eavesdropped at their door. "You'd better go after Reese before it comes to blows. I'll get David."

He sighed. "Right." He ran back toward the house.

CHAPTER 14

*C*oncordia had hoped by the time she returned with David that Nash would have been able to calm Reese sufficiently, but such was not the case. Instead, Reese's raised voice had drawn a crowd to the front parlor: the Gemmers, Maud Wynderhane, and Mrs. Reese were hovering uncertainly on the periphery as Reese and Pickering stood nose to nose, Reese jabbing his finger in Pickering's face as the latter folded his arms and looked on in contempt. At least Nash was the one who had hold of the bat, but his pleas to Reese were ineffectual, as were those of Reese's grandmother.

"Stop this at *once*," said a deep, authoritative voice. Sir Anthony stood in the doorway, accompanied by Lady Dunwick and Charlotte. Although a bruise lingered at his temple, he seemed otherwise whole.

His brows lowered in a stern expression. "Is this any way to behave as a guest in my house?"

James Reese reddened and fell silent.

"Sir Anthony!" Mrs. Wynderhane, brightening, came toward him. "How are you feeling?"

"Well enough, ma'am, thank you," he said gruffly, self-consciously putting a hand to his head. "If you all would excuse us? I wish to speak to Reese and Pickering alone. I believe the breakfast buffet has been laid." As Nash walked by him with the bat, he added, "I'll take that."

Lady Dunwick hesitated, as if to stay behind.

"You as well, my dear," he said softly, patting her hand. "We'll have this cleared up in no time."

Head held high, Lady Dunwick led the group to the dining room, Charlotte falling into step with Concordia and David as they followed the others.

David looked back over his shoulder as Sir Anthony closed the parlor door. "Has your uncle sufficiently recovered to deal with those two?"

"Indeed," Charlotte said, "the doctor has pronounced him mended. And just in time. Aunt Susan couldn't have kept him in bed a minute longer." She hesitated, waiting until Lady Dunwick was out of earshot. "I heard there was a note."

Concordia nodded. "It accused Reese of striking your uncle. Well, specifically, it said that he 'did it.' As the note was wrapped around the bat, the implication is that the bat was the weapon. I saw stains upon it, but Nash seemed to think that was residue from it having gotten muddy at some point."

"I'd like a closer look at the bat," David said. "Reese thinks Pickering wrote the note?"

"Nash believes it, too." Concordia sighed. "I have to admit, it's the most likely answer. Pickering was listening at the library door the other day, when Charlotte and I discussed Sir Anthony's injury and the lack of a weapon nearby. And we all know the man wants Reese's position. What better way to discredit him in Wynderhane's eyes?" Perhaps someone should have told Pickering long ago that James Reese was leaving Wynderhane for another position in the firm. There seemed no point in keeping it secret anymore.

"If so, it was an absurd stunt by Pickering," David said. "It will be the man's undoing."

Wynderhane returned that afternoon and closeted himself with Sir Anthony almost as soon as he arrived. Concordia and David heard about it later from Charlotte, when she stopped by their cabin.

"Uncle Anthony's funds are not as badly off as they first feared," she said. "Mr. Wynderhane was able to move the remaining shares to a safer place. We suffered some losses, of course."

"Your uncle told you that?" Concordia asked.

Charlotte blushed. "Not exactly. I sat out on the porch beside the library window. You can hear everything there."

"Miss Crandall!" Concordia said in her sternest teacher voice. "Are we to all become Pickerings now?" Of course, she had done some listening at windows herself. *Mercy.*

Charlotte raised an eyebrow. "I suppose you don't want to know what else I heard?"

Concordia glanced at her smirking husband before turning back with a sigh. "All right then. Tell us."

"Pickering was sent for. Uncle Anthony had him repeat what he'd said yesterday. The man unabashedly admits leaving the note on the bat."

David waved a dismissive hand. "I examined the bat in question quite carefully. With your uncle's permission, of course. There was no blood on it at all."

Concordia looked over at him in surprise. "You didn't tell me that."

"You were napping. I didn't want to disturb you." He ducked his head sheepishly. "Then I forgot about it."

"So what were the stains we saw?" Concordia asked.

He snorted. "Smelled like berries to me."

Concordia blinked. *"Berries?"*

"Pickering went to quite a lot of effort to get Reese in trouble." David glanced at Charlotte. "I assume Wynderhane doesn't give credence to his assertion."

She nodded. "Although Pickering's bravado defied belief. He admitted that he has no proof of Reese's guilt—he said it was a strong *feeling*. Then he had the nerve to caution Wynderhane against keeping Reese in his employ and boldly put himself forward as the better candidate for secretary."

David let out a low whistle.

"What happened then?" Concordia asked.

"Wynderhane told him Reese was already leaving his employ for something better, and even if Pickering were the last candidate in the city, he would never hire such an underhanded bounder." Charlotte blushed. "Pardon the language. I was merely quoting."

David leaned forward impatiently. "And then? Did your uncle fire him?"

She shook her head. "That is not his way. He would do it in private, not in front of Wynderhane. Although I'm sure that's what will happen next."

CHAPTER 15

The morning of the fair dawned warm and sunny, burning off the fog from the bay in no time. David helped the stable boy load the supplies on the farm cart as Charlotte eyed the horizon. "The heat is bound to be oppressive later."

Lady Dunwick chuckled. "The ices stand should do quite well."

"I noticed your staff is dressed in their finery," David said. "They will be attending as well?"

"Oh yes," Charlotte said. "We would have a mutiny on our hands otherwise. It is the event of the season."

"Unfortunately, Marie must stay behind," Lady Dunwick said. "The Gemmer infant has the sniffles, and Miss Farraday is obliged to accompany Serena to the fair."

Charlotte raised a skeptical eyebrow. "Mrs. Gemmer cannot take charge of her daughter at the fair?"

Lady Dunwick shrugged, no doubt reluctant to criticize her own. "I promised Marie the week off in recompense, after the guests are gone."

"Is Uncle Anthony still feeling well enough to attend?" Charlotte asked. "Perhaps I should wait for him."

Concordia knew she was worried. *July twenty-second.* Today was the day.

"There is no need to play nursemaid to the man," Lady Dunwick said. "He'll be there." Her brows lowered in severity as Daniel Pickering came through the front door, awkwardly balancing his cases.

He cleared this throat and gave Lady Dunwick a polite bow. "May I request a—a ride to the station? It is on your way to the fairgrounds." Gone was the smug air—the crossed arms, the raised eyebrow, the prideful, jutting chin. In its place were the sagging shoulders, downcast eyes, and hesitant voice of a defeated man. Concordia almost preferred the former aspect, as disagreeable as it had been.

Lady Dunwick's expression softened. "Your train won't arrive for several hours. Are you sure you wish to wait that long on a station bench?"

"It is preferable to lingering here," he answered, meeting her eyes only briefly. "Thank you, my lady."

It took no time at all to pull up to the station, unload his cases, and exchange curt goodbyes. As they pulled away, Concordia looked back at the man who had caused so much trouble this past week. He simply stood there, luggage at his feet, staring after them. She had the strangest sensation that they hadn't heard the last of Daniel Pickering.

Canopies had already been set up in East Hampton's village green, along with patio umbrellas, booths, and roughly constructed viewing stands that flanked the improvised baseball diamond at the far end of the commons.

"The grass looks half-trampled already," Concordia said. There was bound to be a great deal of dust kicked up today.

Lady Dunwick sighed. "Last year there was talk of moving the site, but it has yet to be acted upon."

Concordia caught sight of Miss Winston, already dressed as Julius Caesar, frantically waving from a partially enclosed pavilion along the left side of the field. "I'll stop by your booth later."

Charlotte nodded. "As they say in the theater, 'break a leg.'"

"Let me help," David offered, following his wife. "I won't be needed until after the midday meal."

Concordia smiled, remembering the chaos of play productions at the college. "I'm sure we could put you to use."

Miss Winston was exceptionally organized and had already sorted the necessary props and costumes: daggers, togas, and a few benches on stage for seating the Senate members. There was even a painted backdrop, and an extra curtain had been hung across the back corner for costume changes and to conceal props until needed. Even a dressing mirror had been provided. With David's help, Concordia soon had her Brutus costume in place and had sheathed her dagger on a belt around her waist. "Where did you get all this?" she asked Miss Winston.

"It helps to be in the midst of an artist colony. Several people assisted with set painting. Other items were borrowed here and there. Your 'dagger' is what Captain Decker uses for gutting fish." She smiled. "Don't worry: we cleaned it thoroughly. It looks quite convincing from a distance, don't you think? Be careful with it, though. It's sharp."

The women were finally ready, just as fairgoers streamed across the grounds and scattered toward different booths. David acted as a hawker of sorts, standing beside the open tent to draw in a prospective audience. Concordia smiled from behind the curtain as she listened to his patter: "Right this way, folks! Witness the downfall of the great Caesar, performed by the Ladies' Drama Guild!"

After a few minutes, he stopped. Were they full already? Concordia peeked around the curtain and pushed up her spectacles for a better look. Most of the benches were occupied, but there was still some room.

Then she saw the thin, slightly stooped, gray-haired man

beside David at the front of the rope line, and her pulse quickened. *Rusty.*

David was leaning close and keeping a firm hand upon the old man's shoulder, murmuring to him all the while as they walked away. She let out a breath. Thank goodness her husband had the situation in hand.

"How are we doing?" Miss Winston hissed over Concordia's shoulder.

"I'd say we are full enough to get started. More will be drawn in as we go along, I'm sure."

By the time they had finished a selection of early scenes and were ready for Act Three, scene one—the assassination of Julius Caesar—they had so many attendees that one of the volunteers opened the canvas sides of the pavilion to improve the view of the stage. Concordia tried to ignore her sudden flutter of nerves as she focused upon her cue from fellow assassin Servilius Casca: "Speak, hands for me!"

As she straightened after joining the others in mock-performing the fatal deed, Miss Winston's immortal words "Et tu, Brute?" ringing in her ears, she saw a different spectacle playing out beyond the pavilion: that of Susie, Gwen Ambrose, Mr. and Mrs. Wynderhane, and Sir Anthony clustered together. They were too far away for her to hear, but her heart froze when she saw Susie—face contorted in distress—pummeling the chest of Wynderhane as Gwen drew her away, then Sir Anthony taking a step toward Wynderhane, with a look so fierce it made the broker shrink back—

"*Psst!* Mrs. Bradley!" A sharp whisper from the supposedly dead Caesar brought her back to the task at hand.

Finally, the players were finished for the morning. With a promise to return after the baseball game for their afternoon performance,

Concordia hurried in search of David and Rusty. She found them at the shooting gallery. David handed back his rifle to the volunteer and came over to join her. Rusty, unaware of Concordia, kept his eye on the ducks and squeezed the trigger with enthusiasm.

They stepped out of earshot of the old man. "How is he?" she asked.

David grimaced. "I am running out of activities to keep him occupied. I'd hoped that shooting inanimate objects would prove cathartic."

"Or whip him into a frenzy," she said dryly.

"Well, there is that, I suppose. Were you successful at dispatching the mighty Caesar?"

She wrinkled her nose at him. "Yes, the deed was done." She gestured toward Rusty, who handed back his rifle and was presented with a kewpie doll. "He did well."

Rusty's eyes brightened, and he hurried over. "Your husband said you would be finished soon. Can we talk?"

Concordia nodded. "Shall we go over to the food tent? I'm famished. We can find an out-of-the-way table there, I hope."

"Good idea." David patted his middle. "I need to sustain myself for the game."

David went to the counter to fetch their meals while Concordia and Rusty sat at one of tables, laid with a gaily checked red-and-white tablecloth that fluttered in the breeze.

Rusty set down the doll to anchor one corner. "Your husband is a prudent man. Had I not seen him first, I might have gone after Wynderhane, loaded for bear. He talked me out of it. For now."

She suppressed a relieved sigh. "I regret I was not able to get an answer for you. The situation turned awkward—"

Rusty held up a hand. "No need to explain. Bradley told me."

"Still, I should have persisted."

Rusty's eyes softened. "Your husband said Wynderhane's been out of town until now. You cannot blame yourself, dear."

David returned with a tray. "All right, then! Who's hungry?" He passed out the wax-paper-wrapped sandwiches, plates of potato salad, and cups of lemonade.

They ate in silence. After a few bites, Concordia found her appetite was gone. She pushed the wrapper aside. David raised an eyebrow but said nothing.

"When would be a good time for me to see him?" Rusty asked.

"It would be best to get him alone, I think," David said, "which can be difficult. Now that he's back, his wife dogs his every move."

From what they knew of the man's infidelities, she was not surprised. In fact, she remembered seeing husband and wife together when Susie had flung herself at Wynderhane. What had upset the girl? Had Wynderhane made good on his threat and taken their land from them, after all? Her stomach twisted.

By this time, many of the food tent's patrons had moved on. However, almost as if conjured from her thoughts, she caught sight of the familiar, balding gentleman of barrel-chested physique approaching the food counter. Edgar Wynderhane. "Why not speak to him now?" she said to Rusty, nodding toward the man.

Rusty swiveled his head. "That's Wynderhane?"

"And he seems to be alone," she said.

David stood. "I'll get him."

They watched as David approached Wynderhane, who jumped back guardedly, as if expecting to be struck. David reached out a friendly hand. The broker hesitated, then shook it. David murmured a few words. The man nodded, paid for his food, and followed him back to their table.

"Mr. Wynderhane," David said, "this is Mr. Deighton, former proprietor of Deighton's Books and Miss Lester's grandfather."

Wynderhane gave a cautious nod and sat.

David dropped his voice. "It was his store that was burned down and his granddaughter who was killed."

Wynderhane winced.

Rusty, hands clenched in his lap, regarded Wynderhane in silence.

Wynderhane cleared his throat awkwardly. "I—I regret my role in this tragedy. All I wanted was information on certain... rivals. Your granddaughter wanted money. It seemed an equitable exchange."

"'Equitable' would be telling me who made the call from the Stock Exchange Luncheon Club," Rusty retorted. "Mrs. Bradley says you know who it is."

Wynderhane hesitated. "And what will you do with such information?"

"Go to the police, of course."

The broker shook his head. "I would be ruined, banned from the Exchange for life, arrested for wiretapping."

She started. Here was a motive for Victoria's death that she had not considered. What if Wynderhane was behind her death, after all? Perhaps he'd lied. Perhaps he had indeed contacted her, saw how distressed she was, and feared she would go to the police with the entire story. His wiretapping scheme would then be exposed. He could even have hired someone else to commit the actual murder. After all, he must have known her address.

She shook herself. He was villain enough, to be sure, with his philandering ways and his cold-hearted attempts to take away the Ambroses' home, but she was heaping a great deal more depravity upon the man without proof, first suspecting him of attacking Sir Anthony and now the death of Miss Lester. Still, it was something to consider. If true, it could mean that the death of Victoria Lester and the threat to Sir Anthony were *not* connected. She needed to keep an open mind.

"What if you gave Rusty the name, but he left you out of it?" David's voice broke into her thoughts.

Wynderhane gave him a withering look. "And how exactly is he to do that? How would the police find his story credible without me?" He looked over at the pale-lipped Rusty, his expression softening. After a long moment, he sighed. "If you can think of a way, I'd be willing to—"

"Ah, Edgar, there you are!" a voice exclaimed. Concordia jumped. She had been so absorbed in their conversation that she had not noticed Mrs. Wynderhane and Mrs. Reese, nearly on top of them. Now that she was looking around, she realized this wasn't the best place for such a sensitive discussion. Miss Farraday was seated at the next table with little Serena Gemmer, although she seemed too preoccupied with keeping ice cream from dripping on the girl's dress to have heeded the conversation.

"We have been looking everywhere for you," Maud Wynderhane went on, first giving the group an appraising glance before apparently deciding the interruption wasn't offending anyone important. Or she might have been eyeing the table. Her clenched hands suggested an effort of will to keep from snatching Rusty's kewpie doll from the table corner, where it most certainly did *not* belong, or straightening the salt and pepper shakers in the condiment tray. "Mrs. Reese saw some lovely sculptures she thinks would look perfect in a cottage garden," she went on. "I want you to come see them."

Eleanor Reese tapped Concordia on the arm with her fan. "An impressive performance, Mrs. Bradley. You are to be congratulated. You make a convincing Brutus. I positively shuddered when you wielded that dagger!"

"Oh...uh, thank you, Mrs. Reese," Concordia stammered, her attention divided as she watched Wynderhane get up. She nudged David, who took the hint.

"Perhaps, Mr. Wynderhane, we could talk again this afternoon, after the baseball game? It would give us a chance to consider your...offer and come up with options." David glanced at Rusty, who nodded.

Mrs. Reese narrowed her eyes in curiosity, looking back and forth between them.

"What offer?" Mrs. Wynderhane's voice was heavy with suspicion as she gave Concordia a cold stare. *You are up to something,* her look seemed to say. Concordia suppressed the urge to flinch.

Wynderhane drew his wife's arm into the crook of his elbow. "Merely a business matter, my dear. No need to concern yourself at all." He inclined his head. "Very well, Bradley, I shall see you here, after the game."

Concordia let out a sigh after the Wynderhanes and Mrs. Reese left. "How can we convince him to give us the name?"

"By coming up with a feasible story as to how we got it, leaving out Wynderhane," David said.

She shook her head. What an absurd situation they found themselves in, trying to protect an unscrupulous man in order to catch a murderer. Unless he *was* the murderer. She blew out a breath. What a muddle.

"At least we never told the police that Victoria had tapped the line deliberately," Rusty said. "Perhaps I could say I only just discovered a note she had written, naming the man she had learned was responsible for the call?"

David narrowed his eyes. "How would such a note have survived the fire?"

"You're right. Everything was destroyed," Rusty muttered.

"Not quite everything," Concordia pointed out. "The morning of the fire, Claude gave you the books you'd been waiting for. They had come away unscathed."

"True." David tapped his chin, lost in thought.

Concordia looked up to see a tall, young man in a ball cap running toward them. William Nash.

"Bradley," Nash cried, "what are you doing, lounging here? It's time to get ready."

With a smothered exclamation, David stood up. "Excuse me." He hurried off after Nash.

"Good luck!" she called to his retreating back.

CHAPTER 16

oncordia headed toward the ladies' section, along the left and top of the bunting-festooned grandstand. It wasn't hard to find, as a blossoming of parasols filled the space. There wouldn't be much of a view with so many parasols held aloft, which was why most of the male spectators avoided that section at all costs. But at least there would be shade.

She threaded her way through the vendors striding up and down the bleachers, selling lemonade, cider, frankfurters on rolls, popcorn, peanuts, and chewing gum. She found a seat near the aisle with a slightly better view, sitting behind and to the right of a woman with a large-brimmed hat and her husband, who was obviously sacrificing the joys of viewing the game for the sake of love.

The band struck up a rousing tune as the Hassett Knoll men took the field. Though all sported knickers, tunics, long hose, and baseball caps, it was a hodge-podge of colors, with only some of the players in matching uniforms. The spectators cheered their encouragement nonetheless. Concordia smiled at the sight of David, attired in a striped shirt and gray knickers two sizes too large but held up with a stout belt. She stood and waved, but he was too far away to see her.

"May I join you, Concordia?" a woman's voice inquired. It was Lady Dunwick. Although the slight droop in her shoulders and the manner in which she leaned upon her parasol suggested fatigue, the lady's smile was undimmed.

"By all means," Concordia said, shifting over. "How nice to see you. I'm sorry that I've not had the chance to visit the rummage sale."

Lady Dunwick waved a dismissive hand. "We had plenty of help. I know you've been busy."

"How is it going?"

"Splendidly." She gave the bench a swat with her handkerchief before sitting down. "We have exceeded last year's receipts and have so little inventory that we are closing for the day." She exhaled. "I am at liberty for the rest of the afternoon."

"And well deserved. You have put in a lot of work this past week." Concordia surveyed the stands, craning her neck around parasols for a better look. "Where are Charlotte and Sir Anthony?"

"They got seats early, so as to be close to the action." Lady Dunwick tipped her parasol toward the right-field foul line, nearly taking out the hat of the woman in front of them. "Oh, I do beg your pardon," Lady Dunwick murmured. The gentleman helped her untangle the point from his lady's brim ribbon.

"Ah, yes, I see them," Concordia said. Charlotte and Sir Anthony stood with the rest of the Hassett Knoll contingent of fans in that section, clapping and cheering as the game began in earnest.

For the East Hampton batsmen, the process of preparing to hit the ball seemed to include a great deal of dilly-dallying—intervals of stretching, swinging at the air, and toeing the dirt. Of course, there was an equal amount of stretching, glaring, and ball-into-glove-pounding on the part of the pitcher, too. Then, finally, the ball was thrown and the bat was swung.

To the delight of the home crowd, East Hampton scored three runs before it was finally Hassett Knoll's turn at bat. James Reese, the lead-off batsman, strode confidently to the plate and performed another action peculiar to baseball. And saloons.

"Is it customary for them to spit so much?" Concordia asked. She heard a snort from the gentleman in the next row.

"One strike!" the umpire yelled.

"Oh, dear," Lady Dunwick said.

"Who's the umpire?" Concordia asked.

The man in front of them turned. "Our mayor, Ed Lynch. But don't worry. He's as fair as they come."

Concordia nodded her thanks, and he turned back around.

Finally, when the count was full and Reese seemed reduced to hitting a sequence of foul balls—Concordia despaired of there ever being a second batsman—the ball sailed true, and he made it to first. That opened the door to a succession of gains by the Hassett Knoll team, resulting in a scored run and men on first and second with two outs. She looked down the foul line to Charlotte and Sir Anthony, once again on their feet and cheering encouragement to the next batsman. Concordia's heart leapt in her throat at the sight of David as he came up to the plate, applying dirt to his bat handle and waving cheerfully to Charlotte.

Concordia watched, holding her breath, as the pitcher got two strikes past him. What happened next was confusing. The catcher —whether from eagerness or the assumption that the ball coming across the plate was a strike—stepped in and caught it practically under David's arm. Startled, David checked his swing to avoid knocking the man on the head.

"First base!" the umpire yelled, pointing. What followed was a huddle of conversation between pitcher, umpire, catcher, and both coaches, who had run out on the field. David stood away from the whole, kicking dirt off his cleats with the bat, awaiting the final decision.

"What on earth is going on?" Concordia asked Lady Dunwick, as she watched the pitcher grow more apoplectic as the umpire kept pointing to first base.

Lady Dunwick shrugged. "Arguments with the umpire are common, but I haven't seen it so protracted."

The man in front of them turned around again. "There's a new National League rule that I'll bet most o' them on the field don't know about. Any interference by the catcher that prevents the batsman from hitting the ball gives the player an automatic first base. It's a shame, 'cause our man threw a Jim-Dandy pitch. That would have been a strike."

"Do they change the rules often?" Concordia asked.

He grimaced. "More often than I'd like. But this one makes sense."

Concordia watched as the group broke up, the pitcher stalking back to the mound. She clapped as David took first base and the runners advanced.

As the game went on, David acquitted himself admirably in the outfield, his skill in catching fly balls serving to dispatch several batsmen over the course of the next innings. His batting skills, unfortunately, were not as remarkable, and Concordia found herself holding her breath the next two times he came to bat, as he flied out and struck out, respectively. Reese and Nash had better luck at the plate, and each was able to advance runners. By the lucky seventh stretch, Hassett Knoll trailed five to four.

Concordia fanned herself. "Do they intend to play all nine innings?" she asked Lady Dunwick. "I would think they'd make it a shorter game at such a venue."

Lady Dunwick chuckled. "The locals around here take their baseball quite seriously."

Concordia grimaced. She would have to hurry over to the theater tent afterward in preparation for the guild's next performance, which meant she couldn't attend the follow-up meeting with Wynderhane. She prayed David and Rusty could convince the man to reveal what he knew, so they could catch the killer. Then Rusty would finally have some peace.

She frowned. Where *was* Rusty? She hadn't seen him in the stands. Nor Wynderhane, although she noticed his wife and Mrs. Gemmer chatting several rows behind Sir Anthony. Concordia stood for the stretch with the rest of the company, peering around parasols as best as she could. No sign of either man.

"Lemonade! Popcorn! Peanuts!" A lady with a striped apron trod up the steps, a well-laden, wooden tray on a strap around her neck.

"Would you care for some lemonade?" Lady Dunwick asked Concordia, as they resettled themselves after the stretch. She gestured to the seller.

Concordia brightened. That would be just the thing. "Thank you."

The two of them shared a cone of popcorn as well and chatted about local events.

"There is to be a regatta at the end of the month," Lady Dunwick said, brushing the salt from her fingers with a napkin.

"Oh? Will Sir Anthony be entering the *Susan D* in the race?"

"He hopes to, although he's unsure if she will be ready. He hasn't had much time to take the boat out. The accident set him back."

The accident. Now was the time to say something. Leaning close, Concordia murmured, "Lady Dunwick, are you *sure* it was an accident?"

The lady started, then dropped her eyes to her lap, idling brushing her skirt. "You sound like Charlotte. What would you have me say?" she whispered fiercely. "That one of our guests has suddenly decided to try to kill my husband?"

Concordia's mouth dropped open. Lady Dunwick's bald statement had raised a question she had not considered. The pressed irises had been sent to Sir Anthony for years now, symbolic of a long-standing grievance. No move had been made against Sir Anthony all this time. So why now? What had prompted this newfound resolve?

Should Wynderhane refuse to reveal the name, Sir Anthony was their only recourse for information.

Lady Dunwick shifted uneasily at Concordia's silence. "I regret the sharpness of my tone, dear."

Concordia cast a quick glance at the woman, her blue-veined, knobby hands clasped tightly in her lap. Did she know what the irises meant? Now was not the time to discuss it, of course. "Lady Dunwick, we really must speak in private. There's more—" The crack of the bat and the roar from the crowd brought their attention back to the field. Nash had just hit a hard one to right. The ball went sailing over the outfielders and into the awning of the posy booth beyond, where it stuck.

Lady Dunwick sighed as she watched two fielders run after it, attempting to dislodge the ball by whacking at it from underneath. "I told Charlotte her stand was too close to the field."

"Sam Hill," the man in front of them exclaimed, laughing. "Ground rule triple! What are the chances of *that?*"

Nash took his base. Concordia checked the scoreboard. Hassett Knoll and East Hampton were tied, which meant the winning run was now on third. David was up next.

"How many outs are there?" she asked. Lady Dunwick shrugged.

"One." The man in front gestured to David stepping up to the plate. "Soon to be two."

Concordia gritted her teeth. She wouldn't count her husband out yet.

Apparently at his ease, David strode toward the plate, rubbing dirt higher up along the bat. Concordia marveled at his composure. She was ready to bite her fingernails, just sitting here watching.

David eyed the pitcher, then his teammate on third. Nash gave a nod.

The first two pitches came in high. David let them pass, the bat resting on his shoulder. Concordia took a breath and clenched her hands in her lap.

"Pitcher's getting tired," someone behind her said.

"I'll wager he's gonna throw a low ball next," someone else answered.

The pitcher stepped away from the mound, slapped at some dirt on his knee with his glove, blew out a breath, then resumed his position. David waited.

What happened next was a bit of a blur. If she had blinked, she would have missed it. As soon as the ball was released, David stepped forward in a half-crouch, shifted his right hand up the bat, tapped the ball toward first, then ran for all he was worth, dodging the ball as it bounced. The infielders, caught by surprise, rushed toward the ball as Nash made it safely home.

"Sacrifice bunt!" the man in the next row exclaimed. "Unbelievable! Willie Keeler couldn't have done it better. That's the game!"

Concordia exhaled and turned to Lady Dunwick. "Quite thrilling, wouldn't you say? I must congratulate David before getting ready for the play. Are you coming down to the field as well?"

The woman eyed the surging crowd dubiously. "I believe I'll wait here until it thins a bit. You go on, dear."

Concordia stood. "May we talk later?"

Lady Dunwick held her gaze for a moment, then nodded.

It was a challenge to navigate the crowd that clambered down the stands, then struggle against the tide of attendees as her direction shifted toward the ball field. Eventually she found David, Reese, and Nash propping open the supply shed doors, arms laden with gloves and bats.

"Congratulations, gentlemen!" Concordia cried. "It was an

exciting finish."

David smiled and wiped the back of his hand across his grimy forehead. "Well, more suspenseful than we would have liked."

Nash clapped David on the shoulder. "But I was right, they never expected the bunt. And you belted quite a bouncer there, Bradley. They didn't know what to do with it."

"Good thing I had you and Reese to help me work on it ahead of time," David said.

Reese grinned. "Our pleasure." He dusted off his cap. "We're headed to the Maidstone Club to clean up. They've kindly allowed the use of their facilities. You coming?"

With a meaningful look at his wife, David shook his head. "I have something to take care of first. I'll join you later."

"Don't be too long," Nash said. "The East Hampton gents are treating us all to a round of beers at the clubhouse. You don't want to miss it."

After they had left, Concordia asked David, "Have you thought of a way to convince Wynderhane to reveal what he knows?"

David nodded. "I believe so, though it will mean telling the police a little white lie—" He broke off as Charlotte came running toward them.

"Have you seen Uncle Anthony?" she asked. A frown tugged at her brow.

"I thought he was with you," Concordia said.

"We became separated in the crowd. Now I cannot find him anywhere."

"Perhaps he joined your aunt," Concordia said.

Charlotte shook her head. "I just spoke with her. She hasn't seen him."

"He may be chatting up an old acquaintance," David said reassuringly. "But we'll help you look. He cannot be far."

Judging from the tense set of Charlotte's jaw, Concordia knew she shared her fears. Near or far, Sir Anthony could be in grave danger.

$\mathcal{T}$he three spent the next twenty minutes walking among the crowds, discreetly inquiring about Sir Anthony among his acquaintances. They ran into Miss Ambrose and Mrs. Reese coming away from the puppy pen. Their expressions were troubled.

"Has either of you seen Sir Anthony?" Concordia asked.

"Not recently," Miss Ambrose answered. "We have been looking for Susie. I was sure she would be here. She loves petting the animals."

Mrs. Reese pulled her shawl closer around her and shifted uneasily. "I am not at all fond of crowds. People are always losing one another in these large places."

"Perhaps Susie and Sir Anthony went off together?" Charlotte suggested.

"They do get along well," Gwen said. "Earlier today, he was able to calm her right down, after"—she glanced toward Mrs. Reese, who raised an inquiring eyebrow—"well, never mind that. Anyway, she was upset, and he took her to see the ponies." She brightened. "Perhaps they returned there. That would account for both of them being gone."

David nodded toward Lady Dunwick, who paced restlessly beside the closed rummage-sale booth. Maud Wynderhane was with her, alternating between fastidiously plucking dried grass from the hem of her impeccable white muslin dress and ineffectually coaxing her companion to sit down on the bench. "Let's see if she has learned anything more, about either of them."

"Any progress?" Lady Dunwick asked, as they approached.

David shook his head. "I take it you haven't heard anything, either?"

"No." She looked over at Miss Ambrose and Mrs. Reese. "Mrs. Wynderhane has been keeping me company while we wait for word. I see we have recruited additional volunteers. I'm grateful."

Gwen grimaced. "I'm sorry to say I have lost Susie, too. It's all quite nerve wracking." Mrs. Reese nodded her sympathy.

"Is it possible Sir Anthony felt unwell and went home?" Concordia asked.

"We should see if the pony cart is still here. It should be over in the far lot with the other conveyances," Charlotte said.

"Let's go," Miss Ambrose said to Charlotte. "Susie may have gone back to look at the ponies, so we can check for the cart at the same time." They hurried off.

David glanced at his watch. "I'm afraid I have an appointment I cannot miss, but if Sir Anthony hasn't returned in the meantime, we'll continue the search." He nodded toward Concordia. "And you have to get ready for your drama guild performance."

"You're right. I told Miss Winston I would come early." Concordia hesitated. "Lady Dunwick, we hate to leave you—"

The lady patted her arm and gestured toward Mrs. Reese and Mrs. Wynderhane. "Don't worry, dear, we'll be fine. I'm sure there is an innocuous explanation."

It was with conflicting emotions that Concordia headed toward the pavilion. Despite her worry about being late, she was the first player to arrive. The canvas flaps were still closed, and the rope was strung across the area where the attendance line would form.

Concordia lifted the flap and stepped inside. In the gloom, she thought she saw movement on the stage. "Miss Winston?"

Silence. The back of her neck prickled.

Someone was here, and it wasn't Miss Winston. She opened the flaps wide, anchoring them in place. She needed more light. If she were honest with herself, she also wanted a quick escape route. Something definitely wasn't right. What she wouldn't give for Reese's baseball bat right now.

She walked quickly to the stage, head cocked, listening. A rustle of fabric. "Who's here? Come out."

A slim, blond-haired figure shuffled from behind the curtain, clutching an indistinguishable object. She turned a tear-streaked face toward the light.

"Susie!" Concordia exclaimed. "Your aunt has been looking for you. Are you all right?"

The girl shuddered and ran back behind the curtain, to the makeshift dressing area. Concordia hurried after her, impatiently pushing the curtain aside. "Wait!"

The girl stopped and crouched beside the costume trunk. Concordia sucked in a breath. There was a man's foot, sticking out from behind.

No. Not Sir Anthony. Please.

She reluctantly stepped closer. The man moved. Not dead, thank goodness. "Sir Anthony?" She whispered. No response.

She was aware that she still held the curtain in her hand and gave it a vicious tug to let in more light, feeling it rip in her hands. She sucked in a breath at the sight of the man lying on the stage.

Not Sir Anthony.

Edgar Wynderhane.

A large, dark stain spread beneath his shirt, and his eyes were wide with pain and shock as he struggled to breathe. Susie touched him, tentatively, and looked up at Concordia.

Wynderhane reached up a hand towards Concordia. "She... she..." His hand dropped.

Susie ran to Concordia, flinging her arms around her waist, body shaking in silent sobs.

The next image burned in Concordia's mind was that of her reflection in the backstage dressing mirror, pale with shock, protectively clasping a bloodied girl who clutched a knife in a nerveless grip.

CHAPTER 18

"*H*ello? Anyone here?" A woman's voice. Miss Winston.

"I'm sure I heard someone," another woman answered. "And the flap is open."

Concordia glanced down at Susie, face buried in her shirt-waist. *They mustn't find her here.*

She pulled the girl further into shadows and bent down to look her in the eye. "Susie," she whispered, pointing to the rear flap of the tent, "go find your aunt." She jerked a thumb over her shoulder, toward the approaching voices. "Don't let them see you."

Susie's eyes widened.

"Quickly, now," Concordia hissed.

The girl fled, the knife clattering to the stage as she ran. Once the back flap had fallen into place, Concordia took a shuddering breath and straightened. "Over here!" she called to the ladies, step-ping into the light. "We need a doctor. Mr. Wynderhane is gravely injured."

They rushed forward and joined her on the stage, crouching over the barely-conscious man, still gasping for breath and trying to speak. He kept his eyes fixed on Concordia as Miss Winston loosened his collar and peeked beneath his shirt.

"Sh-she...she," he said, over and over.

"Easy, now, save your strength," Miss Winston soothed. She looked up at her companion. "I saw Doc Travers at the shooting gallery. Go fetch him, quickly."

The woman ran off.

Miss Winston wadded up a cloak and gently slid it under his head. "I remember this man, from the Dunwicks' dinner party. Mr.—?"

"Wynderhane. Edgar Wynderhane," Concordia said.

"What is he doing here?"

"I have no idea." What *was* he doing here? Perhaps he'd planned to talk to her alone? If so, who had followed him here and tried to kill him?

Miss Winston's questions seemed to echo her own. "Who would attack him? Did you see anyone when you first came in?"

Concordia shook her head. She hated the lie, but she had to protect Susie until they could figure out what happened. The image of what she had seen this morning, of Susie punching Wynderhane's chest in a fury, was fresh in her mind. But the idea of the girl stalking him with a knife? She didn't believe it. That didn't mean that others would be so quick to dismiss the notion.

"Mrs. Bradley?" Miss Winston persisted. "I asked, was anyone else here? I thought I heard you whispering."

"No, no—I was trying to reassure Mr. Wynderhane." Concordia looked down at the now-unconscious man. If only he could tell them who did this.

"Hello?" a gruff, elderly man's voice called out.

"That must be Dr. Travers," Miss Winston said. She raised her voice. "Back here!"

"I'll light the lamps," Concordia said, moving away. Her foot kicked something that skidded across the floor. She picked it up.

It was a knife, bloodied to the hilt. The one that had been in Susie's hand.

She heard Miss Winston's stifled exclamation behind her. "Why, that's *your* knife, Mrs. Bradley."

Indeed it was. Concordia recognized the scuffed black enamel handle of the fishing knife she'd been given for the part of Brutus. She hastily set it down.

Miss Winston was giving her an odd look. "Do you have a personal antagonism towards this man?"

"Of course not," Concordia snapped.

She...she... What had he meant? Perhaps he'd been distressed that Susie had caused more harm by pulling the knife out of the wound? Or he was worried about the young girl seeing such a disturbing scene? No, Wynderhane was not solicitous of others, even in the best of times.

Concordia sighed. She was grasping at straws, of course. Wynderhane's *she* more plainly indicated Susie as the attacker. Although now, in Miss Winston's eyes, that female was Concordia. How was she to extricate herself from this mess without implicating the girl?

Mercy, why did she invariably get caught up in playacting, knives, and murder?

CHAPTER 19

*C*oncordia watched David pace the front parlor of the Reading Room, where the doctor and Miss Winston insisted they wait for the sheriff. Wynderhane, still alive, had been transported to Dr. Travers's dispensary nearby for whatever treatment could be provided for the poor man. His wife had been fetched as well.

The one bright spot was that Sir Anthony had been found at the Maidstone Club, celebrating the Hassett Knoll baseball team's victory. Apparently, the youth that he'd paid to deliver a message to Lady Dunwick about his plans had given it to the wrong matron. To young boys, every old woman looks the same.

Charlotte, sitting beside her, heaved an impatient sigh. "They could have at least allowed you to return to the cottage. Do they really believe you would try to *flee?*"

David turned from inspecting the candlesticks on the mantel. "It's absurd in the first place to believe Concordia stabbed Wynderhane."

Concordia looked at the blood on her hand, crusted now. "I would dearly like to wash and change, but Miss Winston was most insistent."

Charlotte snorted. "I wonder if she reads those Sherlock Holmes stories on the sly."

"Well, to be fair," Concordia said, "those were the instructions the sheriff's office telegraphed back to Miss Winston. She showed them to me, with her apologies. You don't have to wait with me, you know. I'll be fine."

"Not on your life," David declared.

There was a tap on the door, and Rusty let himself in. "There's a deputy sheriff on his way to talk to you. Miss Winston says he should be here soon."

"How is Mr. Wynderhane?" Concordia asked.

"The same, I hear." He took off his cap and sat across from her. "You're sure he didn't say anything to you when you found him?"

She shook her head.

"We were so close to getting him to tell us what he knew." Rusty sighed.

She bit her lip. Maybe too close. Perhaps their conversation had made someone nervous. They could have been overheard. Or was it merely the sight of Wynderhane speaking to them—to Rusty, Victoria's grandfather—that had prompted the would-be killer to act?

"So what was he doing there?" Rusty went on. "He was supposed to meet us after the game. Why go to the empty drama pavilion instead?"

"Perhaps someone lured him there," Charlotte suggested.

David pursed his lips. "Possible."

If so, that would clear Susie Ambrose as a suspect. Concordia glanced over at Rusty. "Have you heard anything about Susie?"

Rusty frowned. "Who?"

That's right, Rusty didn't know the girl. "Her name is Susie Ambrose, twelve years old. Her aunt lost track of her at the fair. I was hoping she'd been found by now."

Rusty's forehead cleared in understanding. "Ah yes, the simple-minded girl. I heard folks were looking for her. I don't think she's been found yet."

Concordia bit her lip. She should at least tell Gwen that she'd seen her. Susie might have a favorite hiding place where she went when she was distraught. "Rusty, would you find Gwen Ambrose and deliver a note for me?" She searched in her reticule for pencil and paper.

David started. "Why are you sending a note at a time like this?"

Concordia kept her head down as she wrote, afraid that her expression would give her away. "I have a couple of ideas as to where she might be. I want to pass them along, just in case." She folded the slip over twice and was just about to pass it to Rusty when the door opened. She tucked the paper in her skirt pocket.

Concordia's heart sank as she got a good look at the thirtyish, uniformed man who stepped in. His wide neck, thick hands, and muscled, broad shoulders suggested he would be more comfortable in a wrestling ring than conducting a criminal inquiry.

The man swept the hat from his dark head and gave a little bow as he looked back and forth between Charlotte and Concordia. "Deputy Sheriff Yates." To her surprise, his voice was well-modulated, cultured, and his dark eyes swept over her form in a brisk assessment. "You are Mrs. Bradley?"

Concordia inclined her head.

Yates looked at the others. "And these are acquaintances of yours?"

"No," Concordia retorted, "they are my guards, to ensure I do not escape."

Yates smothered a chuckle. "Fair enough. Before we go any further, ma'am, may I take a closer look at your hands and dress?"

Concordia stood and held out her hands. Smears of blood remained on the right hand, where she had picked up the knife, but the other was clean.

"Not much blood there," he remarked, walking slowly around her, examining her clothing. Concordia had the sense that those sharp brown eyes missed little. She was beginning to reassess her initial impression of the man.

"Have you seen Wynderhane?" David asked.

Yates nodded as he continued his examination and Concordia fidgeted in place. She had never been good at standing still. "The man is unconscious and cannot make a statement. I don't know if he ever will. I have also examined the knife—the doc has it in his keeping—but I have yet to see the place where the victim was found. A constable is over there now, keeping guard. I have collected Miss Winston's statement. There are some points to it that I wish to go over with you." He straightened. "Very well, ma'am, you may sit." He crossed back to the door and opened it, nodding to the others. "If you will excuse us, Mrs. Bradley and I have much to discuss."

Rusty and Charlotte obediently filed out, but David seemed disinclined to budge.

"I will stay with my wife," he said.

Bless the man's protectiveness.

Yates met David's gaze. "I'm sorry, sir, I must speak with her alone."

David hesitated, then looked over at Concordia. "You'll be all right?"

She grimaced. "Your being here won't make this any easier. Go on."

"I'll be right outside if you need me." With one last look at Yates, David left, closing the door behind him.

Yates sat on the ottoman across from her, his large hands smoothing the knees of his trousers in a reflexive gesture. He began his inquiry with questions designed to put her at her ease: how long she had been visiting the area—with congratulations upon the occasion of her marriage—what she knew of Wynderhane, her volunteer duties at the fair. He added a few pleasantries about the highlights of the baseball game he had heard about. "It sounds as if I missed quite an event."

She had just started to take her first few deep breaths since finding Wynderhane when Yates got to the heart of the matter. "Tell me about discovering the man in the pavilion."

Concordia began her carefully amended version of the events, keeping as close to the truth as she could while leaving Susie out of it.

Yates raised a skeptical eyebrow when she finished. "That fits with Miss Winston's account—for the most part. However, I must tell you she is of the opinion that you had a personal grudge against Wynderhane and stabbed him yourself." He squinted at her closely, watching her reaction.

Concordia sat back against the cushions, taking a breath to calm her nerves. "So I gather. May I ask what brings her to that conclusion?"

The deputy pulled out a small notepad and pencil, flipping the page until he found what he wanted. "According to the lady, when she first called out to see who was there, you hid behind the curtain, delaying coming out. She later took that as indicative of a guilty impulse to flee. Further, she heard the victim say 'she' more than once, as he was gasping for breath and looking at you. What other *she* could he possibly mean?" He held up a hand to forestall Concordia's objection. "And, finally, the knife used was the one you were given as a prop for the play."

Concordia blinked. Lumped all together, it appeared to be a solid collection of evidence. She tried to ignore the unease that prickled along her spine. "What possible motive could I have for assaulting the man?"

Yates cleared his throat. "Miss Winston theorizes an assignation gone wrong. Unfortunately, Wynderhane's own wife lends credence to that thinking, as she accuses you of trying to lure her husband into some sort of dalliance on a previous occasion. You are both staying at the Dunwick cottage, I understand." He gestured toward her hair. "Mrs. Wynderhane maintains that you cut your hair in a daring attempt to draw attention to yourself and capture his interest."

Concordia felt her face grow hot. How dare Wynderhane's unwanted advances toward her be used as an assault upon her character and appearance.

Well, she was not going to apologize for any of it. She had done nothing wrong. She straightened.

Yates watched her expression shift and gave a satisfied nod. "And now, I will tell you something else, ma'am. I do not believe it for a moment."

She stifled a sigh. "Thank you for that. I assure you, the last thing I want is the death of Mr. Wynderhane. If you will bring in my husband and Rusty—Mr. Deighton, the other man waiting here with me when you arrived—we can tell you what happened back in New York City, before we came. It's all connected."

David and Rusty were summoned—Charlotte was left to pace impatiently outside—and nodded their agreement as Concordia recounted the story of the call Victoria Lester had overheard at the switchboard, her subsequent death and the bookstore fire, Wynderhane's role as the one who had hired Victoria, and his reluctance to reveal the caller at the Stock Exchange Luncheon Club. Concordia left out the incident where Sir Anthony was injured and the anonymous irises. She was theorizing that those were related, but she had to speak to Sir Anthony first to be sure.

Yates scribbled notes at a rapid pace. "You told all this to the city police?"

Rusty grimaced. "Not all. I'd left out the part about my granddaughter deliberately listening in. And of course, we didn't know at the time that Wynderhane was at the club that day and knew the identity of the caller. That came later." He grimaced at David. "We were so close to convincing him to tell us."

"I take it he didn't want to get in trouble for wiretapping," Yates said dryly. He stood. "All right, that about does it for now. Just one more question for Mrs. Bradley."

"What's that?"

"Did you remove the knife?"

She froze. She hadn't. Susie had. "It's a bit of—of a blur, sheriff. I don't really remember. But I must have, I suppose."

"*Deputy* sheriff, ma'am." Yates folded his arms. "Since the knife was left behind, I doubt it was the killer who did so, which leaves only you. But there's a problem with that supposition." He gestured to her attire. "Not to be indelicate, but you should have more blood upon your clothing if that was the case." He got up and stood beside her chair, pointing to the back of her skirt, near the waist. "Allow me to show you something." He led her over to the mirror above the fireplace and turned her slightly to the side.

He pointed to a dark smudge. "That resembles part of a handprint. See the shape of the fingers, there? Impossible for that to be your own hand, with the fingers pointed up and towards the back."

She felt cold all at once. He was right.

He fixed her with a steely gaze. "You are protecting someone, Mrs. Bradley, and I am going to find out who it is." He gave David a meaningful look. Was he trying to convince him to impose some sort of husbandly authority? At least he wasn't as obnoxious as the other policeman, Lieutenant Oliver.

What she wouldn't give for Capshaw to be on the case. She could trust him not to jump to a hasty conclusion and fix blame upon a child. Although Deputy Yates seemed more competent than she initially had given him credit for, she didn't know him well enough to trust him.

Yates waggled a finger at them. "I want you all to remain at the Dunwicks until I tell you otherwise."

"But I am not staying with the Dunwicks," Rusty protested. "I have already checked out of the hotel and cannot afford to board there longer."

"We'll ask Charlotte if the Dunwicks can put you up," David said. Rusty nodded his thanks.

"All right then," Yates said. "And no trips, not even day excursions. I want to know where to find you when I have additional questions."

Concordia winced at the *when* but knew there was no avoiding it.

"If you disregard my instructions and run off, I shall find you and lock you up in the county jail," Yates went on. "And the next court session isn't until October, so that's a mighty long time."

CHAPTER 20

$\mathcal{T}$he Dunwick carriage was waiting to take them back to
the cottage. It was a quiet ride. Concordia stared out at
the sycamore-lined streets in the growing dusk, praying that Susie
had been found.

As soon as they arrived, Charlotte took Rusty inside to talk to
Lady Dunwick about accommodations. Concordia dearly wanted
to speak with Charlotte's aunt right away, too, but she had a more
pressing concern. Susie.

David helped her out of the carriage. "Let's go to the kitchen
and see if we can get something to eat. You must be hungry. I
know I am."

She shook her head. Her stomach was unsettled by worry. "I
want to see if Susie has been found." Her eyes welled with tears.

David held her close, and she clung to him for a moment
before letting go.

"All right then," he said briskly, "but we can still go to the
kitchen. Marie may know what's going on."

She gave a thin smile as he led the way to the back door. One
way or another, he was going to make sure she was fed.

Marie clucked in dismay when they came through the kitchen

door. "Mrs. Bradley! I heard all about it from the grocer's boy. You poor dear. Come, sit down. Let me get you something."

"We can't stay long," Concordia protested, as David pulled out chairs and Marie placed a basket of rolls on the table in front of them. "Has Susie been found?"

Marie shook her head. "Not yet. The gardener and stable boy have joined a bunch o' them in the search, including Mr. Nash and Mr. Reese."

Concordia started to get up. "I want to help."

"Now, now, there's nothing you can do right this minute," Marie soothed. "You don't even know where they've looked. Wait until they come back, and then we'll see what's to be done. They may have found her already." She clucked her tongue again. "Poor child," she muttered under her breath. She went over to the stove and soon set down full bowls of vegetable soup for them both. The soup smelled wonderful. Concordia realized she had an appetite after all and finished the entire bowl, along with a roll.

Nash and Reese trooped in shortly after, dusty and weary-eyed, brushing nettles from their trouser legs. Marie fetched more stools and bowls and replenished the bread basket.

"Did you find her?" Concordia asked.

Nash smiled as he smoothed his tousled dark hair into place. "We did."

She blew out a breath. *Thank heaven.*

"Where?" David asked.

"By the duck pond in East Hampton," Nash said. "A good thing Miss Ambrose was with us. The girl started to run when she saw us—we're strangers to her—but her aunt was able to settle her down. What a sight she was. We thought she was injured at first. There was a lot of what looked like blood on the front of her dress, but Miss Ambrose checked her over and said there's no sign of a wound. She's taken her home."

Reese checked his watch. "My grandmother has been waiting

at their cottage, in case the child came back home on her own. I should go get her."

Concordia stood. "No, we'll go." She glanced at David, who nodded and rose.

Marie unhooked the lantern by the door and passed it over to David. "You'll need this. There's no moon out tonight."

Concordia and David picked their way along the path by the lantern's small pool of light, the sounds of tree frogs and crickets filling the night air. There was no one else about.

Now was the time.

"David," she began, "there is something I didn't tell you, about discovering Wynderhane."

She heard him sigh. "I had a feeling you were holding back something."

"Well, we haven't been alone since…it happened." She took a breath and told him about Susie.

He stopped so abruptly she almost bumped into him. "You told her to *run*? So you are responsible for all of this?"

"I told her to run and *find her aunt*," she snapped. "I never imagined she would hide from everyone."

"Well, obviously she didn't understand everything you said. You should have realized that what the rest of us readily grasp is not easy for her."

She flinched at the harsh tone. She knew he was right.

He resumed walking, and she followed in silence.

Finally, he asked, "Why did you have her leave to begin with? She obviously didn't do it. She was probably trying to help, in fact, by taking the knife out of Wynderhane."

"I don't think her innocence will be obvious to everyone. She is tall and strong for her age. She's angry at Wynderhane for trying to buy their home out from under them." Had he succeeded? She hadn't had a chance to ask. "I saw her strike him on the chest today," she went on, "right out in the middle of the fairgrounds, for everyone to see. Sir Anthony and Gwen had to pull her away."

"I didn't know about that."

"Well, I'm sure word got around. And the townspeople already perceive both of the Ambroses as 'eccentric.' They certainly consider Susie unstable. For years there have been rumors about the girl being disturbed enough to have started the fire that killed her family and burned down their house."

David didn't say anything for a while. As they came within sight of the Ambrose cottage, he asked, "Do *you* believe she stabbed Wynderhane?"

She bit her lip. She would be lying if she said she didn't have any doubts. Wynderhane's *she...she* echoed in her mind.

She was spared a reply by the sound of footsteps. Gwen Ambrose was hurrying toward them. "You heard?" she breathed.

"Yes. Thank goodness," Concordia said. "Is she all right?"

"Yes, we got her cleaned up and fed. She's sleeping now." Gwen shook her head. "I simply do not understand what prompted her to run and hide. She's never done that. Oh, occasionally she chases after a cat or a duck and wanders off, but this is different."

David cleared his throat. "Concordia has something she wants to tell you." He passed her the lantern. "I'll wait inside with Mrs. Reese."

Concordia saw Gwen frown in the dim light.

"Tell me what?"

Concordia repeated the story of discovering Susie near the gravely wounded Edgar Wynderhane, the knife in her hand.

"Heavens." Gwen sucked in a breath. "I'd been out this whole time searching. I knew nothing about an attack on the man. You say he's alive?"

"As far as I know, but the wound looked mortal."

"You know she couldn't have done it, but whatever was she doing there?"

Concordia shook her head. "She was in no position to tell me, even if there had been time."

Gwen grimaced. "True. So that's why there was all that blood on her dress. But what happened then? Is that when she ran away and hid?"

Concordia winced. "I'm afraid I have to take responsibility for that. I didn't want anyone to see her there and think the worst, so I told her to run and find you."

Gwen started. "You told her *what*? You knew I was already looking for her, and you sent her back out? She isn't capable of the critical thinking necessary to go about finding me. In her shocked and frightened state, your instructions caused her to wander alone for hours. She could have been hurt in the time it took us to find her."

Concordia looked down at her hands. Her throat constricted. "I'm sorry," she whispered.

Without another word, Gwen Ambrose turned on her heel and walked away.

Concordia fumbled for her handkerchief.

"You have had a difficult day, my dear," a quiet voice said. It was Mrs. Reese.

Concordia took off her spectacles and dabbed at her eyes. "You heard, I suppose?"

The lady shrugged. "Well, it saves you from having to re-tell it."

Concordia let out a croak that passed for a laugh. "I've done enough re-telling for one day."

"I assume you lied to the—what sort of law enforcement do they have in this backwater—police?"

"A deputy sheriff, actually." She groaned. "Oh, I've made a terrible mistake."

Eleanor Reese patted her shoulder. "There isn't any other kind, is there? We all make mistakes, dear."

Concordia straightened. "But I've caused harm to a vulnerable young girl, when my intention was the very opposite." She'd thought at the time she was doing the right thing. How could she trust her judgment anymore?

"Not irreparable harm," the woman pointed out. "Susie will be fine. Although your efforts will likely come to naught."

Concordia stiffened. "What do you mean?"

"The searchers couldn't help but notice all the blood on the girl's dress when they found her. I saw blood on her hands, too, when Miss Ambrose was cleaning her up. Word is bound to get out."

nfortunately, Mrs. Reese's prediction proved correct. The deputy sheriff arrived shortly after breakfast the next morning to speak with Concordia. The parlor was made available to them. David escorted her in and sat beside her.

Yates flicked a glance at David, sighed, and perched his large frame gingerly upon an antique rocker across from them.

"Now then, ma'am, why don't you fill in the gaps of your story from yesterday." Though as polite as before, there was a brittle edge to his voice today. "I will save us time by telling you I have already examined the Ambrose girl's dress and have left a constable on the grounds."

"Surely you don't believe Susie tried to kill Mr. Wynderhane? There must be an innocent explanation," Concordia said. "She could have—"

He held up a hand. "Please. No speculation. Simply recount *everything* that happened. I want the entire story this time."

She sighed. "Very well."

Yates took notes as she related the story, nodding to himself. "That accounts for the handprint on the side of your skirt and the small amount of blood on your clothing, when there should have been more if you had been the one to pull out the knife." He shook his head. "It's vexing that I have two witnesses who cannot tell me anything."

"How is Wynderhane?" David asked.

"Still unconscious. Doc says he doesn't have much longer and probably won't ever wake."

"His poor wife," Concordia murmured.

"Mrs. Gemmer is with her now, keeping vigil," Yates said. "There is not much to be done for him except wait."

"What happens now?" Concordia asked.

"I have to find a way to ensure that the two Miss Ambroses do not skip town. Jail is hardly the place for them, especially for the simple-minded girl."

Concordia sucked in a breath. "Wait—the *two* Miss Ambroses? I can see your concern that Susie might run away again, but whyever would Gwen flee?"

A small smile played along the deputy's mouth. "By the account of two witnesses—yourself and Miss Winston—the victim clearly said *she* several times before he lost consciousness. That suggests a woman attacked him. I have to ask myself: why did the girl go into the tent in the first place? If it wasn't to kill Wynderhane—I consider that unlikely as well—then it was because *she saw her aunt go in there and followed her.*"

Concordia's eyes widened. "You are saying..." She couldn't finish the sentence.

Yates nodded. "I'm convinced that Gwendolyn Ambrose stabbed Edgar Wynderhane. The lady is tall for a woman, young, and strong. She has plenty of motive, too. I know about Wynderhane going to the town council, proposing to pay the back taxes on the Ambrose property and take it over. The council was ready to let him have his way. The family was about to lose everything."

Concordia quivered with indignation. Gwen Ambrose, a cold-blooded killer? Every instinct fought against that conclusion. "No matter the motive, the woman is not capable of murder," she protested, glancing at David.

He clasped his wife's hand in reassurance and turned to Yates. "You must admit, deputy, that's purely conjecture on your part."

Yates reached into his tunic. "There is more to it than that. The doc found this in Wynderhane's pocket." He passed over a slip of paper, the writing upon it formed of crudely drawn letters. Concordia and David read it together.

You win. Meet me in the drama pavilion during the game, so we can discuss your terms in private. ~G.A.

"I don't believe it," Concordia murmured.

Yates tucked the note away. "This is proof that Wynderhane was lured there on the pretext that Miss Ambrose had capitulated about selling her property. She then caught him off-guard, stabbed him, and fled. She likely never knew Susie was there in the shadows." He stood and reached for his hat.

Concordia and David looked at each other in open-mouthed silence. Finally, David spoke. "Wynderhane had other enemies, Mr. Yates. We told you about an equally strong motive. He was about to pass on crucial information regarding Miss Lester's death—"

"We don't need to travel all the way to New York City to find the killer, Mr. Bradley, or a motive. Both are right in our back-yard." He gave a stiff bow. "Good day."

Rusty, his vest misbuttoned and gray hair askew, hurried in after the policeman left. "I just heard. Has he found out who attacked Wynderhane?"

Concordia scowled. "He's on the wrong track completely. He thinks Miss Ambrose did it, to keep Wynderhane from taking her property."

"I wouldn't be so hasty to dismiss the idea, dear," David said. "We saw the note for ourselves. As disagreeable as it is to conceive of Miss Ambrose attacking the man, it is a possibility. This may have nothing whatsoever to do with the murder of Victoria Lester."

Rusty winced.

David cleared his throat awkwardly. "My apologies for speaking so bluntly, sir."

Rusty waved a dismissive hand and turned to Concordia. "I'm beginning to feel as if we're on a wild-goose chase."

"No, we are not. We just have to sort through it all." She stood and began to pace, trying to collect her thoughts. Rusty and David waited, the silence broken only by the ticking of the mantel clock and footsteps in the corridor.

She took a breath. "Here's what we know, starting at the very beginning. Wynderhane was paying Victoria to eavesdrop on calls from the Stock Exchange Luncheon Club. On June the twenty-sixth, she overheard a man from the club telling a woman that his first attempt to kill someone—another man—had failed, and he didn't know what to do next. The woman seemed to prod him on." She paused, to make sure Rusty was following. He nodded, and she continued. "Here's something you may not have known, Rusty. When I later asked Wynderhane what he knew of the matter, he told me that Victoria had tried to see him at his office the day after she talked to me."

Rusty leaned forward, eyes wide. "I had no idea. What happened?"

"He was out. She left an urgent message with the office receptionist asking him to contact her. He says he never did."

"What if he was lying?" Rusty asked. "Maybe they did talk, and she told him she wanted to go to the police. He would be in a heap of trouble for wiretapping if she reported it. He could have been the one who killed her, rather than the man she overheard at the restaurant."

Concordia nodded. "I considered that at one point, but—"

"But then Wynderhane was attacked," David interrupted.

"True, but there's another reason. The night before she died,

Victoria said in her note to me that 'he mustn't know where I live.' Wouldn't Wynderhane already have her address, as a matter of form?"

"Why would Victoria go to Wynderhane about the telephone call in the first place?" Rusty asked.

"She may have simply wanted to pass the problem on to Wynderhane and let him decide how to proceed. In a way, he had gotten her into this predicament."

Rusty shifted restlessly. "How do we know Victoria's killer came here to East Hampton and didn't remain in the city?"

"Because we believe the man he is trying to kill is Sir Anthony Dunwick." She nodded toward her husband. "You had already suspected that his head injury was no accident."

David nodded. "Yes, it does fit together."

Rusty looked from one to the other, mouth open.

"Indeed it does," she said. "Someone has been in anonymous communication with Sir Anthony for some time, most recently last week. And there have been two incidents that could be construed as attacks upon him." She inclined her head towards David. "Besides the blow to the head, do you remember when we met him at the play? He'd injured his hand. Some sort of traffic accident with his carriage, he said."

David straightened. "I'd forgotten that."

Rusty's eyes narrowed. "Could be a coincidence or a string of bad luck."

"Consider the connections to the Stock Exchange Luncheon Club," she said. "That's where the call came from, and Sir Anthony dined there, though we don't know if it was the same day. We can check that. And several employees from the investment firm that does business with Sir Anthony—regulars at the club—are staying here at the Dunwick cottage."

"So you are saying that the man on the telephone was referring to killing Sir Anthony Dunwick," Rusty said.

Concordia nodded.

"Have you spoken with Sir Anthony?"

She shook her head. "Not yet." But she would. Today.

~

She finally found him in the billiard room with Hans Gemmer.

Sir Anthony brightened when he caught sight of her. "Ah, Concordia, dear! I spoke with the deputy on his way out. You'll have no more trouble from him. He says you are free to come and go as you please, with his apologies."

Concordia glanced over at Gemmer, who tipped his bald head in a short bow. She gave a wan smile. "I understand your wife is with Mrs. Wynderhane now."

"Indeed. It is a very grim situation." Gemmer frowned as he stroked his neatly trimmed goatee. "I have already informed our host that we are heading back tomorrow. We left a junior partner in charge during our absence, and he should not be the one to call an emergency meeting of the board."

Sir Anthony shifted uneasily, the creases upon his high fore-head deepening. "It is entirely your own concern, of course, but it seems bad form to be installing new leadership before the man has breathed his last."

"It is a matter of business, sir," Gemmer retorted. "You are a client of ours—would *you* want your investment firm's decision-making structure in disarray, not knowing who is in charge of your accounts? What if there is a volatile market shift—who will respond? Look at what has already happened with one of your investments. Not to speak ill of a man on his deathbed, but the mismanagement of that account was unforgivable." He sighed, adding half to himself, "I was justified in keeping an eye on him."

Sir Anthony flashed a look in her direction. "We must be boring the young lady to death with such talk."

But Concordia wasn't paying attention, her gaze fixed steadily on Hans Gemmer. An idea was beginning to form. "What do you mean, sir, by 'keeping an eye on him'? Was Wynderhane being monitored?"

The man flushed, glancing uneasily at Sir Anthony. "Um, well, you see…" His voice trailed off.

She leaned closer. "You instructed Daniel Pickering to watch Wynderhane, didn't you?"

But that didn't work out as intended. Pickering had an agenda of his own—advancement within the firm, by any means.

Sir Anthony scowled at the broker. "Is that true?"

Gemmer grimaced as he rubbed the back of his neck. "We were uneasy over some of Wynderhane's recent acquisitions— more risky than our usual offerings—and there had also been certain…personal indiscretions." He glanced briefly at Concordia, who wondered if rumors of Wynderhane's behavior on the porch had circulated despite Reese's efforts.

"Why didn't you simply come to me?" Sir Anthony demanded.

"You are a client, sir. That is not how we do things. We clean up our own house. When you invited us all to accompany you here, I had a word with Pickering. I only asked him to keep an ear to the ground, so to speak. I had no idea he'd—well, go off the rails like that." He flushed and turned away. "I should be going. We have a great deal of packing to take care of before tomorrow."

Concordia waited until Gemmer was well out of the room. "May I speak to you, Sir Anthony?"

"Hmm?" It seemed he had forgotten she was there. He put his cue stick back on the wall rack. "Of course, dear. Let us go to the sunroom."

The sunroom, thankfully, was unoccupied, the dust motes barely disturbed, drifting along the sunlight rays as Sir Anthony gallantly helped Concordia to her chair. "So, how are you settling into married life, my dear? Bradley treating you as he should?"

Concordia smiled. "David is a wonderful man. It has been a strange honeymoon, however."

He sighed. "I imagine so. It is regrettable that you were the one to find Wynderhane the other day." He self-consciously touched the side of his head. "And we didn't need all that fuss over my injury last week."

She nodded. This was the opening she was looking for. Why was she hesitating? She wished she had asked David along.

No, she still believed a one-on-one conversation would encourage Sir Anthony to open up.

"My dear, are you all right?" he asked, frowning. "You have been very quiet. If it is married trouble, perhaps Susan would be a better choice—" He started to get up, but Concordia put out a hand.

"I am worried about you," she said.

He blinked. "About *me*? Why?"

"Do you promise to hear me out, without objection?"

"Of course."

She launched into the story of Wynderhane's wiretapping scheme, Victoria Lester's involvement, and what had ultimately happened to the young lady.

Sir Anthony's eyes widened, but he stayed true to his word and didn't interrupt.

Then she explained the connections she was seeing—the "accidents" Sir Anthony had suffered, the current houseguests who had attended the Stock Exchange Luncheon Club the day of the telephone call, and the attack upon Wynderhane just before he could name the caller.

Sir Anthony waved a dismissive hand. "Have you been reading those detective stories Charlotte is so fond of? These are mere coincidences."

She ignored the jibe. "Do you remember the date you attended the club luncheon as a guest of Wynderhane's?"

His brow furrowed as he concentrated. "It was a Monday, I recall." His face brightened. "Ah, yes, the last Monday of June, I remember now. That would make it...June twenty-sixth."

She nodded. "That was the day of the telephone call from the club. Tell me—the carriage accident you mentioned, when we saw you at the play. Was it before or after that date?"

He winced in memory. "It had been only two days before. I was still quite sore but didn't want to cancel."

"As best as you can remember, how exactly did the accident occur?"

"A carriage came up beside ours on the bridge at great speed. Trying to pass us, I assumed. Which meant, of course, that the heedless fellow was traveling in the opposite lane of traffic. He suddenly swerved into ours to avoid a headlong collision. Nearly ran us over the rail." He shrugged. "Unfortunately, such incidents are common enough."

She pictured the would-be killer making his getaway but unsure over those two days if he had been successful, perhaps anxiously scanning the newspaper headlines in the interim. Then, the disappointment of seeing the man back again, with only minor injuries. *He didn't die. I don't know if I have it in me to try again.*

"Common or not, I believe the man who tried to run your vehicle over the bridge—" Noting his blank look of disbelief, she added, "Yes, I'm convinced it was deliberate—attended the same luncheon. When he saw you whole and hearty, or very nearly so, he made a panicked telephone call to his confederate. Do you remember seeing anyone making a call from the restaurant?"

He shook his head. "My dear, you are seeing conspiracies that are simply not there. Many people patronized the club that day, not just those of us in Wynderhane's party. I doubt the call had anything to do with me. And I refuse to believe one of my house-guests is trying to murder me."

She changed her approach. "You received an anonymous iris last week, is that correct?"

He shifted in his seat. "I suppose Charlotte told you about that?"

She nodded. "I also know that there was no postmark of any

kind upon it, which means that someone here on the grounds slipped it in with your other correspondence."

He folded his arms defensively. "There could have been an outer envelope that was discarded before it reached me."

"No. Charlotte inquired among your staff, and no one had removed any outer envelopes from letters that came in. The maids and housekeeper were otherwise occupied with the influx of guests."

"But why would any of them wish me harm?" he protested.

"I suspect the answer lay in the iris. What does it mean, Sir Anthony? We must get to the bottom of this, before anyone else is hurt." Including the Ambroses, she added silently.

He wouldn't meet her eye, instead focusing upon the window, at the graying skies in the distance.

They heard a rustle of fabric behind them and then a woman's voice. "You *must* tell her."

Lady Dunwick crossed the room and perched upon the cushioned rattan chair across from her husband. "My dear, this cannot be kept secret any longer."

Concordia looked back and forth between them. "What is the significance of the iris?"

Sir Anthony ran a hand through his thinning, iron-gray hair. "Iris was the name of my only sister."

CHAPTER 22

"Sister?" Concordia repeated blankly.

He grimaced. "I never speak of her. She was rather...difficult. Stubborn, impetuous. Even as a child. She refused to conform to the proper behavior expected of the women in our family. Frequently got into scrapes and then tried to spin some falsehood to avoid getting into trouble." He glanced over at his wife, who nodded to him to continue on. "As she grew to adulthood, her nature did not improve. I caught her in male company, unchaperoned, more than once. We could see the ruin she was heading towards but were powerless to stop it, short of locking her away. And her ruin came soon enough." He folded his arms. "She stole cash and jewels from the house and eloped with a two-bit card sharp with so many aliases we never knew what his background really was. My father disowned her after that and refused to have any further dealings with her." He sighed and looked down at his trousers, absentmindedly smoothing the creases.

"Then what?" Concordia asked.

"Hmm?" He came out of the dark recesses of his thoughts. "Well, she wrote to me once. Years later. Begged me to help her get back in our parents' good graces—she did not know Mamma had died. Her letter said she was now a destitute widow with a child to raise. I burned the letter and did not reply. That was the last I heard from her."

Concordia looked at the hard lines of his face, the grim set of his jaw. This was a Sir Anthony she had not seen before—cold, harsh, judgmental. Gone was the paternal joviality, the spark of humor.

It was presumptuous, but she had to ask. "Could she not have been helped? At least discreetly, if the family was concerned about its reputation?"

He turned to her, his eyes a cold blue under lowering brows. "Although her account was plausible, she had lied to me too many times. I was reluctant to become involved again."

Lady Dunwick gave her husband a pitying glance. "But that is not the real reason. Tell her."

He looked at his wife for a long moment. "You are relentless. Very well. It was because of our mother. The woman grieved for Iris for months afterward. She died of a broken heart. That I could never forgive."

Concordia bit her lip. Perhaps Sir Anthony's sister was plotting revenge against him for shunning her. How old would she be now? Quite elderly. Did anyone in the household fit the description of an old lady?

One person did: Mrs. Reese. "Is Iris your older or younger sister?" she asked.

"She *was* my younger sister," Sir Anthony corrected. "She has died since."

So much for that theory. Concordia sighed. "How did you learn of her death?"

"Oh, that was years ago. I received a letter."

"A letter? From whom?"

"It was unsigned. A pressed iris was enclosed in the envelope, along with the obituary clipping. That was the first flower."

"When did she die?" Concordia thought she knew, at least part of it.

"July twenty-second."

She nodded. "Of what year?"

Lady Dunwick shifted restlessly when her husband didn't respond. "More than a decade ago. 1888. We received the first letter, with the flower and obituary, a year after her death."

"Was a threat made at the time?"

"No direct threat, *per se*," Lady Dunwick answered, looking over at Sir Anthony, lost in thought. "There was a vague warning about justice and the workings of Providence. The tone was quite bitter. The writer laid the blame for Iris's death squarely on my husband's shoulders."

"Has he received an iris on the anniversary of that date, every year since? That was ten years ago. You told Charlotte it was only the past three."

"I didn't want to worry her." Lady Dunwick clasped her hands tightly in her lap. "Whoever is sending them has kept track of us. The letters first came to our Hartford brownstone. After we bought the summer cottage, they followed us out here." She shivered.

Concordia raised her voice to get Sir Anthony's attention. "How did Iris die?"

He pressed his pale lips in a stubborn line and shook his head.

Concordia tried another tack. "Do you know anything about the letter writer? Was the hand a man's or woman's?"

Lady Dunwick shrugged.

"Let me tell you what I think," Concordia said. "We are looking for a man. After all, it was a man who made the phone call from the Stock Exchange Luncheon Club, a man who was following Miss Lester, a man who would have the strength to carry out these attacks. Perhaps he was a close friend of Iris. Or a relation—you mentioned she had a child. Did she say it was a son?"

"I don't remember," Sir Anthony said. "I only glanced at her letter before burning it."

Lady Dunwick frowned.

Concordia didn't believe him, either. "Well, whatever the man's connection to Iris, he must work in the investment business in order to have been at the club, and we know he has been here at the cottage. Before the attack on Mr. Wynderhane, I had suspected that either he or Mr. Pickering was involved, but neither of them makes sense now."

Sir Anthony shifted in his seat. "I am extremely uncomfortable with this line of speculation. It is hardly decorous."

"It is hardly *decorous* that Wynderhane was stabbed and is dying," Concordia retorted. "We must learn who is behind it."

"Whom do you suspect?" Lady Dunwick asked. Her tone was even, but the tightly clenched hands, buried in the folds of her skirt, told a different story.

"There are three men the deputy sheriff should question: Mr. Nash, Mr. Reese, and Mr. Gemmer. But for that to happen, you must tell Yates your story, Sir Anthony. He can learn more about the background and actions of these men."

Sir Anthony shook his head vigorously. "I will not bare my soul to the local constabulary and turn him loose upon my guests for such an unseemly inquiry. The Dunwick name would be dragged through the muck by scandal-mongers."

"Surely you must know it is a necessary inquiry," Concordia said. "Miss Lester's murder remains unsolved, the Ambroses stand unjustly accused of attacking Edgar Wynderhane, and the attempts upon your life will continue."

Sir Anthony stood, face ashen. "If you will excuse me." He stalked out.

With a murmured apology, Lady Dunwick hurried to catch up to him.

Concordia watched them leave, mouth open. Now what?

∾

She longed to talk to David, but he had gone to visit Captain Decker. She would have to settle for a quiet walk to consider what could be done. Not about protecting Sir Anthony, though naturally she was concerned for his welfare. However, he was a grown man who could look after himself. Susie could not.

The thought of the girl consigned to a mental institution or some such place if her aunt was convicted of stabbing Wynderhane was unbearable, as was the possibility of never knowing who had killed Victoria Lester. Concordia was sure the same person was responsible for both.

Rusty was in the library, awaiting word of her conversation with Sir Anthony. Well, he would have to wait a little longer. She needed time to consider what could be done next. Feeling guilty nonetheless, she slipped out the door that led around the back of the house to avoid running into him.

She very nearly ran into someone else. Mrs. Reese, coming along the path from the kitchen, dodged out of the way of the screen door just in time.

"Oh! I'm so sorry." Concordia caught the wicker basket that slipped out of the lady's hands. "Where are you off to?"

"Taking some treats over to Susie and her aunt. They aren't allowed off the property. A constable was been positioned at the crossroad." She snorted in disapproval. "That deputy—Yates, is it? —is completely out of line. Susie wouldn't hurt a fly or her aunt either."

"Do you mind if I come along?" Concordia asked.

Mrs. Reese frowned. "Miss Ambrose is still upset with you, but we can try, can't we?"

They followed the path to the Ambrose cottage. A stiff breeze had picked up. Concordia held onto her hat, watching the shore birds that swooped against the iron-gray sky. "A storm's coming."

The lady nodded vigorously. "The gardener says they're

expecting a big one. Could be a hurricane." She gestured toward the upper marshes off to their right. A number of men, clad in overalls and stout boots, were harvesting the salt hay and loading tied sheaves onto a cart. They moved quickly.

Gwendolyn Ambrose was sitting on the porch swing, her mending idle in her lap. She glanced up as they approached and scowled in Concordia's direction.

Mrs. Reese shifted the basket upon her arm. "I'll put these in the kitchen. Where's Susie—by the rabbit pen?" She went inside and left them alone.

"She's quite patient with Susie," Gwen mused.

"May I speak with you?" Concordia asked.

Gwen halfheartedly waved toward the rocker.

Concordia sat. "I deeply regret sending your niece away like that. I was trying to protect her. It all happened so quickly, I had no time to think it through."

"I would think you'd be more adept at dealing with dead bodies," Gwen said tartly. "Charlotte stopped by this morning and told me all about your *lady sleuth* exploits. You seem to stumble over victims with alarming frequency."

Concordia winced. "Charlotte has a tendency to exaggerate, although there is some truth to it. But it is not something one grows accustomed to."

Miss Ambrose's face softened. "I suppose not."

Concordia gave a slight nod, looking to shift the conversation to a more comfortable topic. "What are those?" She pointed to a stack of paper scraps in the mending basket.

Gwen pulled them out. "Recent drawings of Susie's. Sketching and spending time with her animals seem to be the only activities that soothe her these days."

Concordia held up one of them, drawn in lead pencil. She could make out a scribbled-in circle, an *x*, a long, squiggly line. The arrangement seemed random. She turned it sideways. No, it still didn't make any sense. "I can't make it out. What's it supposed to be?"

Gwen sighed. "I don't know. She's drawn the same set of figures a number of times."

They lapsed into silence, looking out across the bay.

"I do hope Charlotte wasn't exaggerating about your ability to discover the truth," Gwen said finally. "Heaven knows we need your help now."

Concordia dragged her attention from the calming view and back to the task at hand. "I will do everything I can."

Gwen rubbed her temples. "Yates thinks I stabbed Wynderhane. He showed me the note. I never wrote that, Concordia. You believe me, don't you?"

"Of course I do. We don't yet know who lured Wynderhane to the pavilion and stabbed him, but David and I have told the deputy sheriff our theory about the motive."

Gwen sat up straighter. "What motive is that?"

Concordia sketched out what had happened to the unfortunate Miss Lester before they arrived at East Hampton and the possible connection to Sir Anthony, leaving out the specifics of the Dunwick family scandal. She stifled a sigh. If only Sir Anthony would tell the deputy sheriff about Iris.

Gwen's eyes widened. "You mean to say, you already had a murder to deal with *before* coming here? And a young lady you were close to. I'm so sorry. Now we have a dying man and Sir Anthony still in possible danger." She patted Concordia's hand in sympathy. "Oh, my dear, you are not having a very good honeymoon, are you?"

Concordia's grimace softened to a smile as she glimpsed David on the path, coming toward them. "It has had its bright spots." She stood to greet him, reaching out a hand as he approached.

He clasped it warmly. "I thought I might find you here." He leaned in closer. "I just spoke with Lady Dunwick. She caught me up on your conversation." He straightened and nodded toward

Miss Ambrose. "If you will allow him, Sir Anthony wants to represent you in court. Let us hope it doesn't come to that."

Gwen inclined her head. "That is very kind. Please thank him for me."

"You can do that yourself," David said. "Lady Dunwick asked if they can call upon you tomorrow."

At least Sir Anthony was not leaving the Ambroses to fend for themselves, Concordia thought. But with all the guests leaving in the next day or so, how were they to figure out who was behind all of this? She stood and brushed her skirt. "We should go." She looked through the open door into the empty kitchen. "Do you suppose Mrs. Reese wishes to walk back with us?"

"She tends to make a longer stay of it." Gwen glanced at the lowering clouds. "I'll make sure she heads back before the storm." She stood and followed them off the porch. "Will you do me a favor, Concordia? Tell me if you learn anything more. I feel so helpless here."

"Of course."

They strolled back along the path to Crosswinds, Concordia with her arm hooked through David's. He drew her closer, nodding toward the mouth of the bay in the distance. "The fishing boats are coming in early. I think this is really going to turn into something."

She wasn't paying much attention and mumbled a noncommittal reply. She wished Charlotte hadn't shared her *lady sleuth* history with Gwen Ambrose. *Mercy*, what if any of the other locals heard of it? Between that and her new hairstyle, she may as well be wearing trousers, at least for those of Maud Wynderhane's mindset.

At least Gwen wasn't angry with her anymore. That was one consolation. She glanced at David, endeared by the dimple in his cheek when he smiled back at her. The warmth of his muscled arm by her side made her feel safe. Gwen's words, *You are not having a very good honeymoon, are you?* echoed in her mind. Well, perhaps there was something they could do about that when they returned to the cottage. She smiled to herself.

As they took the fork in the path that brought them to Cross-winds, they caught sight of Rusty sitting on the porch step, batting at his dusty trousers with his cap.

So much for time alone with her husband. She pasted on a smile.

Rusty stood politely and looked at her with narrowed eyes. "G'afternoon. I waited for you this morning, but you never showed up."

"I'm sorry. The talk with Sir Anthony was a distressing one. I needed a walk to clear my head."

"Why don't we all sit down?" David suggested.

Concordia perched upon the swing. "Sir Anthony confirmed that there is a...history in his family that might justify someone holding a grudge against him. Someone has been in anonymous communication with him over the years, though nothing overtly threatening has been expressed." She was about to lay out the suspects she had talked to the Dunwicks about, but Rusty was too quick for her.

"So we are assuming it is someone here, because of the letter without a postmark and the attack on Wynderhane—which must be related. We can assume it is a man, because of what Victoria told you about the call—and only brokers and their associates can go into the club to begin with. So that leaves us with Nash, Reese, and Gemmer, correct?"

"And Pickering," David pointed out. "Although I imagine he was on the train back to the city by the time Wynderhane was stabbed."

Concordia started. She hadn't thought of that. What if Pickering hadn't left when he was supposed to? Was he still nearby? Perhaps Yates could find out.

"Well, then," Rusty said, breaking into her thoughts, "we

should search the rooms of the other fellows—and soon, before they leave!"

David put up a hand. "Whoa there, you can't go sneaking into bedrooms and going through a man's personal effects. Besides, what would you be looking for?"

Rusty fell silent.

Concordia leaned forward eagerly. "There *could* be items that would give away the culprit. Correspondence, for example, with that woman Victoria heard him talking to on the telephone. One does not unburden oneself to a casual acquaintance. They must have exchanged letters. And then there are the irises."

"Irises?" Rusty interrupted.

"A single pressed iris was enclosed in each of the letters Sir Anthony received."

Rusty frowned. "What does it signify?"

She shook her head. "I don't have permission to share that. But if the latest note—the one without a postmark—was written by someone staying here, perhaps he has brought more of these pressed irises with him."

David frowned. "That's a bit of a stretch."

She shrugged. "The most damning evidence, of course, would be clothing that had been bloodied from the attack on Wynderhane." She hesitated, not wanting to seem indelicate. "I doubt the attacker would be able to…wash it off completely, and he certainly cannot give it to the Dunwicks' laundress. So what could he do with it? Hide it somewhere—"

"That's enough talk of *blood*." David folded his arms. There will be *no* searching of rooms. You are not a sneak thief, my dear, nor do I relish the prospect of retrieving either one of you from the town jail." He gave them each a stern look.

Rusty put his head in his hands. "I'll never know who killed my darling girl."

"Chin up, Rusty," David said, his look softening. "With this storm coming, no one is going anywhere for a while. Perhaps something will develop in the meantime. We will keep our eyes and ears open."

Concordia bit her lip. What about Wynderhane? Would they ever learn who had attacked him? The lives of Gwen and Susie depended upon it. If only she could convince Sir Anthony to talk to Yates.

Well, she wasn't about to give up now.

CHAPTER 23

$\mathcal{T}$he storm swooped in with a vengeance, the rain and wind lashing the trees and rattling the parlor windows that evening as the maid turned up the lamps. The ladies soon followed, gathering for their after-dinner coffee and cordials. Mrs. Reese—having made it safely back from the Ambrose cottage before the rain started coming down—gave the windows a sideways glance before pulling out her knitting needles. Concordia sat beside her on the settee, with Charlotte and Lady Dunwick arranged in chairs on the other side of the coffee table.

Lady Dunwick poured from a delicate china pot and passed the cups. "I think you'll enjoy this. It's a favorite of ours, Sumatran Mandeling."

Concordia breathed in the fragrance of the rich, earthy coffee. It should help perk her up after the fatigue she'd been feeling today.

"I do hope the elm beside the portico doesn't come down," Charlotte said, nervously contemplating the view through the windows, illuminated in lightning flashes. "Uncle Anthony was the first to notice it was leaning and said he would speak with the groundskeeper, but I suppose he never got around to it."

Mrs. Reese chuckled. "Oh, my dear, that is so very like my first husband. The man would make the grandest plans, promising to arrange, or repair, or complete something or other, and hardly ever followed through." She inclined her head toward Charlotte. "You'll find, once you are married"—then her glance turned to Concordia —"and you, Mrs. Bradley, are no doubt catching on to this fact, that it is often easier to simply take matters into one's own hands."

Lady Dunwick chuckled. "Our husbands *do* mean well."

"Excuse me?" a voice broke in. It was Miss Farraday, hovering in the doorway. "Do you mind if I join you? The children are asleep, and Marie is within earshot if they wake."

"Not at all," Lady Dunwick answered. "We haven't seen much of you, dear." She indicated an empty chair next to Charlotte. "Have you heard anything from your mistress? She is still keeping vigil with Mrs. Wynderhane, is she not?"

Miss Farraday nodded as she seated herself. "She returned briefly to pack an overnight case and check on the children. The doctor thinks the crisis will come tonight. She plans to stay the night at the infirmary with Mrs. Wynderhane." She jumped as a boom of thunder sounded nearby. "It's best that she not navigate the local roads tonight, anyway."

Lady Dunwick waved a hand toward the windows. "The curtains should have been drawn already. Charlotte, dear, would you mind? It will muffle the noise."

After that, the room fell quiet, save for the clicking of Mrs. Reese's needles and the now-muffled thunderclaps.

Concordia groped for a suitable topic, but unknown assailants and long-held grudges were uppermost in her mind. "I understand that Sir Anthony has offered to be Miss Ambrose's advocate, should charges be pressed against her. That is quite kind of him."

Miss Farraday's eyes widened. "Charges? I seem to have missed a great deal in the nursery."

"Miss Ambrose is suspected of attacking Mr. Wynderhane at the fair," Concordia said.

Lady Dunwick winced at the blunt statement. "Perhaps we should—"

"Miss Ambrose?" Miss Farraday exclaimed, incredulous. "Why would she do such a thing?"

"It is the deputy sheriff's theory that Miss Ambrose harbored animosity toward Mr. Wynderhane, who wanted to buy the Ambrose property." Concordia struggled to modulate her bitter tone. "When Gwen would not sell, he tried to use a legal scheme to rob them of house and home." Although the man lay dying, it was difficult to check her anger. The entire affair was giving her an aching head and a queasy stomach.

Lady Dunwick shifted uneasily. "It is unseemly to speak ill of a man on his deathbed. Perhaps we should talk of other things."

Concordia flushed and fell silent.

The gentlemen joined them soon after: Sir Anthony, Gemmer, Reese, and Nash, with David and Rusty following. Concordia stood. "If you'll excuse me." She approached David and lowered her voice. "May I speak with you a moment?"

They stepped out of earshot of the room. "My dear, I'm feeling distinctly unwell," she said. "I think it would be best for me to go back to the cabin and lie down."

He frowned. "Can you wait until the storm abates? It's too dangerous to go out now."

A wave of dizziness hit her. He grasped her as she swayed. The ever-perceptive Charlotte jumped up and hurried over, and they helped her take a few steps into the corridor.

"I feel terrible," Concordia heard herself say.

"Let's get her to my room," Charlotte whispered. "She can rest there. Can you walk, Concordia?"

But David was already scooping his wife into his arms and heading for the staircase. Concordia sighed and rested her head against his shoulder. "I'm sorry to be such a bother," she mumbled into his shirt.

"*Shh*," he said, against the top of her head.

Once she was settled into bed, Charlotte left them, promising to return to check on her later.

"I feel so silly," Concordia said, looking up at David. "I hope I didn't make a spectacle of myself."

He smiled. "Not at all. Everyone else was too engaged in conversation to notice. It might be a good idea to have the doctor come by and check on you tomorrow." He gently let go of her hand to pour water into a tumbler on the nightstand. "Here, drink this."

After a few minutes, she passed the empty glass back and rested against the pillows.

"Feeling better?"

"As long as I don't have to stand up," she joked weakly.

He chuckled. "Good thing you're in bed, then. Would you mind if I return to the parlor, dear? I want to keep an eye on Rusty and make sure he doesn't get up to any mischief."

She nodded. "Good idea. You'll make my apologies to the Dunwicks?"

"I'm sure Charlotte is doing that, even now." He lightly kissed her forehead. "I'll be back."

She took off her spectacles, put them carefully on the table, and closed her eyes.

When she awoke, the room was dark save for a single hurricane lamp on the nightstand. It took her a moment to orient herself. Charlotte's bedroom. She grimaced. What an inconvenient time to be indisposed. She was beginning to suspect what it might be, but pushed the thought out of her mind for now.

She fumbled for her spectacles and checked her lapel watch.

Nearly one in the morning. Where was Charlotte? Where was *David?* He'd said he would return.

She gingerly slid out of bed, put her shoes on, and stood. Her head felt clear now, her legs steady. She was also hungry. It wouldn't hurt to check the larder on the way to finding David and Charlotte.

She went down the back stairs to the empty kitchen, poured herself a glass of milk, and gazed out the window as she drank. The wind had died down, but a steady rain lingered. By the glow of a lamp from the stable, she could see a number of limbs had come down in the orchard beyond. She wondered if the oak Charlotte had mentioned was still standing.

She applied the hand pump to rinse out her glass and set it on the drying rack.

The sound of male voices drew her to the billiard room. Sir Anthony looked up from watching Mr. Gemmer complete his shot. "Concordia! Feeling better, my dear?"

She looked around self-consciously, but they were the only three in the room. "Yes, thank you. Have you seen Charlotte and David?"

"Charlotte is playing *Euchre* in the parlor with Nash, Reese, and Miss Farraday," he answered.

She nodded. Poor Charlotte was probably impatient to get to bed. She should find her to let her know she was up.

"I believe your husband and that Deighton fellow are getting a breath of air on the porch," he went on.

Gemmer winked. "More likely, enjoying those cigars you handed out after dinner." Obviously, he and Sir Anthony had mended fences.

Concordia grimaced. The stink of cigars might make her queasy all over again. Nevertheless, she excused herself and went to find David first.

But David and Rusty weren't on the porch. Or in the sunroom, the library, or the study. She frowned. She should check the parlor next. Perhaps they had joined the card game.

Then she heard the creak of footsteps overhead and a man's murmur. She tipped her head to listen. Was it her imagination, or had she just heard *her husband's* voice? The Dunwick bedrooms—including Charlotte's—were in the other wing, so he wasn't upstairs checking on her. She hurried down the hallway, climbed the main staircase, and turned toward the right wing. Aside from the rain drumming upon the roof, the only other sounds were her footfalls sinking softly into the deep carpet runner. She leaned in toward each door along the way, hoping to catch that murmur again. Heaven save her from the embarrassment of someone pulling open a door and discovering her creeping about.

A faint glow showed beneath the second door from the end, and she thought she heard another whisper. After applying her ear to the door to be sure, she checked the knob. It was unlocked. She eased it open.

Quite a spectacle greeted her: David and Rusty, in separate parts of the room, opening drawers and groping under the bed. They hadn't yet noticed her.

"David!" she hissed, quickly closing the door behind her. "What in the *Sam Hill* are you doing?"

David, who had the misfortune to be under the writing table at the moment, gave a stifled yelp as he hit his head on the pulled-out pencil drawer. "Ow!"

"*Shh,*" Rusty whispered. "Mrs. Reese is in the room right next to this one." He crept over to the door and opened it a crack, then closed it. "All right, all's quiet."

David stood and brushed off his knees. "I hope she sleeps soundly," he murmured and turned to his wife. "Are you feeling better, Concordia dear?"

"Don't *Concordia dear* me," she retorted, hands on hips. "You were supposed to keep Rusty from searching the rooms, not join him in the enterprise."

David made a face. "I know, I know, that *was* my original intent. He had gotten away from me and had already searched two other rooms before I caught up to him. He was just slipping into this one."

Concordia glared at Rusty, who cleared his throat quietly and looked down at his feet.

After a long moment, she suppressed a sigh. "Well, did you find anything?"

Rusty shook his head. "Nothing in Reese's or the Gemmers' rooms, no."

"But we found something just inside the door here," David interjected, "so we decided to continue the search." He nodded to Rusty, who groped in his vest pocket and opened his hand in the light of the lamp. There lay a crumbled piece of a pressed flower. An iris.

She sucked in a breath. "You found it *here*? Whose room is this?"

"Nash," David said.

Nash. Was he the one responsible? If so, how was he connected to Sir Anthony's sister? Her son, perhaps? He would be the right age.

There was another possibility: Nash was romantically attached to Miss Farraday, who was also the right age to be a child of Iris Dunwick. Could Nash have acted on the lady's behalf?

"Have you searched through his correspondence?" she asked.

David nodded. "I found nothing of a personal nature. Only copies of Gemmer's dictated letters and office memoranda."

"Any clothing with bloodstains?" she asked.

Rusty shook his head.

"We may never find something of that sort," David pointed out. "An article of clothing could have been buried in the woods or tied around something heavy and dropped off the end of the dock."

"That's not as easy as it sounds," she said. "The person in

question—we're talking about a guest, not a regular member of the Dunwick household—would have to obtain a shovel for digging or a length of rope to tie around a rock. Besides, the attack on Edgar Wynderhane took place only a day and a half ago. How many opportunities would there have been since then to dispose of bloody clothing unseen? It would more likely be hidden away in the house, but somewhere that couldn't be traced back to him." She took a breath. *Wynderhane's dressing room.* What better hiding place than among the victim's effects? Was there an outside lock on that door or just an inner latch? They should check on that.

"You've thought of something?" Rusty broke into her thoughts.

"A possib—" She broke off. Was that a noise? She put a finger to her lips. Then they all heard it: the swish of skirts and a heavy tread in the corridor. The sounds grew closer.

Rusty quickly turned down the lamp while David moved toward the door. Concordia huddled behind him, breathing quietly over his shoulder.

"I really shouldn't be following you here," a soft voice whispered on the other side of the door. Concordia's eyes widened. Miss Farraday.

They heard a soft chuckle. "How else am I to steal a kiss without anyone seeing, my dear?" It was Nash.

Concordia felt her face grow warm in the silence that followed.

"Now, I'll be but a minute while I get the book," Nash said, "and then you can return to the nursery and no one the wiser."

Concordia and Rusty exchanged a look of alarm. How could they possibly explain their presence here?

David reached for the knob, quietly holding it in place. They heard the key in the lock, then the jiggle on the other side. He kept a firm grip on the inner knob.

They heard Nash mutter under his breath.

"What is it?" Miss Farraday asked in a hushed voice.

"Knob's stuck, drat it," he said. "These old places—you never know what's going to break down next."

"I'd better go," she whispered. "You can give it to me tomorrow."

Nash sighed. "I'll see if the staff has something that can loosen this knob."

Their footsteps faded.

"That was close," Concordia whispered.

David cautiously peeked out. "All right, hallway's clear. Let's go."

With a silent wave, Rusty headed for his bedroom while Concordia and David slipped down the servants' staircase to catch up with Charlotte. They found her reading alone in the parlor.

Her face brightened when they entered. "Feeling better, Concordia?"

She smiled. "Yes, thank you. I'm sorry to keep you up so late."

Charlotte waved a dismissive hand. "No problem at all."

"We're going back to the cabin," David said. "Goodnight."

"Goodnight."

David unhooked a porch lantern to light their way. The cloud cover still obscured the stars, although the rain had stopped.

Concordia could hold it in no longer. A laugh bubbled out of her when they reached a turn in the path.

"What's so funny?" he asked.

She stopped to catch her breath and quoted, "'You are not a sneak thief, my dear, nor do I relish the prospect of retrieving either one of you from the town jail.'" She folded her arms and gave him a look of mock-sternness for good measure.

He chuckled. "I will never call you to account in that regard again, my dear. I admit I succumbed to the temptation of the chase. Once we'd found that flower..." He hesitated. "Does that mean Nash is the man we're after?"

"Maybe, though one flower is not much to go on," she said. "It could have been dropped by someone else passing by and was kicked under the lintel. It's a shame nothing else turned up. But there's another hiding place we can explore." She told him her idea about Wynderhane's dressing room.

He grunted in appreciation. "That would be clever, indeed. However, if we find something—a shirt, perhaps—but can't identify who it belongs to, how does that help?"

"It would at least clear Susie and Gwen Ambrose of blame," she said. "Neither of them has access to the upper floor of the Dunwick cottage, certainly."

"Yes, that's true. And it would bring police attention back to the cottage's occupants."

"Who won't be occupants much longer." With everyone scattering, they might never know who stabbed Edgar Wynderhane or killed Victoria Lester.

But if the Ambroses were left alone, that would be some comfort.

She grimaced in the dark. Not for Rusty.

CHAPTER 24

$\mathcal{T}$he Dunwick houseguests were not to leave for New York City the next day, or the day after that. It took the entire first day after the storm to clear the fallen trees that blocked local roads to Hassett Knoll and the East Hampton Station, only to find the railway closed while a one-hundred-year-old sycamore was being cleared from the tracks along the line to Bridgehampton. Telegraph lines were also down, making quick communication to New York City impossible.

Gemmer alternately chafed, sulked, and spent his time with Nash, dictating telegrams and letters he could not send.

William Nash took the extra workload with ill grace, casting dark looks at Reese, at leisure to play billiards and smoke cigars with David, Rusty, and Sir Anthony.

The one bright spot was the respite they all had from Deputy Sheriff Yates. Concordia and Mrs. Reese were finally able to navigate the path to the Ambrose place the second day after the storm to check on them and found Gwen and Susie busy repairing the chicken coop behind the cottage. Susie promptly dropped her hammer and ran into the house at the sight of them.

Mrs. Reese glanced at the girl's retreating form, a frown tugging at her brow. "I thought she would be used to me by now."

Gwen brushed off her apron. "It's surprising, I'll admit. She's been in brighter spirits these past few days without that policeman underfoot."

"It could have been my presence that startled her," Concordia pointed out. There had been only the one time Susie had run to her for comfort, prompted by an event neither one of them cared to endure again.

"I wouldn't worry about it," Gwen said. "She gets in a mood sometimes."

Concordia passed her a basket of rye loaves. "Marie wanted to send these along, with her love." She pointed to their still-intact roof. "I see you weathered the storm with very little damage. You should see the Dunwicks' gazebo."

Gwen nodded, plucking distractedly at the blue-checked napkin covering the basket. "Any word about Mr. Wynderhane?"

"I haven't heard anything," Concordia said. "Have you, Mrs. Reese?" The lady liked to gossip with the staff and was a surprising fount of information.

Eleanor Reese, still looking at the door to the cottage, roused herself. "Hmm? No, but I expect we'll hear something today, now that the main road has been cleared." She turned to Miss Ambrose. "Would you mind if I go inside and keep Susie company?" She pulled out a small, hand-knitted stuffed bear from her bag. "I made her a gift."

Gwen smiled. "How kind! Of course."

Concordia watched her go in. "She seems quite fond of your niece."

"Yes, she—"

"Ho, there, ladies!" a man's voice called. Coming along the path that led from the main road was the craggy-faced Captain Decoy —*ahem*, Decker—carrying a wood toolbox. His thinning gray hair ruffled in the breeze as he waved his battered cap enthusiastically. "Thought I'd see how you folks were getting along. Everyone all right?"

Concordia nodded. "Right as rain. How is the village doing?"

"Nobody hurt, thank the Lord, but it's a real mess." He shook his head. "A'least those ne'er-do-well boys who're always hanging 'round the general store and plaguing Mrs. Ginnis will be put to work. Though I doubt they know how to swing a hammer proper." He swatted at a fly with his cap. "Back in my day, we was carrying our own tool boxes by the time we was eight." He inclined his head toward the coop. "Lemme give you a hand wi' that, miss."

"Any other news?" Concordia asked, watching him crouch down and reach for a pair of pliers. "We're a bit out of touch."

"I hear the train tracks've been cleared, but the telegraph lines are still down—those'll be a while, I 'spect." He looked up at Gwen, his brow creased. "An' that city fella died last night. The one who was stabbed at the fair."

Concordia's stomach twisted as she glanced at the now-pale Gwen Ambrose. "Wynderhane has died?"

"Yes'm." Decker shook his head. "Poor fella. When *I* go, I hope it don't take me three days to do it." With a low, tuneless whistle, he went back to his work.

"Yates will come for Susie and me," Gwen whispered through pale lips. "I know it."

Concordia clasped her trembling hand. "I'll go fetch Sir Anthony."

Gwen gave a mute nod, and Concordia hurried away.

She found Sir Anthony with Lady Dunwick, David, and the gloomy-expressioned groundskeeper standing beside the splintered gazebo roof that lay at their feet.

David noticed her first. "What's wrong?"

"Mr. Wynderhane has died," she panted, turning to Sir

Anthony. "Can you come to the Ambrose place right away? Miss Ambrose is anxious about what will happen next. Now that the roads are clear, Yates may—"

"I'll get my jacket." Sir Anthony turned, taking the steps up to the cottage two at a time, calling over his shoulder, "We'll deal with the gazebo later, Marcus."

Lady Dunwick bit her lip. "That poor family. I'll go as well and see what more can be done."

Concordia watched her follow her husband.

"Should we accompany them?" David asked.

She grimaced. "A large group descending upon the family might scare Susie." She put a hand through his arm and dropped her voice. "Besides, there is something we need to do, before it's too late."

～

The upstairs hall of the east wing was empty, and they had no trouble getting into Wynderhane's dressing room. As Concordia had suspected, the door had a latch that only locked from the inside for privacy.

"I feel like a ghoul, going through a dead man's personal effects," David murmured.

"I know, but if we don't do it now, everything will be packed up by the maids and sent on," Concordia said.

They worked in silence, sifting through tidy stacks of collars, socks, shirts, trousers, and nightshirts. Concordia moved on to the shoes.

"Not having any luck here," David said, watching her thrust her hand into a riding boot. "We should probably go before someone comes."

She sucked in a breath. "Wait, I feel something." David joined her as she brought the boot over to the light of the window and pulled out a wadded cloth. It was a white cotton shirt. She spread it out for a better look, heart pounding faster at the sight of the brownish splotches on the front. Tiny pearl buttons ran down the back, the bib was ruffled, the sleeves were puffed… "David," her voice quavered, "this is a *woman's* shirtwaist."

~

David fetched Rusty and brought him back to the dressing room. The old man's eyes went wide when they showed him the blood-stained shirt.

"A woman?" he said incredulously. "We were so sure it was Nash."

Concordia nodded. Wynderhane's *she…she* echoed in her mind. At least now they could refute Yates's contention that Gwen Ambrose—who could never have gained access to Wynderhane's dressing room—was responsible. "We have to show the deputy sheriff, so I'm putting it back where we found it. But we need your help."

Rusty straightened. "Anything."

"Stand guard over the dressing room. Don't let anyone in—not the maid, or even Mrs. Wynderhane, if she comes. No one is to take anything from here. Can you do that?"

"You can count on me." The old man hesitated. "But wasn't it a man who killed my Victoria?"

"I'll explain later," Concordia said. "We'll be back as soon as we can."

They hurried along the path to the Ambrose cottage.

"I'd very much like to hear that explanation now," David said. "Are we back to the two deaths being unrelated?"

She picked her way through the storm debris still cluttering the path. "They *are* related. I believe the shirtwaist belongs to Miss Farraday, along with the iris Rusty found last night. There were no other irises in Nash's room. Where else could it have come from? At the risk of sounding indelicate, we heard for ourselves that she is no stranger to William Nash's bedroom door. She must have dropped it earlier without realizing."

David's eyes widened. "You are saying the *nursemaid* killed Wynderhane and sent the irises to Sir Anthony? Why?"

"The logical explanation is that she is Iris Dunwick's daughter. With the help of William Nash, she is seeking revenge for the treatment of her mother by Sir Anthony."

Miss Farraday had said she was an orphan. Not quite a full-fledged lie. By Concordia's estimate, the nurse would have been thirteen or fourteen at the time of her mother's death in 1888. According to Sir Anthony, the father had died some time before. Concordia tightened her grip on David's arm as she stumbled over a flagstone.

"She had charge of two children during the fair. How could she have done it?" David asked, helping her to her feet.

"One child. The baby had the sniffles and stayed home with Marie, remember? Miss Farraday only had five-year-old Serena to look after. Perhaps she slipped away when the girl was watching the puppet show or was occupied at the animal petting corral. It would have been a risk, I grant you," she added, noting his skeptical frown, "but not an impossibility."

"All right. For the sake of argument, let us say she managed it. *Why* kill Wynderhane?"

"To protect Nash. She feared Wynderhane would give him away. I noticed her nearby—close enough to overhear—when you and Rusty were trying to convince Wynderhane to reveal the name of the caller at the club. What if it was Nash, calling Miss Farraday?"

David stopped short. "You are suggesting that Nash strangled Rusty's granddaughter and set fire to her rooms?"

She grimaced, not wanting to believe it of the young man. Or of any of them, really. "It's only a theory. But Nash works in the same office and may have intercepted Victoria's message to Wynderhane and feared the worst."

"But Reese and Gemmer work there, too, as did Pickering," he said.

"True, but the shirtwaist indicates we're looking for a connection to a woman."

"Gemmer has a wife staying here, and Reese has a grandmother. Those are all connections to women."

Concordia shook her head. "We know Reese is guiltless—Pickering tried to frame him with the berry-stained bat in order to advance his own position. Neither Mrs. Reese nor Mrs. Gemmer is the right age to be related to Iris Dunwick. If we go with the theory that Iris's child wants revenge, then the child cannot be older than her mid-twenties. Only Miss Farraday is connected to Nash."

"You're making a great many assumptions without proof."

Concordia sighed. "I know." Right now, a stained shirt and a dried flower were the only clues they had to go on. But those should be enough to clear the Ambroses of guilt, at least, and allow them to could go on with their lives. Although it was uncharitable of her to even think it, she was grateful they wouldn't have to worry about their property being taken away by Wynderhane.

Yes, definitely an uncharitable sentiment. The poor man wasn't even in the ground yet.

The angry voices were already audible—amidst the noise of Captain Decker's hammering—as Concordia and David approached the fork in the path leading to the Ambrose cottage.

"You will have to knock me down and tie me to a chair before I allow you to take me away and leave Susie alone." Gwen Ambrose's voice held the shrill tinge of hysteria. Anxiety tugged at Concordia's abdomen. The woman sounded close to her breaking point.

"She will not be left alone. The girl will be placed in someone else's care for the time being." The voice of Deputy Sheriff Yates, calm though it was, had the steel-hard edge to it that Concordia recognized from her own encounters with the man. "I don't wish to use force, Miss Ambrose, but I will if necessary."

"We have to hurry," Concordia urged, letting go of David's arm and picking up the pace. Finally, they emerged from the path and came within sight of the group, Concordia panting, "Wait! We found something!"

Sir Anthony, Deputy Yates, and a police constable stared at her, open-mouthed. Concordia flushed from more than exertion. *Mercy,* she was acting as hoydenish as her students, who routinely yelled down the stairs to their cottage mates, ran full-tilt to their classrooms, and flung themselves akimbo into chairs. Some staid matron she was turning out to be.

Gwen broke away from the group and reached for Concordia, clasping her hands eagerly. "What have you found?"

"Possibly the evidence we need to clear you of blame, but I want the deputy to see for himself and decide." She inclined her head toward the men. "Where is Susie?"

"In the house, with Mrs. Reese and Lady Dunwick." Gwen frowned. "She's hiding under the bed and won't come out. They are keeping an eye on her to make sure she doesn't come to harm."

Concordia put her arm around Gwen's waist and led her back to the group. Yates watched them, brown eyes narrowed in caution. "Did I hear you say you found some sort of evidence, ma'am?" His eyes flicked to David, who had caught up to them.

David nodded. "I'll let my wife tell you. She is the one who reasoned it out."

Concordia flushed with gratitude at the tone of pride in his voice.

"Very well," Yates said reluctantly. Concordia imagined he would have preferred a male explanation. Of course, after her own experiences with some of Mother's friends and their rambling accounts over the tea table, she couldn't say she blamed him.

She tried to make her account as succinct as possible. Sir Anthony's eyes widened when she described the bloodstained shirtwaist stuffed into the riding boot. Even Yates seemed to have lost his skeptical expression and leaned forward in interest.

"And where is this evidence now?" he asked.

"We put it back where we found it," she said.

"Mr. Deighton is standing guard outside the dressing room to make sure no one disturbs it until you get there," David added.

Yates nodded toward the constable. "You remain here with the girl. Make sure she stays put. The elder Miss Ambrose will accompany us back to the Dunwicks."

The man tipped his cap. "Right, sir."

Yates turned to Concordia. "Lead the way."

No one said much as they walked along the path from the Ambrose property to the Dunwicks'. Concordia and David walked side by side, with Yates following right behind—too wide-shouldered for anyone else to comfortably walk the narrow path beside him—and Sir Anthony and Miss Ambrose bringing up the rear. Concordia could hear snatches of whispered conversation between those two, but most of it was legal terminology she didn't understand or knew she shouldn't be eavesdropping upon.

Rusty, pacing in front of the door to Wynderhane's dressing room, hurried toward them as soon as they reached the top of the stairs. "The maids are anxious to pack up his belongings. I've had quite a time keeping them out, including a heated discussion with Mrs. Gemmer, who has just returned." He held the dressing room door open for them.

Bless the man, Concordia thought, giving him a smile as she went in.

Yates was close behind her, practically breathing down her neck. "Where?" he asked gruffly.

She pointed to the left riding boot, beside its mate on the floor in the corner. He picked it up and carried it to the window. Gwen and Sir Anthony crowded around as he spread out the garment.

"The laundry mark has been cut out," he observed, turning it over. He glanced at Sir Anthony. "And you would definitely say that Miss Ambrose and her niece have no access to this upper level? One or both of them couldn't have sneaked up here?"

Gwen stiffened as if to retort, but Sir Anthony put a hand to her arm. "In the summertime, when the house is occupied, it would be impossible for either young lady to come up here unobserved. Miss Ambrose comes to the kitchen to deliver produce from her garden, and that is only upon occasion. She leaves by the same route. If you want confirmation, speak to our cook, Marie."

Yates pulled out his notepad, scribbled in it, and put it back in his tunic. "I shall do so, thank you."

As the deputy continued to examine the shirt, Sir Anthony shifted impatiently. "Well? It should be obvious now that neither Miss Ambrose nor Susie is responsible for the murder of Wynderhane. You should drop all charges against them and turn your attentions elsewhere."

The policeman roused himself. "Hmm? Ah, yes, the charges. May we use your parlor, Sir Anthony? It's much too cramped in here to discuss the matter." He picked up the shirt and tucked it under his arm.

Once they were settled in the parlor—Rusty being permitted to accompany the group—and the door closed behind them, Yates addressed Sir Anthony. "You say I should drop the charges against the Misses Ambrose. I had already resolved to do so in the case of young Susie Ambrose. I originally considered the possibility that she assisted her aunt in stabbing Edgar Wynderhane, but after spending time with the girl it's obvious that malice aforethought is beyond her. It's more likely her dress was bloodied by her pulling out the knife in an attempt to render aid."

"What of the murder charge against Miss Gwendolyn Ambrose?" Sir Anthony asked.

Yates ignored him, looking at Gwen with narrowed eyes. "If you would stand please, Miss Ambrose, and turn your back to me."

Gwen complied, glancing nervously over her shoulder at him.

He shook out the shirtwaist and held it lightly against her back. "You see that the size is correct." He nodded toward her. "You may be seated, miss."

"But that signifies nothing," Concordia protested. "Other women staying here have a similar build. Wynderhane's own wife, along with Mrs. Reese, Mrs. Gemmer, and Miss Farraday."

Gwen fixed Yates in a glare. "The shirtwaists I wear are much more plain, sir. You are at liberty to examine what passes for a wardrobe at my cottage. You will see it is quite sparse."

Sir Anthony cleared his throat. "Miss Ambrose, we shall get this sorted out without resorting to a search of your personal effects. Mr. Yates will speak to Marie and confirm that you could not have gone upstairs. Try not to worry."

"I would like to go home," Gwen said wearily. She glanced at the deputy sheriff. "I assume you have no further need of me for now?"

Yates inclined his head in acknowledgment, then moved over to the writing desk and drew out some paper. He scribbled a brief note and passed it to her. "Give that to the constable. I want him back here to help me search the rest of Mr. Wynderhane's belongings before they are packed away." He fixed her with a stern look. "I trust that you and your niece will stay put at your residence." Gwen nodded.

Concordia stood. "David and I will walk you back."

"Thank you."

Yates and Sir Anthony stood politely as they took their leave.

As Concordia passed by Sir Anthony, she leaned in to whisper. "Now is the time. You must tell him—everything—before it is too late."

She could feel his troubled gaze at her back as she closed the door.

CHAPTER 25

*O*nce they had seen Miss Ambrose safely to her door and showed Yates's note to the constable, Captain Decker drove the rest of them back to the Dunwick cottage in his farm cart: the police constable, Concordia, David, Lady Dunwick, and Mrs. Reese. Lady Dunwick and Mrs. Reese shared the driver's bench with Decker—poor Lady Dunwick getting squeezed in the process, seated between the stocky Decker and the buxom Mrs. Reese. Concordia, David, and the constable perched atop hay bales in the back.

"Hang on back there, folks!" Decker called, flicking the reins. "Storm runoff has rutted this road somethin' awful."

But the three of them needed no encouragement to cling to the sides for dear life. The captain drove with abandon. Concordia nearly lost her hat in the process and finally tucked it under her arm to keep it from flying away. She landed in David's lap more than once.

The passengers drew a collective sigh of relief when the cart pulled up to the Dunwicks' portico.

"Thank you for the ride, Captain," Lady Dunwick said politely, as he helped her down.

"My pleasure, ma'am." He ran a hand self-consciously through his grizzled hair and resettled the cap. "You think I could be speakin' wi' Sir Anthony a moment? It's about the regatta."

"Regatta?" Lady Dunwick echoed.

"Yes'm. He sent in his entry form last week but never put down who his crew would be."

"Ah, yes. I remember. Unfortunately, Captain, I doubt my husband would be equal to participating, with all that has been going on..." Her voice trailed off. Sir Anthony and Yates were stepping out on the porch. Yates caught sight of his associate and motioned him over, while Sir Anthony came over to clasp his wife's hands. "My dear, we have much to dis—" He broke off when he noticed Decker. "Hello, Captain."

"Captain Decker gave us a ride home," Lady Dunwick explained.

"Ah, much obliged."

"Not a'tall, sir, not a'tall," Decker said. "I was coming over here, anyway, hoping to be speaking wi' you about the regatta."

Sir Anthony raised an eyebrow. "That's in two days' time, isn't it? I assumed it would have been canceled. The storm must have caused a lot of damage to the local boats."

"Nothing so terrible, sir, though a few had to drop out of the race. How did your boat fare?"

"Oh, she came through the storm with just a few cosmetic scrapes on her hull. Nothing serious," Sir Anthony said.

"Well, then! Splendid. We need a minimum number of boats in the race in order for it to continue." The captain dropped his voice and leaned forward. "My vessel is the current favorite. That prize money could go a long way for me, sir. I know you've been having a bit of personal trouble lately, with your guest killed an' all, but I'd be ever so grateful if you'd stay in the race."

Sir Anthony's expression reflected a progression of emotions: guilt, indecision, loyalty, and the hopeful prospect of a day out in his beloved boat, something he had not yet had much opportunity for.

David straightened. "If you need a hand at the tiller, Sir Anthony, I'd be happy to help. I'm sure Reese and Nash would pitch in, too, if they don't have to return to the city right away."

One look at Sir Anthony's face, and Concordia knew the matter was decided. She touched David's sleeve. "I'll be at the cabin." It had been a most trying day. She needed peace and quiet in which to think.

Concordia wound up falling asleep much earlier than she planned and barely stirred when David joined her sometime later. At first her sleep was deep, restorative, and dreamless, but that changed. Night sounds—her husband's soft snore, the hoot of an owl, the chorus of crickets, the wind soughing in the trees—roused her briefly before she drifted asleep again and began to dream.

A woman stood at a distance, too far to see the particularities of her shape: short or tall, thin or stout. She was staring out into the bay, her form rigid in watchful stillness. What was she watching for? Concordia didn't know. The wind whipped the woman's hair around her face, and she clutched her shawl closely, protectively around her, bunching it in one hand. Her other hand held something that Concordia could not make out but very much wanted to know.

Suddenly, Concordia herself was out in the wind as well, pushing with heavy legs to approach the woman, struggling for a better look as the strong and hostile gusts made her eyes water and nearly wrenched the spectacles off her face. Any attempt to call out, and the words were forced back down her throat. She applied a kerchief to her mouth and nose as she got closer and looked again, this time focusing upon the woman's hand.

She recognized the knife, the one she had brandished as the

treacherous Brutus. The one Susie had pulled out of Wynder-hane's chest. The one used to gut fish. The one turned towards her now, ready to strike...

"No!" She yelled herself awake, heart pounding. She was in her bed, David beside her.

"Darling, darling, *shh*, it's all right," came his soothing murmur. He drew her to him as she turned and sobbed on his shoulder.

∾

She awoke to the sun shining in her eyes and an empty pillow beside her. She wandered out to the tiny kitchen and found a note propped beside an amply loaded breakfast plate of fruit and muffins.

Dearest:

I didn't want to disturb you. I'll be at the dock, helping Sir Anthony get his boat in order for tomorrow's regatta. I hope you are feeling better.

Love, D.

As she ate and then dressed, she thought of last night's dream. Not surprising, given the discovery in Wynderhane's dressing closet, but something about it nagged at her. She stepped out to the porch to put on her hat and shoes, grateful for the warm sun on her face and the soft breeze that fluffed her hair.

The woman in her dream could have been anyone. So much about it was indistinct—the face, the figure—while other images were quite sharp in her mind's eye. The knife. The shawl. The rigid posture.

She shook herself. Dreams were fickle things, not worth lingering upon. She would be better served thinking about who might have owned the bloodstained shirtwaist. She closed her eyes to better recall the details of the garment. Eggshell white. Lightweight, fine cotton. Ruffled front. Pearl buttons. Leg o'mutton, three-quarter sleeves. She sighed. In other words, any shirtwaist a woman of average means would wear in warm weather. She herself owned two such.

Miss Farraday would be her first choice, given the other circumstances. And the size would be about right, Concordia thought, remembering Deputy Yates holding it up against Gwen Ambrose. Miss Farraday was tall and broad-shouldered for a woman, just like Gwen. Of course, a blouse of that size could also fit several matrons of their group: Mrs. Reese, Mrs. Gemmer, and Mrs. Wynderhane were each on the stout side.

Even if she were to consider Charlotte and Lady Dunwick— which she most certainly did not—both women were of a petite or medium build.

Four women. Each had attended the fair. Any of them could have had a note delivered to Wynderhane, supposedly from Miss Ambrose, luring him to the empty pavilion with the promise of settling the dispute and selling her property to him.

Miss Farraday's motives she had already explored. She set her aside to consider again later. She reviewed the other possibilities, one by one, trying to be open-minded to the idea that the deaths of Victoria Lester and Wynderhane might be unrelated. What about other motives for killing Wynderhane?

Mrs. Gemmer was relatively unknown to her. As the wife of the dead man's partner, there *could* be some sort of financial gain that Concordia could not begin to guess at, but even so, why wouldn't Hans Gemmer have done the deed? And why attack Wynderhane at the East Hampton Fair, of all places? Gemmer and Wynderhane worked in the same office and socialized with the same people in the city. There would be ample opportunities to commit murder on one's home turf. Why wait for a beach holiday? The false note, the weapon at hand, the short time frame in which he was stabbed before someone might have come along... these suggested a sudden urgency, a spur-of-the-moment decision.

Mrs. Wynderhane was a stronger possibility than Mrs.

Gemmer in that regard. Perhaps she had tired of her husband's infidelities and had looked for a way out that didn't involve the expense or scandal of a divorce. Susie's fit of fury out on the fairgrounds could have suggested the idea of killing her husband and fixing the blame upon Miss Ambrose.

Concordia bit her lip as she thought. While it seemed plausible, there was something she was missing about that notion. She would have to go back to that.

Then there was Eleanor Reese. As James Reese's grandmother, she must be in her sixties. Could the woman wield a knife? Her fingers were strong and nimble, kept agile from decades of knitting. She could clutch it easily. But was she powerful and determined enough to actually plunge it into Wynderhane's chest?

Assuming it was physically possible, what motive could she possibly have? Concordia frowned, trying to recall any interactions between Mrs. Reese and Wynderhane. Dinner exchanges, tea-time conversation...polite, meaningless. The woman's grandson, of course, spoke continually with his employer, and Eleanor Reese spoke with James, but she had seen no interchanges of substance directly between the old lady and the dead stockbroker. Had Mrs. Reese even addressed Wynderhane with anything but a polite hello?

Well, there was the embarrassing incident on the back porch, when Wynderhane had tried to take liberties. Concordia flushed at the memory. David and Mrs. Reese had both rushed in when she screamed, just after she had kicked the man away. The old lady had been quite reproving: not of Wynderhane, actually, but of her grandson's excuses for the man.

Yes, that's right, Mrs. Reese said she'd been in the library and had heard the whole thing...

The whole thing. Concordia sucked in a breath. At the time, she and Wynderhane had been discussing Victoria's murder and the unknown man who had made the phone call from the club. What if Eleanor Reese's motive was the same one that Concordia had ascribed to Miss Farraday? What if Mrs. Reese killed Wynderhane to protect someone she loved—in this case, her grandson—from discovery?

Mrs. Reese and Mrs. Wynderhane had been standing nearby the lunch table at the fair, when David and Rusty were trying to convince Wynderhane to give up the caller's name. Wynderhane had initially refused but promised to think about it. Had Eleanor Reese overheard that as well? If her grandson was the guilty one, she couldn't take a chance. Her beloved James was in danger.

Concordia sighed. No, that couldn't be right. They'd already eliminated James as the one who had struck Sir Anthony. There had been nothing but berry stains and dirt on the bat, and Pickering had admitted as much, all the while maintaining that Reese was responsible.

She couldn't believe she was even considering this, but what if Pickering was right? What if the man's petty motives and despicable behavior to make Reese look bad had confused them all? Whatever Sir Anthony was struck with was more likely to be at the bottom of the bay than lying around for someone to find.

She shook her head. She didn't like considering the Reeses at all. Eleanor was such a kindly old lady, James a charming, engaging gentleman.

Well, she should continue exploring the possibility, at least to find the flaw and return to her original theory of Miss Farraday. Not that she liked that line of thought any better. Madeline Farraday was an appealing young woman, even if her amorous behavior left something to be desired.

What had happened just before discovering Wynderhane? The baseball game had finished. They were all looking for Sir Anthony and Susie. The deed must have already been committed by then. Mrs. Reese was standing beside Mrs. Wynderhane and Lady Dunwick, each looking perfectly calm and expressing concern for Susie, wanting to help. Concordia remembered them both, Mrs. Wynderhane with her charming muslin dress...

Just a minute. Mrs. Wynderhane could *not* have killed her husband. The image returned to her now, of Maud Wynderhane, in a cap-sleeved white dress of sprigged muslin, plucking dried grass from the hem. There was not a spot of blood on her clothes.

What about Mrs. Reese? Concordia closed her eyes to concentrate. Yes, the lady had no blood upon her, either. But...her rose-paisley fringed shawl had been wrapped around her shoulders. Despite the warmth of the afternoon. Her shirtwaist had been completely covered below the neck.

That was the detail she had missed. Her dream *had* been trying to tell her something. The dream's image of the fringed fabric of the shawl, clenched in a fisted hand, was still fresh in her mind. It had been a detail she had vaguely noticed during the fair but hadn't ascribed any significance to. Who thought twice about an old lady wrapped in a shawl, albeit on a warm summer's day? We assume old people are always cold.

She jumped to her feet, notions of Miss Farraday forgotten. With any luck, Mrs. Reese would be out of her room by now, and she could look around.

Concordia returned the breakfast plate and napkin to the Dunwick kitchen, where Marie was occupied chopping vegetables and throwing them into a pot.

"Good morning, Mrs. Bradley," the cook said, with barely a glance over her shoulder.

"The muffins were delicious, thank you."

Marie smiled as she stirred. "Ah yes, Mr. Bradley said you'd like 'em. You can jus' set the plate down in the sink. I'll take care of it."

"Are all the guests up and out-of-doors on this lovely morning?" Concordia asked.

The cook nodded. "You husband went with the master and the

two young fellas to work on the boat before the race tomorrow. Mr. Gemmer went into East Hampton—the telegraph line's been fixed—to send a telegram and arrange for their baggage at the station. Mrs. Gemmer, along with the missus and Miss Charlotte, rode with 'em to do some shopping in town. Oh, and Mr. Deighton—that friend o' yours?—he went along, too." She put the lid back on and rummaged in the pantry.

Concordia was assuming that Marie's "young fellas" were Nash and Reese, so that left only Eleanor Reese out of Marie's account. "Do you know where Mrs. Reese is? I had a question for her."

Marie grunted under the weight of a sack of flour. She plunked it on the counter and wiped her hands on her apron before answering. "Out for a walk, I think. At least, that what she usu'lly does after breakfast." She gave Concordia a pointed look. "It's right quiet around here, so I can get my work done."

Concordia took the hint. "Well, I'll leave you to it."

Marie barely murmured a reply as Concordia left.

Mindful that staff might be upstairs making beds and cleaning rooms, Concordia quietly climbed the steps and glanced along both hallways from the upper landing. She didn't see anyone, but off to her left she heard a girl humming as she worked.

Concordia scurried down the hallway of the right wing, mercifully empty, counting doors as she went. Yes, there was Nash's door, which meant—according to Rusty—that Eleanor Reese's room was just beside it. She tested the knob. *Drat.* Locked.

A couple of hairpins would have been indispensable right about now, but with her short hair...well, she would have to improvise. She pulled out her hatpins, laid aside her braided straw, and set to work bending the pins the way Penelope Hamilton, a Pinkerton friend of hers, had shown her last year during their cross-country train trip. She hoped this worked. Her practice at lockpicking at the time had been abysmal. A covert operative she was not.

After twice having to interrupt her task to hide in a nearby alcove when she heard the maid moving to another bedroom, she finally felt the lock release. She opened the door and slipped in, remembering just in time to retrieve her hat.

The drapes had been opened to let in the light. She latched the door behind her as a precaution before starting her search for the shawl. If Mrs. Reese had put it around her immediately after fleeing the scene, there might be smudges of blood on the fabric.

She searched the armoire, bureau drawers, and beneath the bed. She checked chair backs and hooks. The shawl wasn't here. She sighed. Mrs. Reese must have taken it with her. Still, Concordia drifted aimlessly around the room, not even sure what she was looking for. She pulled out desk drawers, hoping for a letter, a journal...*something* that would point to Eleanor Reese's guilt. Or her grandson's.

At the moment, all she had were suppositions. She needed proof.

Footsteps approached. Heart pounding in her chest, she tiptoed to the door and leaned in to listen. The maid must have finished with the bedrooms along the left wing. The sound seemed to be coming from the set of bedrooms two doors down. She didn't have much time.

She bit her lip and looked around the room. What had she missed?

She spied a white enameled box upon the vanity table. It was about the size of a small sewing basket. A jewelry case, most likely. Although she doubted it contained anything of interest, she opened it anyway. The red-velvet-lined interior revealed the usual pins, chokers, rings, and bracelets. She lifted the tray to look beneath and sucked in a breath. There lay a bulky, white envelope.

Heart beating faster, she slid her thumb under the flap and looked inside.

Irises. Pressed and dried long ago, but unmistakably irises. Nearly a dozen of them.

The envelope trembled in her hands. This she would not leave behind. It could be hidden or disposed of too easily, if the woman grew nervous. She tucked it in her pocket, restored the case, and slipped out of the room as quickly as she could. She had to find David. And Deputy Yates.

CHAPTER 26

*I*f anyone had caught sight of Mrs. Bradley hurrying toward the dock, clutching an unpinned hat in one hand and fistful of skirts in the other as she navigated the slope, muttering to herself all the while, he or she would not believe her a sober, composed matron of the newly married ranks, but rather a harum-scarum hoyden—one of those college girls, perhaps, who wore bloomers, played lawn tennis, and stayed up past their bedtimes reciting Latin poetry to their fellows.

Fortunately, no one was on hand to witness the spectacle, including anyone on the dock. In fact, the boat was gone as well. She stopped to catch her breath. Where were they? She adjusted her spectacles for a better look. *Ah.* She could make out the mast of the *Susan D*, with its green-and-yellow-striped tell-tales, well out in the harbor and beyond shouting range. She waved frantically. A few of the men on the boat—she couldn't make out exactly who—cheerfully waved back.

She blew out a sigh. Now what? No one was at the house besides the staff.

Gwen Ambrose might know how to reach Yates. He could be there now, in fact, although she hoped for Gwen's sake he was leaving them alone. If Yates wasn't around, Gwen might know what to do.

Concordia retraced her steps and headed for the Ambrose place.

~

She had become so accustomed to the black, hulking structure of the burned-out Ambrose mansion that she almost passed it without a second glance, but then she noticed movement out of the corner of her eye. She turned for a better look. Gwen Ambrose stood gazing at the structure, hand on hips.

"Gwen!" Concordia called. "What are you doing there?"

Gwen looked up, startled. She must have been so occupied she hadn't noticed her. Gathering her skirts, she joined her on the path. "Susie is gone again," she panted. "I was considering where to look next."

Concordia's stomach twisted. "How long?"

"Could be as long as a couple of hours. She was sleeping when I went out to take some photographs by the shoreline. I leave my empty case by her bed so she knows that's where I am."

Apparently Gwen was no longer a suspect if she was allowed to scramble along the shoreline again. That was one bright spot, at least. "But you say she does wander away at times, to explore."

Gwen shook her head. "This is different, Concordia. Something is wrong. Every morning when she wakes up, she feeds the animals. It's a chore she loves. But they haven't been fed."

"Show me."

Gwen led the way to the backyard, where the goat pen, chicken coop, and rabbit hutches were. Sure enough, the feeding troughs and bowls were empty. The chickens wandered around the pen, pecking futilely at the ground. Gwen pulled out a sack from a stout tin box and scattered grain for them.

Concordia was crouched at the gate to the goat pen, which gaped slightly. "Has this latch always been bent?"

Gwen stifled an exclamation and came over to see. "There was nothing wrong with it last night." She glanced at the goats inside the pen. "Speckles is missing! He's Susie's favorite. It's a wonder the others didn't escape." She reached for some twine to secure the gate for the time being. "Well, now we know why she's gone. She's trying to find the goat."

Concordia frowned. She wasn't at all confident the animal had gotten out by accident. "Before we conduct a wider search, let's take a look around and see if anything else is out of place." She didn't know exactly what they were looking for, but her neck prickled with unease.

Gwen raised an eyebrow in inquiry, but agreed.

As they searched, Concordia told her what she'd discovered in Mrs. Reese's room and its significance.

Gwen's eyes widened. "Eleanor Reese? You think she killed Wynderhane? She's just a harmless old lady."

"We should have Deputy Yates look into it, nevertheless. Do you know how to reach him? He needs to see what I found. He can also help us look for Susie."

Gwen sighed. "I'd hoped we were finished with Yates, but yesterday he said he'd return today for some final questions. He showed particular interest in Susie's recent drawings."

Concordia was interested in Susie's drawings, too. What if the girl had been trying to tell them, in her own way, what she had seen?

Concordia remembered one of her sketches, a collection of odd symbols: a crude X, a wavy line that trailed down, a scribbled circle. It didn't make sense. But if it was supposed to portray Mrs. Reese...

Of course. Knitting needles were the X. And a trailing ball of yarn would account for the rest of it.

Mrs. Reese had no doubt recognized the meaning of Susie's

drawings right away but had made the bold decision to stay close to the girl, visiting often on the pretext of motherly concern, when in reality she was assessing how much of a threat she was.

And now, apparently, Susie had been judged too much of a threat. They had to find her before it was too late.

Concordia was about to share her thoughts aloud when they reached the shed that housed Gwen's photography supplies. Gwen impatiently flung the door open.

Both women gaped at the goat inside, chewing on a leather camera strap. At the sight of them, Speckles bleated plaintively.

"What a mess," Gwen said, picking her way through the debris scattered on the floor. She went over to a high shelf. "At least he couldn't reach my chemicals—"

"What is it?" Concordia asked, watching Gwen push bottles this way and that, searching for something.

"A bottle's missing. Bromide of potassium."

"What's that?"

"I use it when I make collodion emulsion plates, along with—" She broke off at Concordia's confused expression. "Never mind."

"Is it poisonous?"

Gwen bit her lip. "In large enough doses."

Surely, Mrs. Reese wouldn't be so wicked as to kill an innocent child. Concordia's stomach clenched at the thought. The truth was they just didn't know what the woman was capable of.

"What is it, Concordia?" Gwen asked impatiently. "What aren't you telling me?"

"I believe Mrs. Reese is responsible for Susie's disappearance," Concordia said. "Susie saw her in the pavilion, either in the act of stabbing Wynderhane or as she was fleeing. Your niece has been trying to tell us ever since, with her sketches."

Gwen paled. "Oh, dear Lord. But why was Susie in the tent to begin with? It seems unlikely she would follow Mrs. Reese in there."

"We may never know. My guess is she was chasing after a

kitten or puppy that had wandered off from the animal pen at the fair."

Gwen sighed. "Possibly." She shook her head. "How could I be so wrong about the old lady? I don't understand it. Mrs. Reese has been a frequent visitor here since the attack on Wynderhane. Why wait until now to harm Susie?"

"Perhaps Yates's repeated visits were making her nervous? We must find them."

Gwen urged the pony at as brisk a pace as it could manage, Concordia clutching the bench seat of the cart. The terrain was beginning to look familiar to her, after several excursions to Hassett Knoll and East Hampton. The fork in the road was coming up. The left would take them on to the village, whereas the right...

She touched Gwen's sleeve. "Isn't the windmill that way?" She pointed. "Maybe we should check it first."

Gwen nodded and slowed the cart. With a twitch of the reins, they changed direction for the abandoned windmill.

The graveled road soon became so clogged with weeds they had to jump down and lead the pony around the worst spots. "It would be quicker if we continued on foot and left the cart here," Gwen said.

Concordia agreed, and Gwen unhitched the animal and set it loose.

"Aren't you worried it will stray?"

Gwen shook her head. "He'll be perfectly content to nibble the grass. He won't go far."

Soon the dilapidated windmill structure and house came into view. Gwen dropped her voice to a whisper. "If they are here, they must be in the house. There isn't much in the windmill itself besides the mechanism."

If Mrs. Reese was here, whispering wouldn't help them avoid detection. The lady had only to look out any window on this side to see them. The surrounding field in between was flat and treeless, with wild grasses not nearly tall enough to hide anything larger than foxes and woodchucks. In fact, they were making quite a bit of noise in pushing their way through the vegetation on the barely discernable path to reach the building. The place looked as if no one had been here for years. The roof was missing a great many shingles, window panes were broken, and the porch sagged atop rotted ground supports.

They tested each step carefully until they reached the front door, which listed at an angle, hanging by a single, bent hinge. Concordia took a breath and looked at Gwen. "Ready?"

She nodded.

After a quick tour of the ground level yielded nothing, they cautiously started up the rickety stairs. Gwen sucked in her breath with a hiss as she picked up a small black object on a lower step. "Look! Susie's shoe."

Concordia squared her shoulders. There were two of them, younger and stronger than Eleanor Reese. They should be able to gain control of the situation. Mrs. Reese was alone. Or was she? Could James be with her? No, Marie had said he'd gone to the dock to help Sir Anthony with his boat. And the boat was gone, presumably with him on it.

Concordia met Gwen's eye. "All right," she said quietly, "let's get your niece and bring her home."

CHAPTER 27

For an old lady who had just been caught kidnapping a defenseless girl, Eleanor Reese was exceedingly calm. But of course, she had been expecting them. They found her in the bedroom, sitting in a creaky antique chair beside the old, broken-down bed, placidly knitting. Susie lay sprawled upon the mattress, not moving.

"Don't worry," Mrs. Reese said cheerfully, "she's alive. I mixed something into a bit of tea I brought with me to put her to sleep. Poor girl was quite thirsty after our fruitless search for her goat."

Gwen started to cross the room, but the old lady held up a hand. "No closer, if you please." The words were polite, but the tone was brittle and threatening.

Concordia watched in shock as the woman whipped out a pearl-handled derringer from her bag and put it against Susie's forehead. "Do as I say," she said sharply.

Gwen retreated.

Mrs. Reese nodded her approval. "That's better. Sit in the chair by the armoire." Gwen sat, eyes fixed upon Susie.

"Good. Now then, Mrs. Bradley, you are to pick up that rope and tie your companion to the chair." She waved the pistol.

"Quickly, now. No, no—wrists *behind* her back, dear. And do a good job. I'll be checking your work."

Concordia gritted her teeth and complied. Though she tried to be gentle, Gwen winced as she bound her wrists together. Concordia tugged down Gwen's cuffs so they were beneath the rope and tied an underside knot—harder for the old lady to see—making it a little less tight, hoping it would escape detection. "I take it the weapon is one of Sir Anthony's?" she said over her shoulder.

"Indeed, the man has quite a collection. James took it from the display case last night and passed it along to me. Sir Anthony was so busy with the yacht this morning he never noticed."

"How can you possibly believe you'll get away with this?" Concordia asked, glancing back.

"You won't be around to see that part," the lady said. "James has come up with a clever plan—the poor boy is *so* underappreciated at the firm—I have only to keep you securely here for him to take care of later." Her eyes narrowed. "Resume your task, young lady. No lollygagging."

"Was it also part of your grandson's plan for you to kill Edgar Wynderhane?" Concordia asked tartly. She was crouched at Gwen's ankles now, tying them together. She couldn't see Mrs. Reese's expression, but she heard her sigh.

"James considered himself safe for the longest while, even after Wynderhane realized it was James who had called from the club and silenced the young lady. After all, Wynderhane couldn't reveal the wiretapping arrangement without considerable risk to himself. But I heard you at the fair—you and your husband wouldn't let it go. Wynderhane was close to capitulating. Eventually, he would have told your husband and that other man—Dusty?—that James had made the call. Something had to be done, quickly. There was no time to consult with James."

Concordia straightened, now finished with the rope. She flashed a look of apology to Gwen before turning back to Mrs.

Reese. "So you improvised, forging a note to Wynderhane from Miss Ambrose, to lure him to the tent."

Mrs. Reese nodded in approval. "Very good, my dear. I knew the greedy man would not pass up such an opportunity."

"But you didn't count upon Susie seeing you. That was rather clumsily done, as was having to cover your stained shirtwaist with your shawl in ninety-degree weather and then needing a place to hide the garment later."

Mrs. Reese glared but didn't answer.

"Then you feared that Susie, despite her limited speech, would somehow communicate that you were the murderer. Through her drawings, perhaps. There was always the risk of someone catching on. You kept close to her, gauging her reaction to you."

The old lady glanced at the girl sleeping on the bed. "She didn't see me do it. She came in just after. We locked eyes for a moment, and then I escaped. I had hoped she wouldn't understand. But those drawings and her recent aversion to me—we couldn't take a chance." She swallowed.

Concordia softened her voice. "You aren't a cold-blooded killer, you know, Mrs. Reese. You panicked when it came to Wynderhane. Do not add this to your crimes. You can put a stop to it, right now. We can tell you are fond of Susie. But if you go through with your grandson's plan, how will you feel, knowing you had a hand in murdering a defenseless girl? The remorse would eat you alive."

Mrs. Reese sucked in a sharp breath. The words, when they came, were forced out through clenched teeth. "Remorse? You don't know...what you are talking about." She took a moment to compose herself, carefully set the pistol on the bed within easy reach, and picked up her knitting once more. "Now, take that other piece of rope, sit down in the second chair, and tie your ankles together. I will do the rest."

Concordia eyed the weapon on the dirty mattress beside

Susie's head, wondering if she dare lunge for it. She was on the other side of the room. Was it too far to risk?

She may as well have said it aloud. Mrs. Reese raised an eyebrow and gave a small smile. "I wouldn't try it. Do as I say, Mrs. Bradley."

Concordia worked on keeping the woman distracted as she picked up the rope and surreptitiously slid the second chair closer to Gwen. "I concede there are things about this situation that I do not know. For example, how did James learn that Victoria Lester had eavesdropped on his telephone call from the club? The call was to you, was it not?" She recalled the old woman's words. *It is often easier to simply take matters into one's own hands.* For reasons as yet unknown, she was the driving force behind all this.

Eleanor Reese nodded.

"How did James learn of Miss Lester's involvement?" Concordia asked again.

"The girl came to the office to speak with Wynderhane while James was in the filing room. When the receptionist told her Wynderhane wasn't in, the young lady grew agitated. Her voice was loud enough for him to overhear. After she left, he struck up a conversation with the receptionist, who assumed he already knew all about Wynderhane's eavesdropping scheme. He *is* Wynderhane's secretary, after all. He should have been told. If the man hadn't been so close-mouthed and secretive, all of this could have been avoided," she added bitterly.

"How did James find Miss Lester?"

"It was a simple matter to look up her address in Wynderhane's files."

Concordia suppressed a sigh. Poor Miss Lester. She'd never had the chance to evade him. He'd known where she lived all along. "Why did he set fire to her room after he struck her?"

She grimaced. "When he found out from the receptionist that Miss Lester kept logs of her conversations for Wynderhane, James feared there could be something incriminating in her room he'd overlooked."

Concordia fought the wave of anger that threatened to steal her breath away. James Reese and his grandmother had much to answer for, but if she succumbed to her emotions, they would never get out of here. She kept her voice level. "Does James want to kill Sir Anthony because he turned James's mother away when she needed help?"

Mrs. Reese's hands stilled, and she clucked her tongue. "*Ahh.* You've made me drop a stitch." She looked up. "So, Anthony Dunwick told you about that, did he? I thought he'd take the secret of his dishonored sister to his grave. How would the Dunwick lineage survive such a scandal?" She chuckled to herself. "Fear has a wonderful way of loosening the tongue."

Gwen inclined her head toward Concordia. "Tell her about the irises."

Mrs. Reese started.

Concordia suspected she'd dropped another stitch. "Yes, I found the envelope of pressed irises in your jewel case this morning. You've been sending one to Sir Anthony, each year, with Iris's death date."

Eleanor Reese sighed, her expression introspective. "It was her funeral bouquet. I preserved them."

"You were fond of her, then," Concordia said.

Mrs. Reese's expression softened. "She was the daughter I'd never had. A kind woman, a loving mother, and a good influence on my son. He finally turned his life around because of her, giving up the shadier pursuits of his youth. She managed what I could not. He abandoned his aliases, his schemes, his restless moving around from place to place. He settled down at last, became an accountant."

Concordia marveled at the drastically disparate portrayals of Iris Dunwick. Fallen woman, or saving angel? How sad that Sir

Anthony could not have seen the positive side of his sister's nature.

"But my son died when James was fourteen years old," Mrs. Reese went on. "After that they moved in with me, but I was a widow myself and the three of us struggled to make ends meet." She fell silent, lost in her own thoughts.

"Is that when Iris wrote to Sir Anthony?" Concordia asked.

The woman roused herself. "It wasn't easy for her to ask for help. She had a touch of the Dunwick pride herself. But she had her son to think of. For months, she waited for her brother's reply, sinking further into a melancholia we couldn't pull her out of. Between her husband's death and her brother's rejection...it was all too much for her." Mrs. Reese's knitting lay still in her lap as she stared into nothingness.

Gwen, no stranger herself to family tragedy, broke the silence. "What happened then?"

Mrs. Reese glanced back at her, but not really seeing her as she mused aloud. "Iris wanted, more than anything—more than money or security—to be reconciled with the Dunwicks, to introduce her only child to them." Her expression contorted in anger. "But all she got from them was stony, condemnatory silence. What was her unforgivable sin? Marrying my son, the man she loved."

"Did she...take her own life?" Concordia asked hesitantly. It would explain a great deal about Sir Anthony's reticence. Yet another scandal for the Dunwick family.

Mrs. Reese's eyes gleamed with unshed tears. "James found her. They would not allow us to bury her in consecrated ground. The irises I cut from my garden were her only flowers, and James and I her only mourners."

"I'm sorry," Gwen Ambrose said.

The old lady's expression hardened. "Save your pity. It won't help us now."

"Neither will revenge that destroys the innocent along with

the guilty," Concordia pointed out. "It has been eleven years. Why exact retribution now?"

"Some wounds never heal. When James met Sir Anthony for the first time last month and saw for himself the privileged life the man led—theater tickets, fancy clothes, the deference of underlings and peers alike, only the best hotel accommodations, a summer house in the Hamptons—he felt all the more keenly the deprivation of his younger years and his mother's last, desperate act." She scowled. "We could have had a different life if not for Sir Anthony's rejection."

Concordia grimaced. They could, indeed.

"Have you finished with your ankles, Mrs. Bradley? Well then, let's get this done." She set her knitting aside and plucked another length of rope from the foot of the bed.

Was it Concordia's imagination, or had Susie moved her hand slightly? She didn't know whether she wanted the girl to stay asleep so she'd be spared the terror of their predicament or wake up to help them. But what help could she give?

"I want to be back at the Dunwick cottage before they rescue James," Mrs. Reese added briskly, coiling the rope to keep from tripping over it and moving toward Concordia.

Concordia frowned. "Rescue?"

"James will have his revenge upon Sir Anthony at last. He convinced him to take them out in the boat today. I prepared a special flask of cider for them, when they get thirsty."

Gwen shot Concordia a look of alarm. "The bromide."

"Oh, that was yesterday," Mrs. Reese said complacently. "I had hoped it would take you a while to miss it."

Concordia's heart raced, and her mouth had gone dry. She could barely get the next words out. "My husband is on that boat."

Mrs. Reese grimaced. "Such a nice man. That Nash fellow, too. It's unfortunate, to be sure, but it can't be helped. James will capsize the boat once everyone is...incapacitated and hold on until someone comes along. Everyone else will appear to have drowned. Including Sir Anthony."

Concordia felt as if she were drowning herself. *David. Not David.* She struggled to get a full breath, her chest tight, her ears ringing.

As Mrs. Reese reached for her wrist, Concordia saw motion across the room. Susie was waking up. *The gun was still on the bed.*

In one swift movement, Concordia yanked her own wrist, which caused the old lady gripping it to lose her balance and tumble face-down across her lap. Concordia couldn't stand with her ankles tied to the chair, but she hunched over Mrs. Reese and clasped her tightly. The woman squirmed and screamed invectives at her, but still Concordia held on.

The one benefit of the noise was that it fully roused Susie, who sat up in confusion and alarm.

"Susie! Are you all right?" Gwen called.

The girl's eyes widened when she saw her aunt. She gave a slow nod.

Gwen breathed a relieved sigh. "Thank heavens. All right, dear. We need some help over here. Come and unknot my ropes, there's a good girl."

Susie slid off the bed onto unsteady feet, grasping and lurching her way over to Gwen, alternating between holding furniture for balance and putting her fingers in her ears to block out the sound of Mrs. Reese's yelling.

"The knots aren't that tight," Concordia gasped out, still wrestling with the writhing old lady. "She should be able to—to undo them."

"I wish we could keep that one quiet," Gwen said. "It's the noise that's scaring Susie the most right now."

Concordia briefly loosed a hand to fling her skirts over the woman's head, which muffled things a bit, rather like quieting a cranky bird.

Soon Gwen was freed and hugging her niece tight.

"I'm all in favor—of—of family reunions," Concordia huffed, struggling to maintain her grip on the old lady, "but could someone—please—untie my ankles?"

Gwen, carefully maneuvering around the flailing limbs of Eleanor Reese, untied Concordia's ankles.

Still, Concordia didn't get up, though her arms ached with the exertion of holding onto the surprisingly strong old woman. She inclined her head toward the gun on the bed. "Grab that first before I let her go."

Gwen gingerly took possession of the derringer.

"Don't point it at us!" Concordia said sharply. "Put it in your pocket for now. Carefully."

As soon as the weapon was secured, Concordia released Mrs. Reese, who sprawled to the floor. Without a backward look, the lady got up and ran out the door faster than Concordia would have expected possible.

"We're just going to let her go free?" Gwen asked incredulously.

Concordia no longer cared about Eleanor Reese. She was harmless now and wouldn't get very far. "We have to intercept the *Susan D* before Reese kills them all."

"We need a boat for that," Gwen said.

Concordia remembered Captain Decoy...Decker, who boasted about having the fastest boat in tomorrow's regatta. "I need to borrow your cart. Is Susie up to walking back to the Dunwicks with you? They can send for the doctor to look at her."

Gwen smoothed her niece's hair. "Susie? Do you feel well enough to walk?"

The girl hugged her close and nodded against her chest.

"Make sure to send for Yates as well," Concordia said, as she ran for the stairs.

"Where are you going?" Gwen called after her.

"To find Captain De-Decker." *Drat.* She almost said it again.

CHAPTER 28

*C*oncordia didn't even bother to look for Eleanor Reese as she rushed back to the road. What that woman did from now on meant nothing to her.

The pony, mercifully, was munching contentedly on the grass within sight of the cart, and Concordia was able to lead it over and buckle it back into its traces. Soon they were on their way down the fork in the road leading to Hassett Knoll.

As they rattled past the Main Street shops, the patrons stopped to stare. She knew why, of course—hatless, short hair all in a tumble around her head, skirts filthy from grass, weeds, and the dusty house, spectacles sliding down her nose—it was a wonder they had stayed on her face at all—the pony lathered and panting. She must look like an asylum escapee.

She pulled up to the café and jumped down, leaving the pony to its own devices. "Is Captain Decker here?" she called, as soon as she set foot inside. "I must find him—"

"Over here, ma'am!" Decker stepped out of the gift shop alcove, cap under his arm. He frowned as he got a good look at her. "What's wrong?"

She drew a breath. "The *Susan D*'s in trouble, or soon will be.

We need your boat to catch them." She prayed it was as fast as he claimed.

Bless the man—instead of time-wasting exclamations or demands for an explanation, he steered her by the elbow out of the shop. After one look at her pony's quivering flanks, he dug out a coin and tossed it to a youth loitering nearby. "Make yourself useful. Take this poor animal and the cart 'round to my place. Give him some water and a good rubdown."

The boy caught the coin in the air, then hesitated.

"Look lively, son!" Decker said gruffly. He held out his arm for Concordia. "My cart's across the street. You can tell me what's happened on the way."

As they bounced and jolted along the rutted streets toward the village dock, she recounted Susie's kidnapping and their discovery of James Reese's plan to kill Sir Anthony and the rest of his crew while they were out on the bay.

Decker let out the occasional low whistle as he listened, concentrating upon maintaining his speed while dodging ruts deep enough to take a wheel clean off the cart. Finally, when she had finished her account, he made a *tsking* sound. "What kinda times are we living in! It's gettin' to be that you can't even trust little old ladies anymore."

They came to a rolling stop at the dock, and Decker flung the reins toward an ill-kempt fisherman smoking a cheroot. "Who's out right now?" he asked the man, squinting into the bay's horizon. He pointed. "Is that Hardwin's oyster sharpie?"

The man spoke around the pipe stem clenched in his teeth. "I reckon."

"Dang it, I need a mate. He's the best one around these parts," Decker muttered. He turned to survey the pier. "Where is everybody?"

"Hardly anyone out today," the man said, scratching the stubble at his chin. "Most folks still clearing fallen trees and fixing their roofs from the storm. And they's busy fixin' nets at the fishery."

"Well, we're gonna need some help. The *Susan D*'s in trouble."

The man squinted skeptically at the still waters of the bay. "Huh?"

Obviously, this was a gentleman sadly lacking in imagination.

Decker glowered at the dim-witted man. "Take my cart, go 'round to Nickerson's place, then to Fitch's. Tell 'em they need to get out their boats and catch up to us. I don' know exactly where we'll be, but I 'spect somewhere near the east end of the bay, toward the Dunwicks' dock." He gave him a sharp look. "Got it?"

He straightened. With a "Yessir," he jumped into the cart with alacrity.

Despite her fear and worry, Concordia couldn't help but admire Captain Decker's commanding air.

Decker led her farther down the pier, where his sloop was tied, a sleek vessel of oak and yellow pine. She looked at the name emblazoned on the back. *The Decoy.* Under less-dire circumstances, she would have enjoyed a private chuckle over that.

"You know anything about boats?" he asked.

She shook her head.

"Well, you're gonna learn today. S'long as you can tug a sheet or hold a tiller, you'll be fine."

"Well, I've *heard* of a tiller. It's that thing in the back, right?"

He rolled his eyes and handed her in to the boat. "I'm gonna have my hands full," he muttered.

DAVID

David Bradley had not been out on the water in ages. A confirmed "city boy," opportunities such as these didn't come his way often. Sir Anthony, Will Nash, and James Reese made agreeable enough companions, although he would have preferred the solitary company of his wife and a more leisurely excursion. He was spending most of his time either trimming the sail or manning the tiller, as Sir Anthony climbed over him to secure the lines. Nash and Reese had initially helped with hoisting the sails, but now sat at relative leisure near the bow, idly coiling line and conversing.

Ah well, it was a glorious morning to be out on the bay. A good, stiff breeze filled the *Susan D*'s sail, the sun sparkled upon the waves, and the blue sky stretched endlessly overhead. He could make out the sails of other pleasure boats in the distance, though there seemed to be fewer fishing boats on the water than one might expect.

"Where are the fishermen?" he asked Sir Anthony, who shrugged.

Reese spoke up. "The groundskeeper said the fishery, that way"—he pointed west—"suffered damage in the storm. They're still repairing the boats and nets that got torn up."

"Speaking of fishing," Sir Anthony said, "I know a good spot for striped bass. There's a quiet cove not far from here."

Reese looked up, a gleam in his eye. "Perfect."

By the time they had reached the spot, David was spent. They'd had to tack upwind to reach the cove, and his arms and shoulders ached from the unaccustomed exertion. He took off his cap and mopped his forehead and neck with his kerchief.

"We can drop anchor here," Sir Anthony said. He nodded toward Reese and Nash. "You two mind taking care of that? Bradley and I could use a rest."

Once Nash and Reese secured their position, Reese reached under the seat and pulled out a hamper. "I had a feeling we'd be out on the water for a while, so I took the liberty of bringing along some cool cider and comestibles from Marie's kitchen."

Sir Anthony gave an approving nod.

Reese pulled out the carafe, gave it a vigorous shake, then started pouring and passing around the cups.

David hadn't realized how thirsty he was until he lifted the cup to his lips and drank deeply.

～

"No, no," Decker said impatiently, "*leeward*, Mrs. Bradley—away from the wind! Pull on the jib sheet *away* from the wind."

She dropped one rope—though Decker kept insisting upon calling it *line*—and picked up another, which to her mind was quickly becoming the definition of sailing.

"Better. Now, trim it 'til the edge stops luffing."

"Luffing?" What language were they speaking?

He rolled his eyes. "Flapping, ma'am. Until it stops *flapping*. Watch it get tight, but not too tight."

She nodded, keeping her eye on the jib sheet. They began to pick up speed.

"All righty, then, I'll take over the sails, you grab the tiller." He pointed to the long, wood handle protruding into the aft section of the boat. "It controls the rudder. Don't worry, I'll tell you which way I want you to move it."

She picked her way carefully over ropes, boxes, and other detritus.

"Watch the boom!" he yelled, as a sudden shift in the wind yanked the sails and tipped the boat sideways. She crouched as it swung across the cockpit to the other side. With the sloop's bottom tilting under her feet, she made a mad, lurching scramble for the tiller.

"Starboard, forty-five degrees!" he called.

She grasped the long handle. "Which way is *starboard*?"

"Right!"

The tiller moved easily under her hand, and the boat stabilized.

"All right, hold it steady, right down the middle. We're headed toward the Dunwicks' dock. Keep an eye out for 'em along the way."

But Concordia was already scanning the sailboats in the distance, willing her traitorous stomach to behave. *We're coming, David. We're coming.*

~

DAVID

David felt decidedly unwell. The sun hurt his eyes. His limbs felt heavy. And the world was spinning too fast for his liking. Perhaps it was the bright light, the motion of the water, the exertions of the morning. All he wanted to do was curl up and go to sleep.

But a distant portion of his mind nagged at him that this was not a normal kind of unwell. He lifted his head to look around. Nash was hanging over the side, retching. Sir Anthony, slumped upon the cockpit seat, wasn't moving at all.

Where was Reese? David languidly turned his head toward the sound of a chain rattling. *Ah*, there he was, pulling up anchor.

Reese gave him a worried look. "I thought it best to get us back to the dock. Everyone seems indisposed."

"Except for you," David managed to croak. Why was Reese the only one unaffected? Something was definitely amiss. But this overwhelming feeling of lethargy made it difficult to string his thoughts together. He almost didn't care.

Reese gave a hollow laugh. "Lucky me, eh? At least one of

us is able to get us back. Just relax. I'll take care of it."

David closed his eyes with a sigh.

~

"I see them!" Concordia cried, pointing to the right.

Decker squinted. "That's them, all right, coming out of Gull Cove. Good fishing there." He gave her a skeptical look. "Are you sure there's cause for concern, ma'am? Seems like a harmless excursion to me."

"I told you what Mrs. Reese tried to do to us," Concordia retorted. "Her grandson has masterminded a plan to bring a great many people to harm. Why do you doubt me?"

"Okay, okay." Decker held up his hands in a placating gesture of surrender. "Far be it for me to argue with a woman. Nothin' but grief comes o' that. We'll go see what's going on."

The tension in her shoulders eased somewhat. "Thank you."

"Not a'tall. Ready to come about? Twenty degrees to port, Mrs. Bradley, nice and easy." He released the jib sheet from the cleat, neatly ducking the boom as it came across.

Concordia kept her grip on the tiller as if her life depended upon it.

~

DAVID

A voice, filled with pain and rage, penetrated the fog of David's consciousness. "It is *your* fault my mother is dead! You may have just as well have fed her the poison yourself!"

David opened his eyes. Reese had Sir Anthony by the collar, shaking him, dragging him off the cockpit seat toward the starboard side of the boat. Sir Anthony lifted his head, gazing at Reese with horrified eyes, unable to get his legs under him to resist.

David pushed himself to stand, then promptly fell to his knees. "Stop!" he yelled, though he couldn't seem to put much power in his voice. Had Reese even heard him? Where was Nash?

He crawled towards them.

Reese had Sir Anthony's head and shoulders dangling over the lifeline by the time David reached them. Reese gave a yelp of surprise as he felt David's arms wrap around his knees and pull him down. Sir Anthony, having again lost consciousness, was pinned under them both, as the struggle between James Reese and David Bradley began in earnest.

"Something's wrong!" Concordia cried. They were a hundred yards away now, and she could see three men clustered together, arms and legs flailing, at the edge of the sloop. Then she recognized the head of wavy black hair. *David.* He was still alive. She held her breath as she watched him grabbing at Reese to keep him from pushing Sir Anthony overboard. There was no sign of Nash.

Then the wind shifted, and the *Susan D* abruptly listed to starboard, sending all three tumbling toward the hatch.

Decker sucked in a breath. "She's gonna go over in this wind! I'll make a jump for it when we're close enough. If there's time, I'll ease this sheet"—he pointed—"but if not, you'll have to do it. Then drop anchor." He nodded toward the weight and chain in the corner. "Got it?"

"Right." She tried to look more confident than she felt, but her stomach was in knots at the sight of her husband, fighting for his life while she was out of reach.

He raised a shaggy eyebrow. "You're no shrinking violet, that's for sure. Bradley's a lucky fellow."

Just as they were pulling up beside the *Susan D*, a gust of wind sent it tilting in the other direction, so far to port—and toward *The Decoy*—that Concordia feared it would either capsize or the mast lines of both boats would become entangled. She saw David grab for a stanchion to keep from being flung off the deck, but Reese and Sir Anthony tumbled overboard.

"I'm going in. Drop anchor!" Decker released the line, grabbed a life ring, and jumped in the water.

She tossed the weight over the other side, keeping her feet clear of the chain.

"Ahoy, Decker!" a voice called in the distance. She turned toward the sound, shading her eyes for a better look. Three other boats were approaching. Two men on the closest one waved. She waved back.

Sound carries well across water. She heard a whistle, then a throaty laugh. "That's a purty lady! Doin' well for yoursel', are you, Decker?"

"Ne'er you mind," Decker yelled back, grabbing a sputtering Reese by the back of the collar after making sure Sir Anthony was clutching the life ring. But Reese fought Decker for all he was worth, twisting and thrashing, trying to land a blow. Decker gave him a couple of good dunks to settle him down. "Jes' get over here quick, afore we all go under."

CHAPTER 29

*A*mong the boats to join in the rescue was one commandeered by Deputy Sheriff Yates, accompanied by two uniformed constables. Concordia stayed aboard *The Decoy*, anxiously watching the proceedings.

Yates flashed a steely look in her direction as he climbed into the *Susan D* and helped haul Sir Anthony, Reese, and Decker out of the water.

She could see David struggling to get to his feet in an attempt to offer assistance, but Yates waved him back. "You're obviously in bad shape, sir," she heard him say. "We'll have plenty of aid in a moment." Thank goodness the *Decoy* was close enough that she could see and hear what was going on. She was sorely tempted to jump across to the *Susan D* and gather her husband in her arms, leaving Decker's boat to drift.

"David!" she called. "Are you all right?"

David gave her a grateful look and a quick nod before he turned back to Yates. "There's a man missing. Will—Will Nash." He pointed to Reese. "*He* put something in the cider. Knocked us out. I awoke, and he was—was trying to push Sir Anthony over —overboard."

Yates grabbed Reese by the shoulders, his expression fierce. "What did you do with Nash? Did you throw him over?" Reese merely glared and wouldn't say a word.

The deputy turned to Decker. "We're going to need help searching for the missing man, but Sir Anthony and Mr. Bradley need a doctor right away."

"Fitch here has fitted the *Sea Maiden* with an auxiliary gas engine that can get 'em back quick," Decker said. "The rest of us will stay and help you search and keep an eye on your prisoner."

Yates gave a grunt of assent and called over to Concordia. "You hear all that, Mrs. Bradley?"

She nodded.

"When you get to the Dunwick cottage, stay there. I have many questions for you when we're done here."

Concordia, David, and Sir Anthony were put on the *Sea Maiden*, the wet and shivering Sir Anthony tucked in with blankets. Concordia clutched David's hand tightly and stroked his hair as his head rested in her lap. He gave her a long, reassuring look, then closed his eyes and slept until they reached the Dunwicks' dock.

Lady Dunwick and the rest of the party had returned to the house long ago and, after hearing Miss Ambrose's story, had been anxiously awaiting them. Lady Dunwick cut short the clamor of exclamations and questions, from Charlotte and Rusty in particular. "We must get the men taken care of at once. Beds are being made up in the study. That will make it easier on the poor doctor when he returns." She sighed. "Two calls in one day. The man may very well drop us from his practice."

So the doctor had already come to check on Susie. Concordia had a dozen questions of her own, but she wanted to stay with her husband. She asked only one before following David and Sir Anthony into the study. "How is Susie?"

"She's fine," Charlotte chimed in, "but wanted desperately to go back home. The doctor said she was all right. Where are the deputy sheriff and the others?"

"Mr. Nash has not yet been found," Concordia said. "They are searching the area."

Charlotte put a hand to her mouth. "Oh, dear. Poor Miss Farraday. You know the two have an understanding."

There seemed to be no good answer to this, so Concordia merely sighed and hurried to the study.

She stayed with David—who promptly fell asleep again as soon as he lay down—until the doctor arrived. The man looked quite harried. "More bromide poisonings?" The doctor shook his head. "Despicable."

"Will they be all right, doctor?" Concordia asked. "Lady Dunwick said Susie has recovered. Will be the case for them as well?"

The doctor was crouched over the unconscious Sir Anthony, feeling his pulse. "Why are you still here? I must examine these men."

Concordia stood, hands on hips. "One of these *men* is my husband. I want an answer."

His expression softened. "They look to have ingested more bromide of potassium than the girl did. I need to examine them further to be able to tell you more."

She sighed. "I'll be in the parlor."

He was already turning back to his patient. "I'll find you there when I'm done," he called over his shoulder.

Lady Dunwick waited with Charlotte in the parlor, a tray of tea and toast untouched in front of them.

Lady Dunwick looked up, her face pinched and pale. "How are they?" Despite the woman's obvious anxiety for Sir Anthony's welfare, her voice was steady.

"They seem to be resting comfortably. The doctor's examining them now." Concordia wanted to offer more words of encouragement, but Lady Dunwick's trembling hands and rigid posture denoted a woman on the brink of losing her composure. For a lady of her breeding, such a display would be most embarrassing.

"I'm sure you can do with a strong cup of tea after your time on the water," Charlotte said, reaching for the bell pull. "I'll ring for a fresh pot."

Concordia gave a tired nod. Her shoulders ached with chill and dread. As she sat beside Charlotte, she felt the lump of the envelope in her pocket and pulled it out. "I found this in Mrs. Reese's room earlier today." Was it really the same day? It felt so long ago. She passed it over to Lady Dunwick. "Mrs. Reese said these were originally the flowers from Iris Dunwick's funeral. She preserved them and later decided to send them to Sir Anthony every year, on the anniversary of her death." Concordia hesitated, unsure if she should tell her the rest.

But Lady Dunwick was made of sterner stuff than she realized. "How did Iris die?"

Charlotte leaned forward as well. Concordia bit her lip. "According to Eleanor Reese, Iris had suffered from melancholia for some time. She committed suicide."

Lady Dunwick clenched the envelope tightly in her lap. "So Anthony *is* responsible for her death," she whispered.

"You cannot say that," Charlotte put in quickly.

"I agree," Concordia said. "His action—or lack thereof, more precisely—may have *contributed* to the decision she made, but it was by her hand."

"If Uncle Anthony had known how desperate she was," Charlotte said, "I'm sure he would have helped her."

A muscle in Lady Dunwick's jaw twitched. "I am not so sure."

CHAPTER 30

*T*he doctor arrived in the parlor just as the tea was being brought in. "My lady." He bowed.

Lady Dunwick inclined her head and waved him into a chair. "How is he?"

The doctor sat gingerly, as if unaccustomed to any moment of leisure. "He will survive, as will the younger gentleman—Mr. Bradley, I believe?" He turned to Concordia, who nodded mutely, her heart too full to speak. She took her first easy breath since this morning.

The doctor turned back to Lady Dunwick. "Because of Sir Anthony's age, the recent blow to his head, and the severity of the assault upon him—which ended in exposure to the colder waters farther out in the bay—he will require a longer time to recuperate. But he *will* recover," he added quickly. He passed a slip of paper to Charlotte. "Instructions for his care this coming week. I will come by daily to check on his condition, but do not hesitate to call if you observe anything of concern." He stood, glancing out the window. "Do you wish me to remain, to see to *that* man?" He inclined his head.

Concordia and Charlotte jumped up and went to the window.

On the path leading to the portico, Yates and Decker were restraining a purple-faced, apoplectic Rusty Deighton. The gray-haired bookseller had apparently just flattened the damp and bedraggled James Reese, to judge by the latter clutching his nose with manacled hands and writhing on the ground. Decker, grinning, let his hands slip and Rusty nearly broke loose from Yates to go at Reese again.

"What is it?" Lady Dunwick said.

"A mere scuffle," Concordia said, watching as a constable stepped in and hauled Reese to his feet.

"Indeed. No need for your ministrations, doctor," Charlotte said.

Charlotte and Concordia exchanged a look before turning away.

CHAPTER 31

*Y*ates whipped off his hat as he joined them in the parlor. "My men are waiting in the carriage to take the prisoner to the East Hampton jail for tonight. We'll be transporting him to Riverhead in the morning. What's left of that cider flask is headed there, too, for examination. Lady Dunwick, have I your permission to search Mr. Reese's room before I leave?"

Lady Dunwick sighed. "Of course."

Yates nodded and turned to Concordia. "I want to take your statement, ma'am—along with your husband's, if he's up to it. Captain Decker already told us what he saw before our arrival on the scene, so you don't have to repeat that part."

Lady Dunwick indicated a chair. "Please sit down, deputy."

"Thank you, my lady." He pulled his notepad and pencil from his vest as he seated himself.

"Did you find Mr. Nash?" Concordia asked.

Yates scowled. "Yes, the poor fellow drowned. A couple of the fishermen have taken his body back to the ice house until arrangements are made. Reese has much to answer for."

277

"Including the death of Victoria Lester," Concordia reminded him.

He nodded. "I will telegraph the city authorities once we return to East Hampton. A lieutenant..." He flipped back a few pages in his pad. "Ah, here it is...Oliver. Fifteenth precinct."

"What about Eleanor Reese?" Concordia asked. "She has much to answer for as well: killing Wynderhane, kidnapping Susie, attempting to tie us up and leave us for her grandson to dispose of. Has she been found?"

Yates sighed. "I've had no time to send anyone to chase her down. She cannot have gone far." He squinted at her closely. "How did you figure out she was responsible for Wynderhane's death?"

Concordia blew out a breath. "I hardly know where to begin."

Lady Dunwick held out the envelope of irises in a trembling hand. "It began with this, Mr. Yates." He took it, and she stood. "If you will excuse me, I will leave Concordia and Charlotte to explain."

Once she had gone, Yates looked inside the envelope. "Where did this come from?"

"I discovered it in Eleanor Reese's room," Concordia said.

He shook his head, muttering to himself, "Heaven save me from inquisitive females. Hunting through closets, guests' rooms, old windmills..."

Charlotte gave a soft chuckle. "You don't know the half of it," she murmured. Fortunately, only Concordia heard her.

Yates leaned back as if settling in for a cozy chat. "Care to explain why you searched Mrs. Reese's room, ma'am? Or is that a customary practice of yours?"

"Hardly, sir," she retorted. Perhaps he *had* heard Charlotte. "I must admit, I at first suspected poor Mr. Nash and Miss Farraday —they had a secret courtship going on—" She stopped. "Oh, dear. Someone has to break the news to Miss Farraday, before the girl hears the gossip. She is bound to be distraught."

Charlotte stood and smoothed her skirt. "I'll go."

Yates stood politely. "Please convey my condolences to the young lady as well."

With a quick nod, Charlotte left.

Concordia watched the deputy's broad shoulders sag as he re-seated himself. "This must be difficult for you, Mr. Yates. I doubt so many deaths come your way at once."

Yates gave her a grateful look. "We have our share of tragedies —accidents, an occasional saloon brawl gone wrong—but not cold-blooded, deliberate murders." He sighed. "A typical summer day on my watch is generally spent chasing down scofflaws who haven't bought a bicycle license. Mundane, to be sure, but I'll be glad when things return to normal." He set the envelope aside and pulled out his notebook. "Sir Anthony told me yesterday about his sister. I barely had a chance to make sense of it all before I find you chasing after Reese and his grandmother." He lowered his brows. "Let us return to my original question. How did you come to focus upon Mrs. Reese, of all people, as Wynderhane's assailant?"

"The discovery of the bloodstained woman's shirtwaist got me thinking about what women I might have seen at the fair, just after the deed was committed but before I found Wynderhane. None of them, of course, would be walking around with a stained blouse for all to see, but Mrs. Reese had been draped in a shawl. I didn't realize until later how incongruous it was that she would be wearing it on such a warm summer's day."

Yates nodded. "To cover the bloodstains."

"Exactly. My original intent this morning was to search her room for the shawl, in case there were bloodstain traces on the garment. I stumbled upon the irises."

Yates looked up from scribbling on his notepad. "Does your husband know about your predilection for...uh, snooping, ma'am?"

She flushed. "He knows everything about me that he needs to

know." Besides, David had done some snooping himself during this trip. She smiled to herself.

Yates wisely decided not to continue that line of inquiry. "What did you do once you found the envelope?"

"No one was around—the men had already left in Sir Anthony's boat—so I went to Miss Ambrose for help in finding you. She was hunting for Susie. The rest Miss Ambrose has no doubt told you." She shuddered at what might have happened if the Reeses' plan had been successful.

His brow darkened. "I regret to have been so mistaken about Miss Ambrose and her niece." He shook his head. "I wish there was something I could do to help that family."

Concordia sat up straighter. A plan was beginning to form. "Actually, I believe there is." She told him her idea.

He frowned. "We'll need a good bit of help for that."

"I'm sure Captain Decker can be pressed into service."

Yates nodded. "Let me see what I can do, but it won't be until next week. By then, this business should be in the hands of the county prosecutor." He stood. "Now, if you'll excuse me, I'm going to see if your husband is well enough to make a statement."

"Thank you, Mr. Yates." She smiled. "For everything."

To Concordia's surprise, he gently clasped her hand, practically enveloping it in his large one, and made a gallant bow over it. "I am indebted to you, Mrs. Bradley." He straightened, and his eyes gleamed with barely concealed amusement. "Don't take this the wrong way, ma'am, but I hope you and Mr. Bradley consider a different locale for your vacation next year."

"Honeymoon," Concordia muttered to his retreating back.

EPILOGUE

Over the next few days, the Dunwick cottage was cleared of its guests. Rusty was the first to go, pressing Concordia's and David's hands in gratitude before stepping into the waiting carriage. "At last, I'll have justice for my girl. Thank you."

Concordia couldn't help but notice that the knuckles of Rusty's right hand were still swollen, and he winced as David returned the handshake. That must have been quite a punch.

The Gemmers left soon after, including Miss Farraday. Concordia pulled her aside as the children were being bundled into the carriage. She pressed a slip of paper in her hand, containing her Hartford address. "Write to me when you can. And let me know your decision, regarding what we discussed last evening."

Miss Farraday had been surprised by Concordia's offer to speak on her behalf to the lady principal at Hartford Women's College about possible enrollment and a scholarship.

Her eyes had misted. "I thought my future would be with Will."

"Your future is what you make of it," Concordia had said. "I know you consider yourself too old. But it is not too late. I believe you would be well-suited for it."

Miss Farraday smiled and tucked the paper in her glove. "Thank you, Mrs. Bradley. You have given me a great deal to consider."

It was much a quieter household now, especially with no deputy sheriff coming for regular visits. Such tranquility was more conducive to Sir Anthony's recuperation. As the doctor had predicted, David had made a rapid recovery from his unfortunate experience and was soon back to normal activities. Sir Anthony, however, remained confined to his bed. Lady Dunwick dutifully tended to her husband, but according to Charlotte, her chilly demeanor toward him was plain to see.

"I wonder if they will ever be reconciled," Concordia said to David, as they sat on the porch at Crosswinds. They had been spending most of their time here, wanting to stay out from underfoot until they were due to leave the day after tomorrow. "She is still quite angry at Sir Anthony for putting honor above family."

"For some families, honor is all they have left," David said.

Concordia sighed.

"I'm sure they will find a way through this," he said. "They are both reasonable people."

"And both stubborn," Concordia added. She was about to pick up her book again when she saw a pair of figures on the path. It was Gwen Ambrose and Captain Decker, who carried a small burlap bag.

After an exchange of greetings, Decker gave Concordia a smile that lit up his craggy face. "We're all set for tomorrow."

"Wonderful!" Concordia exclaimed.

"He won't tell me what's going on," Gwen said, with a sideways look at her companion, "only to expect some company in the morning and to be prepared for an outing."

"It's a surprise," Concordia said with a twinkle.

Captain Decker nodded to Gwen. "I'll be taking you and Susie out for the day—some fishing and a visit to see Ike's horses. That way the girl isn't troubled by the commotion."

"Commotion?" Gwen turned to David for clarification, but he merely grinned.

Decker passed the bag to David. "All done. I finished it with linseed oil. It came out beautifully."

"What's that?" Concordia asked, as David thanked him and tucked it aside.

"It's a surprise," David said, with a twinkle of his own.

Decker threw his head back and laughed. "You and the missus make a charming couple, I must say."

The next day dawned clear and warm as Concordia and David, hamper from Marie's kitchen over his arm, headed for the Ambrose property. Even from the path set well back from the road, they could hear the rattle of wheels as the carts began to arrive.

As they passed the hulking ruins of the old mansion, Gwen ran over to greet them.

"I see your company is arriving," Concordia said.

Gwen laughed. "It looks as if all of Hassett Knoll is arriving on my doorstep. The captain tells me they are here to take down... this." She waved a hand toward the old blackened house.

Concordia nodded. "It's a welcome surprise, I hope?"

"I cannot believe it. I thought no one cared about us. To have so many... How did you do it?" Gwen dabbed at her eyes with the corner of her apron and gave Concordia a hug.

Concordia smiled as she recognized the broad-shouldered figure approaching them. "Thank the deputy sheriff and Captain Decker. They organized the entire enterprise. I merely made the suggestion."

Gwen turned to the deputy, attired today in suspendered twill trousers and a faded-plaid work shirt. "I cannot begin to thank you, sir."

Yates grimaced. "It was the least I could do, miss, after putting you and your niece through a grueling investigation. I deeply regret the distress I caused."

"You were only doing your job," Gwen said. "I know that."

Across the clearing, a team of men had already set to work, backing their carts up to the old house, pulling out saws and crowbars.

Captain Decker and Susie stood at the end of the path, waving frantically. "Susie is rarin' to go, miss!" Decker called. "We should be off."

David passed her the hamper. "For your picnic."

Gwen took it with a lighthearted laugh. "I feel like such a lady of leisure!"

"We head back to Hartford first thing tomorrow morning, so we should say our goodbyes now," David said. "We wish you all the best, Miss Ambrose."

"You must write to us, and let us know how you are getting on," Concordia said. "I enclosed our address in the lunch hamper."

Gwen gave her a quick hug. "I will miss you, dear. Thank you so much, for all you have done." With a final squeeze of Concordia's hand, she hurried off to join Decker and Susie.

Concordia swallowed the catch in her throat as she watched her go. With a sigh, she turned back to Yates. "Any news of Mrs. Reese?"

Yates frowned. "One of the fishermen found an empty rowboat adrift near his dock, about thirty yards from the mill. He thought the storm had tossed it out in the current, but there was a lady's shawl inside. We've searched the likely areas where Mrs. Reese might have launched it but haven't found anything. Yet."

Concordia shivered, and David pulled her close.

"We told Reese about it, hoping that might prompt him to make a full confession," Yates went on.

"Were you successful?" David asked.

Yates rubbed his hands in satisfaction. "Indeed we were. Apparently, the man first attempted to kill Sir Anthony in the city and make it look like a traffic accident. When that didn't work, he followed him out here—thanks to his employer—and tried again.

He thought he had succeeded, in fact, with that blow to the head when Sir Anthony was alone in his sailboat. The boating excursion was his third attempt. He plied you all with the bromide-tainted cider, knowing it would be welcome after a warm morning out on the water, and waited until everyone was incapacitated. His plan was to dump Sir Anthony and the rest of you overboard and leave you to drown, then capsize the sailboat and wait for rescue, with a tale of woe about how he couldn't save the others when the boat went over. Fortunately, Captain Decker and Mrs. Bradley were able to thwart his plan. Your efforts helped as well, Mr. Bradley. Reese didn't count on a struggle."

David grimaced. "But Nash lost his life. That must have happened while I was still unconscious."

Concordia was feeling distinctly ill, listening to Yates recount the cold-blooded plan. "Can we go back to the cabin?" she asked in a thick voice.

David looked down at her pale face. "Of course." He extended his hand to Yates. "Congratulations, sir. Nicely done."

Yates smiled and hitched up his suspenders. "Time for me to get to work. Good day to you both."

Leaning heavily upon David's supportive arm, Concordia barely managed to reach the cabin hedges before she lost what little breakfast she had consumed that morning. He put her to bed with a cool, wet cloth to her forehead and let her sleep.

She awoke to the sound of twittering birds in the rose bushes outside her window. Cautiously, she sat up. Much better. The queasiness and fatigue were gone. She checked her watch. Noon! *Heavens*, she had slept the entire morning. She straightened her shirtwaist, put on her shoes, and brushed her hair.

David was sitting out on the porch swing, reading. He looked up with a smile as she sat down beside him. "Feeling better?" She nodded and clasped his hand. He squeezed back and searched her expression with anxious eyes. "Is there anything you want to tell me?"

Mercy, he must think women come equipped with an infallible "with-child" barometer. Although that would certainly be a time-saver. She chuckled. "Only after the doctor tells *me.* I'll make an appointment when we get home. It may be too early to know. I want to be sure before we make any announcements."

He gave her a wide smile as he gently brushed back her hair from her forehead. "I love you so. You will be a wonderful mother."

She smiled. She wasn't entirely confident about that, but the prospect didn't frighten her as it had before.

"By the way, while you were sleeping, Charlotte stopped by with something." He passed over a parcel wrapped in tissue paper.

She pushed aside the layers to find the ivory-and-lace layette she'd seen during the rummage sale sorting. "Oh, David! Isn't it lovely?"

He smiled as he watched her smooth the delicate folds of the gown. "Charlotte said her aunt tucked it away for you when she noticed you admiring it. There's a note."

"So kind," she murmured, plucking the card from the folds.

My dear Concordia,

I am grateful for all of your efforts on behalf of Sir Anthony. His life has been spared and the threat lifted from our family. The newspapers may still get wind of it, but we will face that difficulty if it comes.

I regret that you suffered unpleasantness during what is supposed to be the joyous occasion of your honeymoon. Please accept this small token of my appreciation, in anticipation of the next stage of your life. The child will be in for an adventure.

Yours Sincerely,

Susan

David leaned over the arm of the swing, reaching for the burlap bag Decker had dropped off the day before. "And here is something else, from me."

Concordia lifted out the smooth, wood object whose much

rougher form she'd wondered about for the past few weeks. It was a maple teething rattle, its rings interlocked on a stem that was knobbed at one end and had a small duck shape on the other.

"I carved it from a single piece of wood," he added.

"It's beautifully done."

"I can't take all the credit. Decker showed me how."

"Your wood-carving skills have come a long way, Mr. Bradley." She looked up at him, a gleam in her eye. "I'm sure there are a number of projects back home that would benefit from your newfound abilities."

He laughed. "A cradle, perhaps?"

Concordia leaned against him with a contented sigh, looking out upon the bright, sparkling waters of the bay in the distance, listening to the cry of the gulls and the lapping of the waves.

What a perfect honeymoon.

THE END

AFTERWORD

It's a great time to be a historical author, with the wealth of digitized historical material available on the internet. For anyone interested in the background research that went into the writing of this book, I've shared some wonderful primary and secondary sources on my website, kbowenmysteries(dot)com. I'd love to see you there.

I hope you enjoyed the novel. Please consider leaving a review on your favorite online book venue. Word of mouth is essential to help readers find books they will love, particularly those written by independently published authors. Thank you!

To order other books in the Concordia Wells series, please visit KBOwenMysteries(dot)com and click on the "Books" tab. Purchase links to all of the online venues are provided.

ALSO BY K.B. OWEN

ACKNOWLEDGMENTS

~

Many people have had a hand in bringing this book into the world, and I want to express my sincerest thanks to them here. Among those who helped were specialists in their respective fields. Any errors found are solely mine, not theirs.

To Luci Zahray, the "Poison Lady," who helped with a crucial question.

To historical dining expert Jan Whitaker, because a lady has to dine out from time to time, and we cannot have Concordia patronizing any questionable establishments.

To Paul Owen, USNA '82, who helped with the sailing scenes.

To artist Melinda VanLone, who never fails to create such wonderful covers. I am grateful for her time and talents. Melinda can be reached at BookCoverCorner(dot)com.

To Kristen Lamb, Cait Reynolds, Piper Bayard, and the generous community of fellow writers known as WANAs, for their advice and support. We are truly not alone.

To Jami Gold, for her assistance with certain aspects of the story's plot structure.

To Kassandra Lamb, for her spot-on edits, and to Julie Glover, for her meticulous proofreading of the manuscript.

To my dad, Steve Belin. Although you aren't with us anymore, I know you are still cheering me on. I miss you, Dad.

To my mom, Agnes Belin, to whom this book is dedicated. You instilled an abiding love of reading ever since I was little, and you continue to share your enthusiasm for my writing career. Thank you!

To my sons, Patrick, Liam, and Corey, who encourage me and make me laugh.

To Paul Owen, my husband and my love. None of this would be possible without you.

K.B. Owen
November 2017

ABOUT THE AUTHOR

K.B. Owen taught college English at universities in Connecticut and Washington, DC and holds a doctorate in 19th century British literature. A long-time mystery lover, she drew upon her teaching experiences in creating her amateur sleuth, Professor Concordia Wells. *Unseemly Haste* is the fourth book of the series.

Contact:

kbowenmysteries.com
contact@kbowenmysteries.com